MAN ON A
RED HORSE

MAN ON A
RED HORSE

A WESTERN STORY

FRED GROVE

Five Star
Unity, Maine

Copyright © 1998 by Fred Grove

Five Star Western
Published in conjunction with Golden West Literary Agency.

May 1998

First Edition

Five Star Standard Print Western Series.

The text of this edition is unabridged.

Set in 11 pt. Plantin by Minnie B. Raven.

Printed in the United States on permanent paper.

Library of Congress Cataloging in Publication Data

Grove, Fred.
    Man on a red horse : a western story / by Fred Grove.
— 1st. ed.
        p.   cm.
    "Five star western" — T.p. verso.
    Published in conjunction with Golden West Literary
Agency" — T.p. verso.
    ISBN 0-7862-1157-1 (hc : alk. paper)
    I. Title.
PS3557.R7M26   1998
813´.54—dc21   98-2607

MAN ON A
RED HORSE

Chapter One

Jesse Alden Wilder found the Río Mimbres as inviting as expected, a sweet-water godsend in this high, arid land, which a U.S. Army map showed flowing out of the rugged Black Range miles away to his right. Making camp under towering cottonwoods, he unsaddled and picketed the red horse and the brown pack mule on waist-high grass and strolled about to view his surroundings.

Over there were the blackened remains of a long-dead campfire. Plenty of deer tracks were among the willows along the river, but no fresh horse tracks — good, for this was Apache country. He'd seen no one since departing Fort Cummings that morning by way of Cooke's Cañon. Upriver, he'd been told, scattered Mexican families farmed the river valley.

Placing his Spencer carbine close by, he kept a sharp lookout while he noisily bathed in the running stream. The grazing horse raised his blazed face at the splutters and splashings, fox ears twitching. *Always a sentinel,* Jesse thought, *day or night.* The red horse was always alert, listening, watching, ever suspicious of the world around him, survival ways learned as a wild horse on the Texas plains before being captured and purchased by Jesse out of a bunch of horses in El Paso. He had the eye of an eagle and the step of a deer. A shame he'd been gelded. What qualities he could have passed on as a sire: durability, speed when needed, sure-footedness, moving fast and light, looks, temperament, and that never-ceasing wariness. *El Soldado* — the Soldier. So Ana had named him. A battle-tested horse, flinching at the first crash of musketry, but never bolting. A fading red ribbon still adorned the coal-black mane,

Ana's loving handiwork. It would stay there until it wasted away. Ana was gone forever. He couldn't bring her back. Eventually, he realized, he'd have to say good bye, but he couldn't yet. He needed more time. It was too soon. The past wouldn't let him go.

Afterward, he washed his clothes and spread them on bushes to dry and aired two sleeping blankets, which made his bedroll with the rubber poncho. Then, taking a small hatchet, he gathered and chopped wood for an evening fire, liking this place more by the moment. Just by chance, he'd found a temporary Elysium. So he would stay a while, resting his stock and himself for the footloose, though punishing, days ahead.

The remainder of the afternoon he spent cleaning the seven-shot .56-50 Spencer, an eight-shooter with one in the chamber, and a Colt Navy .36 revolver, and checking the Blakeslee Quickloader, which was a leather-covered wood case with a hinged lid holding ten tin tubes of seven metallic cartridges each. While doing this, he considered what lay ahead of him to the west. Along the old Butterfield Overland Mail Line, abandoned before the War Between the States, but still the main trace across southern New Mexico and Arizona into Tucson. Fort Bowie, in Arizona, was the nearest westward post.

It occurred to him while he relaxed, watching his stock graze, that the mule, which he had bought from a Mexican farmer on the way out of Chihuahua, had no name. In his hurry, Jesse hadn't thought of that. The mule wasn't the big type you saw back in Missouri and Tennessee — he was small but well knit, tough, nimble as a mountain goat, an ideal pack animal to travel the far Southwest. Every creature loyal to man deserved to have a name. Jesse mulled that over: *El Diablo* . . . or Chico? *El Diablo* was too harsh, too mean. From now

8

on the mule's name would be Chico. It fit his independent, sometimes devilish, temperament that went with his hybrid nature. It behooved any man to be mindful of flying hoofs when approaching a mule's hindside. Chico. It fit. Besides, he liked the little mule.

Toward evening, he led his four-footed friends to water and picketed them for the night within a few rods of where he would sleep under a cottonwood. Twilight lingered while he cooked bacon in a small frying pan and boiled coffee in a can sometimes used for stew. For a change, he enjoyed biscuits and dried fruit from the fort, carefully rationing the latter.

The fire died down to cherry-red coals, and a breeze, springing up through the trees, became a garrulous visitor. Presently, back in the mountains, a coyote lifted its falsetto yips, joined by another and another, producing a high-wailing, drawn-out chorus. Jesse smiled. He was being treated to a serenade. Now an Apache, he mused, could tell whether the wild, high notes meant rain or dry weather. To newly arrived Anglo-Americans in the Southwest, it was mere howling, a disturbance, a lonely sound in a lonely land. To a *mestizo* Mexican — a mixture of Spaniard and Indian, predominately Indian, and, therefore, more in harmony with nature — it was singing. And to Jesse, no longer a stranger to this border country, it was singing.

He lit his pipe with a coal from the fire and leaned back. By now, more coyotes had added their voices to the evening concert. In this clear weather, the singing would likely continue off and on all night, maybe until after sunrise. He didn't mind it at all; it was company, same as the copper-colored horse and the mule were company. Thus thinking, he asked himself in a roundabout way — *Why am I here?* — a question he had asked before in other alien places, and he always came back to the same vague, nebulous answer: instinct. He wasn't

9

running from anything. He wasn't a wanted man back there in Tennessee or down in Mexico. In his wanderings and warring after the War Between the States, some people might call him a mercenary, yet he was not, because he'd always followed his heart. He was looking for something he could not define — it was out there somewhere, always beyond him. *Peace of mind? Security?* The first, he sensed, would come in time, after much time. He'd passed up the second when offered the job of post scout at Cummings because he was weary of warfare. So far, war had determined his place in life. Would the violence ever end for him?

He stopped himself abruptly. He was thinking too much again, almost brooding — too much looking back. A little more and he'd be on the verge of sickening self-pity, which he detested for its weakness. He should have crossed the gap between sorrow and self-control by now, he told himself. A period of mourning was needed and reasonable, but he should stop thinking of the past so much. Yet it still seemed so close. *How long ago had it been? Five . . . six months? Five, it was, since her death, then the continual fighting as the Juáristas drove the stubborn foreign enemy toward Mexico City.* Getting up, he walked the perimeter of the moon-washed camp and prepared for bed.

Just before he dropped off to sleep, he could still hear the coyotes singing and, last, the comforting movements of the horse and mule cropping the good grass.

Far into the night something aroused him. Some change in the fusing rhythm around him, some nearness, some presence. The night was dead still. The coyotes had quit. He froze, listening. The steady grazing sounds also had ceased, which concerned him. He reached for the Colt Navy and drew it to him. Now he caught what had broken his sleep, a sniffing and the awareness of something physically close upon him.

As suddenly he relaxed, wide awake, feeling not a little foolish. He should have known at once, seeing the long, blazed face peering down at him, so near Jesse could smell the warmth of the grassy breath. He stayed motionless. The horse leaned in, now sniffing Jesse's hat brim, but seemingly careful not to touch his face. Then, apparently assured that all was well, he turned and moved away and quietly resumed grazing, and the night was as before.

A strange vigil. Perhaps the horse didn't do this every night, but Jesse suspected the horse did it often when he wasn't aware of it. As long as he'd owned the red horse, and as much as they'd been through together and survived, night was the only time *El Soldado* would come to him. Never in daylight, even for feed, even when feed was scarce.

Then Jesse remembered: his nightmares, his demons. After leaving him in peace for some time, they had returned this night, of all nights, flashing through his mind in savage bits and pieces. . . . He was Captain Wilder, back in the shrieking, smoking hell of Franklin, charging the Yankee trenches, seeing the powder-black faces of his fallen friends, hearing their tearing cries. He was clubbing with his musket in the furious, milling, man-to-man fight in the yard at the Carter House, in his ears other wild rebel yells with his own: *"Yee-haaa! Yee . . . haa . . . haaa . . . haa!"* Then he was in the Yankee prison at Camp Morton. His recall was so real he could smell the stink of the cold barracks, hear the coughing at night of the sick and hungry men, some near death. . . . He was astride the red horse, rushing with the Juáristas for the camp in the Sierras too late, hearing the ripping crash of French musketry, and then seeing the littered camp and finding Ana. . . . Shattered days that never seemed to end. Scenes that stayed alive in his mind. Somehow, through all this, he'd always been the survivor, and not without feeling guilt. Strange, in a way.

11

He was in a cold sweat. Maybe he'd cried out? Maybe that had drawn the red horse? He could only guess as he drifted off into sleep, always intrigued by such feral vigilance.

He slept past dawn, his usual getting up time, and woke to bird song and to find the horse and mule eyeing him accusingly for his lie-abed indolence and their neglect. "You're both spoiled," he told them and, pulling on boots, led off to water. From his pack he rationed them shelled Fort Cummings corn in nose bags. A light feeding. Grain was always scarce and, therefore, a treat while traveling. Besides impressing an animal that man was looking out for it, Jesse hoped feed would serve to keep an animal near camp in event it broke picket. Left afoot in desert country would be courting disaster.

A fine, bright morning after a troubled night. A breeze moved along the singing river. Mourning doves called. Yes, he would linger here a while. A man couldn't find a more suitable camp on the edge of desert country: wood, water, forage, shade, and cool nights. After breakfast, he took out a small hand mirror and started trimming his beard. The even-featured face he saw was that of a South Carolina Alden, or so he'd been told as a boy. His dear mother's side of the family. The Alden men were often carousers and woman chasers and racehorse fanciers, frequent losers at the track, who spent more time in town than they did farming — so the story went, told in discreet whispers with a rolling of eyes. His was a face burned dark by wind and sun. A full mouth, turned thoughtful now. Likewise thoughtful gray eyes set wide, sun wrinkles at the corners. A straight nose. His snow-white hair, turned so overnight in Mexico at Ana's death, hung nearly to his shoulders. Soon the Mexicans had a name for him, *El Soldado del Palo Blanco* — the soldier of the white hair. He trimmed it shorter. A Minié ball at Franklin had

12

ripped a path along the right side of his head and left naked scalp showing. He was twenty-eight years old, and knew he looked much older. No matter.

Around mid-morning he tied the mule in a thicket and saddled the red horse. But as he started to mount, the horse danced away from him and flung up his head, blowing through his nostrils. Jesse had to chuckle, saying: "I know you ran wild in Texas. Do you have to remind me this morning?" When he tightened the reins and reached for the saddle horn next time, the horse stood still, and they turned upriver. He rode with the Spencer in a saddle sheath, the Colt Navy at his belt.

He rode steadily for some time, the horse in his usual eager, running walk. Their coming flushed deer away from deep pools of shade by the river, vanishing up a juniper-studded cañon. He marked the place in his memory to return early next morning for meat. This was all untouched country through here, no sign of man. *Suitable,* he thought, *for cattle raising and farming*.

After a while, the steady *chock-chock* of an axe broke the stillness. He entered a clearing and saw a sandaled Mexican man dressed in peasant white chopping wood in front of a small adobe house where three children played in the yard. At the sound of the horse, the man jerked and held the axe defensively. Jesse halted and raised a hand. *"Buenas días, señor."*

He started to ride on when the man said: "You are welcome to stop, *señor*. However, all I can offer you is cool water."

Jesse thanked him and dismounted and tied the horse to a juniper branch. A woman, showing a cordial smile, came to the doorway of the adobe. A brush corral held two lean mules. By the corral sagged a much-used wagon. A vegetable garden grew not far from the river. Despite the air of hard times, this seemed a happy little family.

With natural dignity devoid of an obsequious behavior before an Anglo-American, the man shook hands and invited him to sit in the shade of the *ramada*. There they smoked and talked while the big-eyed children watched in silence, in awe of the stranger and his horse.

Jesse smiled at them; shyly, they smiled back.

"How has life been here?" Jesse asked.

"A struggle, *señor*. But it is getting better each season. Two years ago I brought my family here from Chihuahua. Life is much harder there on the big haciendas. A man is no more than a slave to the *hacendados*. Living is bare. Here there is hope. In time I will have cattle. I will bring up a few at a time from *Méjico*. Meantime, there is much to do. Sometimes I sell wood in the little village of San Lorenzo up the river. There is hay to cut."

"Have the Apaches bothered you?"

"There is little here to interest an Indian. Little to take. No fine horses like yours. I stay alert. So does my wife. I keep a rifle by the doorway."

"Fort Bayard, northwest of here, should discourage any raids."

"So you know about the new fort? Sometimes their soldiers ride down the valley."

"This country will attract more people in coming years. When danger is past, they'll come in a swarm. Many Anglos. So you will be wise to register title to your land as soon as you can. Stake out now what you want. I'd say it will take a fair number of acres for each cow."

"*Gracias, señor*. I hadn't thought of that."

"As soon as there is local government, you can do that. Have your land surveyed and the boundaries located. If you don't, somebody may try to take it from you. Some big rancher."

"I will remember. We need no *hacendados* up here." His eyes strayed from the carbine sheath on the saddle and back to Jesse. "*Señor,* there have been rumors in the valley of a big fight in the mountains not long ago. We supposed it was *soldados* fighting Apaches. Perhaps they attacked a *ranchería?*"

Jesse wasn't surprised that he knew. It was strange, on the frontier, how news of a big fight spread so fast, as if carried on the wind, or by some mysterious telegraph. "It wasn't a fight with Apaches," he said. "It was between cavalry from Fort Cummings and a band of thugs. They'd been attacking wagon trains on the trail from Mesilla to the fort, murdering and looting. They had a big camp in the mountains. The cavalry attacked and took prisoners."

He said no more and was glad when the woman brought him a dipper of water. Thanking her, he said: "You have beautiful children, *señora*."

She beamed. "They are taken with your red horse."

"Maybe they'd like a ride? Would that be all right?"

She looked at her husband. He nodded.

The oldest was a boy of about six. Jesse lifted him to the saddle and, mounted behind, sent the red horse off on a circling ride to the river and back, the boy clutching the saddle horn. Then, one by one, the little girls followed, leaving them all in breathless excitement.

"You are very kind, *señor*," their father said. "They've never been on a horse before. You also let them hold the reins, which they will never forget. Now they will be after me to get them a pony. Until I do, they'll have to be satisfied with a poor burro."

"I still remember my first ride with my father," Jesse said. "You feel high above the ground in another world, and the horse seems so big and powerful."

Now it was time to ride on, but, before he could, the father

15

said to the boy: "Ernesto, go to the garden and bring back a melon for our visitor. Be sure it is ripe."

The boy was off with the words and returned with a cantaloupe. As Jesse put it in a saddlebag, his host said: "*Señor,* you have found the valley as beautiful as we have. But you say you will ride on to the west. It is very dangerous that way. Why not make your home here along the river? There is plenty of good land. They have dances in San Lorenzo every Saturday night. Before long you'll find a good wife who will bring you much happiness and many children."

Jesse laughed. "*Señor,* you make it sound inviting, and I thank you kindly. Although I'll go on, I will remember the people and the Mimbres as a place to come back to."

Heading out, he turned and waved when he reached the trail by the river. The entire family waved back, the children jumping up and down. He rode on, his mood suddenly thoughtful and heavy.

Soon after dawn next morning he rode slowly upriver, head swiveling, watching. Approaching the juniper-studded cañon, he tied the red horse and, the Spencer in hand, went stalking ahead.

He spotted them at the murmuring river, among the drooping willows. A little bunch. He must have made a sound, because in an instant they quit drinking and began slipping away for the haven of the cañon, as silent as smoke.

He shot a fat buck, the blast of the .56-50 like a clap of thunder in the early stillness. It took longer than it should have to gut, skin, and butcher the deer, not having done this in a long time. He left one quarter in the high fork of a cottonwood to come back for, and, with all but the head wrapped in the skin, he followed the river, the horse settling down after shying at the blood smell and the new burden.

The sun was high when he rode into the clearing. One look told him that he was late. He halted, feeling a sharp disappointment. The wagon and mules were gone. Sunday, he supposed. Gone to church. Or maybe it was Saturday. Days and dates meant little to him any more. He hung the meat in the *ramada* and rode back the way he'd come. No need to present the gift in person. The family would know.

In camp, he cut thin strips of meat and hung them on a tightly stretched rope. Within two or three days the meat would cure into jerky in the sunshine and dry wind. A man could live on jerky and water.

As if questing man must always see what lies just over the next hill or across the next river, he forded the Mimbres next morning and rode until the up-and-down land began to flatten out, just wandering and looking, seeing no person, letting the horse sort of pick the easiest way. Although he found several springs, no place looked as inviting as the Mimbres. He turned back. It was afternoon when he reached camp.

Something on his bedroll caught his eye. Dismounting, he found a stack of corn tortillas wrapped in cottonwood leaves and a string of green chiles. He smiled, warmed all through. No need to tell him in person. He knew.

That evening he dined on tortillas and venison stew seasoned with fiery, satisfying chiles, while the never-failing coyote chorus serenaded him in falsetto.

Mexico pressed constantly on his mind, and he began to feel restless when several more days had passed, and one morning he packed up and left. If he kept looking back, retracing the unchangeable past, he'd be thinking too much again, mulling, brooding. Idleness did that to a man. He needed to be on the move. He'd rested long enough.

Riding southwest from the river, he came to the ruts of the Butterfield and struck out west, across a broad desert plain, seeing cone-shaped peaks standing like sentinels in the glare of the brassy distance, and a band of antelopes running free, their white rump patches glittering.

Today he rode with the Quickloader's leather strap looped over the saddle horn. He could slip the strap over his shoulder in a moment, and the loader would be ready for use.

As the sun burned away the morning, he spotted dust plumes crossing the trail far ahead of him. He pulled up to watch, seeing distant figures. After a bit, the dust moved off to his right, toward what on the Army map would be the Burro Mountains. Apaches, he figured, returning from a raid into Mexico, headed for their haunts in the mountains, their booty mules, goods, tequila, if they hadn't drunk it all, and likely a captive child or two and as likely a woman or two, destined for the harshest of lives, doomed to become broken-down wretches. The boy captives would grow up to be trained as warriors. Jesse realized that he also made dust. No doubt the Apaches saw that, but deemed him of no importance now.

That afternoon a clump of cottonwoods grew out of the undulating plain: *Ojo de la Vaca* — Cow Spring, according to the map, a virtual oasis in this sun-tortured emptiness. He approached the cottonwoods warily, his eyes sweeping from the roofless stone stage station and the attached stone corral to the skeleton hulks of burned wagons. He rode to the great spring under the trees and stood by, the carbine in hand, watching, while the horse and mule drank. When they had their fill, he got down on hands and knees and drank. The water was sweet. He filled canteens.

Tracks ringed the spring: shod horses and mules, antelopes and coyotes, some tracks he took for wolves, and some still larger he guessed as mountain lions ranging down from the Burros, and fresh moccasin prints that gave him cause for thought. The spring was a junction point. A road slanted in from the northeast, likely from the Santa Rita copper mines, then angled southeast in the direction of Janos in Chihuahua, and the Butterfield showed recent travel. He sensed a going back in time. Early Spaniards likely had watered and rested here on the way to and from Santa Rita.

He counted the remains of six wagons camped in a circle. Going over, he found only charred wood and twisted metal. Not one grave anywhere. Wiped out. Nobody left to do the burying. Animals had dragged off the victims. An old depression came over him. Images flashed through his mind with vivid clarity. Wagons and bodies stripped of everything usable: guns, shells, knives, clothing, bedding, leather, down to cooking pots. He visualized how it had happened, finished in a few savage minutes. The Apaches charging on foot out of the east with screeching cries, the sun at their backs. This didn't look recent, and no burned smell lingered. He crossed to the station. It still held the frame of a bunk bed built against the wall — only that. Nothing more.

He had no wish to camp here, although the fresh moccasin prints most likely had been made by the war party he'd sighted earlier. It was too great a magnet for trouble, the only water within miles. Therefore, he continued on west a way and camped well off the trail among mesquites, feeling more comfortable with open country around him and grass for his stock.

He carried wood in his pack from the Mimbres, but decided on a cold camp tonight, jerky and tortillas and good spring water. He fell asleep with the singing of the coyotes sounding muted and lonely across the cool, windy distance, rising in chorus from the Burros.

Much later, it seemed, a noise snapped him awake. Not the rustlings of the sentinel horse sniffing around his bedroll, this was a different sound. Now he heard it again, the horse stamping nervously. Now a snort of alarm.

Jesse's entire body went tight, his fog of sleep clearing in an instant as old reflexes took over. He picked up the carbine, rose to his feet, and eared back the hammer. He could see *El Soldado*'s dark shape near the end of his picket line. The horse seemed to be staring suspiciously at something. Chico was also watching. Silently, Jesse stepped that way.

The horse snorted and backed off a trifle, but still facing whatever was out there. Bit by bit, a shape materialized, moving soundlessly away in the muddy light, low to the ground.

Jesse's tension dissolved at once. Hell, it was just a coyote sneaking around the camp. He felt like laughing. He watched until the coyote became part of the night, a black and gray shape in the cloudy moon wash — now lost to sight.

He went back to bed, again intrigued by his horse. He watched the stars glitter a long time, waiting for the first smear of dove-gray light. It seemed to loiter behind a wall of clouds. A lulling wind rose. He dozed . . . awaking suddenly, upon him a flood of pink dawn. The bracing desert air swam with odors. His friends were waiting patiently, heads turned his way.

"I know," Jesse lectured them, "you're always hungry. So am I this morning. Let's eat." He then fed them from nose bags before eating his own breakfast.

He rode steadily all morning, pausing only to dig a pebble from the mule's right front shoe, not stopping again until he reached Soldier's Farewell. Once a meal-and-change stop, judging by the size of the station, the walls were ten feet high. And an adjacent stone house and a large corral. Another remnant of the entrepreneur's dream, he thought, dashed by the war. He watered at a spring in a nearby ravine, rested for an hour, and lined out southwest. The proximity of the mountains bothered him, remindful of Apaches. He sought more open country for camping this night, and there was too much of the day left to halt now.

The trail took him through a low pass where the Burros appeared to run out, and before sundown he made camp at Barney's Station, the smallest one he'd seen, including those on the long stretch between the village of Mesilla on the Río Grande and Fort Cummings. This was an adobe house and corral and a dirt tank of stock water. Having covered nearly forty miles today by map memory, he fed extra grain and rubbed down the horse and the mule before putting them on picket and cooking his own supper, since a man, if he was worth a damn, always looked after his stock before feeding himself. An old rule.

Again, he avoided the station and laid out his bedroll off the trail. Tomorrow's stretch would be shorter across to Stein's Peak near Doubtful Cañon in the Peloncillo Mountains. Today he'd pushed harder than he liked in this heat.

He slept later than usual and was cooking breakfast when he heard the rumble of wheels and the rattle of harness chains and a mule-drawn Army ambulance rolled up to the station, flanked by an escort of six dusty cavalry troopers.

An erect individual wearing the gold leaves of a major on his shoulder straps stepped down from the ambulance and stretched, regarding Jesse in yawning surprise. Jesse nodded; the major nodded.

"You're welcome to use the fire," Jesse invited.

"Thank you, sir. May I ask how you managed for firewood?"

"Carry some in my pack."

"Now that's a thought. Corporal, water the horses, then put on the coffee pot, thanks to this gentleman. I guess the water is potable?"

"Is if you boil it," Jesse said. "If a man didn't, I reckon it wouldn't kill him."

21

The major smiled and strolled about restlessly, showing a keen interest in the surroundings, near and far. He was a solidly built, blue-eyed, rust-bearded man of military carriage, obviously charged with driving energy. Strong jaws. Chiseled features. Sizing him up from experience, Jesse took him for a West Pointer, about in his late thirties. Probably a veteran of the war. Campaign tough. Ambitious. On the way up. But promotions were slow now in the peacetime Army, the frontier cavalry offering more opportunity than other branches — observations Jesse had gleaned at Fort Cummings.

The major, strolling back, stopped to look at the red horse with a cavalryman's judging eyes. Turning to Jesse, he said: "I can see, sir, that you are well mounted. I like his conformation and the way he holds his head." He continued to study the horse. "Well-muscled rear quarters. Long underline. Short cannons and pasterns. Sloping shoulder for speed. He's a compact horse. Good balance."

"Thank you. Not big, but tough."

"Tough enough and big enough. It's a misconception in some Army quarters back East that big, heavy, long-coupled animals do better in mountains and rough-country campaigns. Quite the contrary, it's the shorter-coupled, compact horses who make the stayers. Army replacement mounts are coming more and more from the sturdy Western mustang type. By chance is he gaited?"

"Has a nice running walk."

"Ah. Now you are talking about one of the true pleasures of riding, of getting over ground." He eyed the horse in more detail. "I'm trying to arrive at his approximate weight. What do you say?"

"Over eight hundred pounds or so."

"I'd say . . . eight-fifty, sir, and close to fifteen hands high. I believe I also see Spanish blood in this horse."

"Could be. The trader I bought him from in El Paso, who handled a lot of Texas horses, told me he was captured wild. He'd never had a saddle on him, though the man didn't tell me that till later. Threw me sky high twice, pitched like a demon, but soon settled down."

"About how old is he?"

"I figure him for a six-year-old now, because the cups are worn from his two middle teeth."

The major smiled again. "Believe our remount officers could learn from that observation. Furthermore, as a six he has reached his full growth, or close to it, and is able to take the grind of hard use." Nodding, he strolled on, gazing off toward the humped Burros.

The corporal filled a big coffee pot, threw in handfuls of ground coffee, and muttered aside to Jesse: "Appreciate this, sir. Detail's in a rush for Fort Bowie. Special escort from Fort Bliss. Bivouacked last night on the trail . . . cold camp. Major had us up at four o'clock."

"Night travel is safer out here," Jesse said, "and much easier on your mounts."

"And hell on sleep."

As Jesse laid on more wood and built up the fire, the corporal said — "We can cook bacon faster'n coffee can boil at this altitude." — and got busy. Another trooper joined the cooking. Before long, the troopers were drinking coffee from blackened tin cups, wolfing down bacon and hardtack sopped in bacon grease on tin plates.

The major, apart from the others, finished first. Seeing that, the corporal threw out the coffee grounds, sloshed the pot with water from the tank, and the detail made ready to pull out.

"We're obliged for the use of your campfire, sir," the major said as the detail formed, and the driver took his seat.

"You're all mighty welcome, Major," Jesse said, touching the brim of his hat to him. "Enjoyed the company and horse talk. Good luck."

The major snapped an informal salute in return and started to step up into the wagon. At the last moment, he paused, his eyes curiously on Jesse. A question seemed to pass through his mind. He had the impulse to speak, but appeared to think better of it, and entered and sat down, spoke to the driver, and the detail took off.

Jesse watched them go. *I guess he was about to tell me the obvious . . . that it's dangerous for a lone man in Apache country. Guess he wonders, too, how a civilian would know Army rank unless he'd served. In turn, I wonder what's up at Fort Bowie.*

Watching, he saw their dust soon rising in thin ravels across the blazing sky, visible for miles. *One reason,* he thought, *why Apaches often traveled at night . . . to hide their going.* An hour later he could still see the telltale dust, although dimly, when he saddled off from the station.

The mail road led some miles across the highest section of an alkali flat to the barren Peloncillos, where he turned northwest, flanking the mountains, feeling his isolation in the remoteness of this vast sea of desert. By now he no longer saw the detail's dust.

The miles fell away. He shuttered his eyes against the dazzling brightness, the red horse in the tireless running walk, the haltered Chico trailing like the tail of a kite. Time lagged. There seemed no end to the pebbly trail.

Distant sounds shook him out of his lethargy. The horse flicked his ears and lifted his head, staring curiously. Jesse stiffened — that was gunfire! Like a volley. Instantly he thought of the ambulance escort. But he could see no movement. They were too far ahead, by now four or five miles. The guns crashed again. Now a tapering off to scattered shots,

24

then silence. For a short while the stillness held, broken as the firing opened up again, heavier than ever, a steadiness to it, the shots like splatters across the afternoon quiet.

He rode a little faster, more alertly. Just when he thought the gunfire was over, meaning the escort had broken through, it resumed. A pattern settled in. There would be scattered shots, then a lull, and more scattered shots. To him that meant the escort was under siege.

The afternoon was half gone when he sighted the stage station near the base of Stein's Peak; the off-and-on firing sounded much nearer. But he saw no ambulance or horses or troopers. The station looked abandoned, except for the make-shift wooden gate. It was another large stone structure, like Soldier's Farewell, built for defense. Doubtful Cañon would be just beyond.

He crossed a wash, and, as he clattered up to the station, a gray head popped up above the wall. Jesse waved. The head disappeared and a wild-looking old man ran out, a scarecrow of ragged clothes and long hair and bushy whiskers and flowing white beard.

"What is it?" Jesse asked him.

"They're in the cañon," the old man gabbled, hands shaking. "Ambushed!"

"You mean the cavalry escort with the Army wagon?"

"Yeh. The fools! Been Indian sign around here since yestidy. I told the officer to fort up here, but he said they's in a hurry. Figured they could git through. So the fools went on! Only reason the 'Paches don't git me is 'cause they think I'm crazy. Heh, heh." He jumped up and down, showing a toothless grin. "Maybe I am, but crazy like a fox. I'm a miner. They's not only copper in these mountains, heaps of it, they's gold, too. Heh, heh." He started shaking again. "You'd better fort up with me. Put your stock inside."

25

Jesse hesitated. He didn't have to get in the fight, Yankees besides. Should he help or stay out of it? The station would be a safe haven.

"You'd better git inside," the old man warned.

A sudden burst of gunfire crashed. Jesse could make out the banging of Army carbines, intermixed with the crack of rifles. As he delayed, the carbines slacked off, but the rifles did not.

He untied the halter rope from the saddle horn and handed it to the old man. "Mind taking my mule inside?"

"Yer mule? Mean you aim to go down there?"

"I'll take a look," Jesse said, not certain why he was. He drew the Quickloader's strap over his right shoulder and rode on.

Chapter Two

Coming to a spring in a bank of the wash, he halted so the red horse could tarry for a deserved long drink before going on.

The wash extended into the cañon with a swoop, the grade dropping sharply as the rocky road wound deeper into the mountains and the brushy walls of the cañon rose higher.

He rode at a cautious trot, the carbine riding on its sling, the Quickloader swinging easy, not quite understanding himself. He had no real obligation to get involved, yet here he was. He could go back to the stage station and stay out of it, yet he hadn't. That would be the sensible course. He knew these troopers only in passing. Besides, they were Yankees, though once he'd worn the blue, yet only for reasons of survival. He played it all back and forth in his head as he rode warily along.

An occasional shot and yell told him the ambush had narrowed down to a siege type of fight. *A stalemate. Maybe they didn't need help, after all. Maybe there was nothing he could do. Maybe. . . .*

He made an impatient motion with his right hand. To hell with all this mind circling and searching for reasons, this holding back, this trying to sort things out. He heeled the horse faster, already feeling better, freed of doubt.

He rode for several minutes, thinking ahead, projecting, assessing the gunfire sounds and what he would find. Rounding a bend, hugging the side of the cañon on his right, he saw, suddenly, the ambulance in the middle of the road, the mules down, dead. Of course, they had drawn the first shots.

One trooper was down. Others were posted around the wagon and here and there in the brush behind boulders. The Apaches hadn't killed any horses, no doubt anticipating them as booty.

While Jesse watched, a blue-clad figure rose behind the wagon and calmly snapped off a revolver round and unhurriedly crouched down. It was the major, conducting himself, Jesse thought, as an officer should, an example for his men. And damned cool about it. Maybe a little too cool. An Indian fight was no place to be needlessly heroic for effect.

That single round drew a flurry of shots from high on the cañon to Jesse's left. Through the drifting fog of grayish smoke and red flashes he could see the main fire was issuing from a parapet of rocks and small boulders. From the parapet's dimensions, it appeared to have been built for some time, a favorite ambush site. This near, as the smoke cleared, he also could see the paint-streaked faces of the Apaches, their headbands, and long hair.

A sharp awareness flashed over him. His position was scarcely better than the escort's, except he hadn't been discovered. He needed a field of fire if he was to do anything.

At that, he led the horse into the brush and tied him and began a zigzagging climb up the sloping face of the cañon, weaving through brush and behind boulders for cover, pausing often, swiveling his gaze from the Apaches to the escort and back. The Apaches were still firing. The major still crouched behind the wagon. Now and then a trooper would take a quick shot and duck down, apparently without effect. There was little the escort could do from that angle, shooting up at the parapet.

He stopped and sank down, hacking for wind, appraising his position. In his back-and-forth scrambling, he'd covered only some thirty yards. He had to get up higher, much higher. He looked around. Above him was straight up. But slanting upward across from him was a clump of boulders. From there he'd have a fair enfilading line of fire. The best he could do. Trouble was, the rough ground between, ten yards or more, was all open. And the Apaches had stopped shooting. Better wait.

Sudden stirrings across the cañon drew his eyes. More Apaches were slipping along through the brush to join those at the parapet. Others were scattered out in flanking moves. Seeing that, the major alertly shouted, and the escort fired in unison. An Apache stumbled. Immediately the entire Apache line erupted in fire. Powder smoke bloomed.

Now! Jesse knew, if ever he was going. He got up and started angling across, the Quickloader banging against his side. He jumped the beginning of a rain-washed ditch and sprinted for the boulders, sliding in behind them as the shooting dribbled off and ceased.

Looking across the cañon, he found that he was even a little above the parapet, which now lay angled to his left. He could see the painted faces and naked upper bodies quite plainly, even gestures. There seemed to be a good deal of talking going on. With their superior position, they'd become understandably careless of any threat other than the trapped escort. He quickly counted fifteen Apaches strung along the parapet and in the brush on each side. As he watched, more Apaches slipped down from the rim of the cañon.

It was time to do something. He judged the range under a hundred yards, ideal for a carbine. He rested the Spencer between two boulders, adjusted the sight, thumbed back the hammer, picked out a face on the parapet, and pulled the trigger. The face disappeared. He began firing rapidly, yet deliberately, working the loading lever like a pump handle, sweeping the parapet, scoring. He saw the startled reactions there, the Apaches jerking around in astonishment. Where was this coming from? But only briefly. His gunsmoke gave away his position, and they concentrated on him with yells.

The Spencer was empty. Ducking down, he withdrew the magazine from the buttstock, lifted the Quickloader's lid flap, and pulled out a tube of seven cartridges, tilted the tube, and the cartridges slid into the buttstock. He put back the tube and reinserted the spring-loaded magazine, locked the cover plate, and was ready again. All this in the space of a few, practiced moments.

He found fewer targets now, but they couldn't all take cover. As he fired, the carbine grew hot, and he jerked out a red bandanna for his left hand to hold against the barrel. He reloaded again.

Bullets were slamming against the boulders, ricocheting off, snarling and whining. Bits of rock flew by him. Keeping low, he crawled to another position. For a very short interval, he watched for smoke puffs, placing his shots there. The Apaches had spread out, lithe figures firing muzzleloaders. Here and there he saw them reloading, tamping home charges with ramrods. Others, quicker, judging by their rate of fire, seemed to have newer weapons. Whatever, he could maintain a sustained rate of fourteen to sixteen rounds a minute, while a muzzle-loader fighter, jumping around, dodging, could do no better than three.

Picking targets, he fired four quick rounds from there, then changed positions again. As he faced about, it came to him that the rate of fire from the other side had dropped off considerably. At the same time he heard shouts from below, shouts that sounded like cheers. Looking down, he saw the troopers waving back at him while they kept up the shouting. Some waved hats. The major, hands cupped to his face, was calling out something that Jesse couldn't make out above the Apaches' gunfire. The major was pointing furiously down-

30

cañon, and Jesse saw two Apaches working down the face of
the cañon, getting lower and lower. A flanking movement, if
they crossed to this side. The major fired his revolver — missing at that range.

Jesse adjusted sights fast, settled on the lead Apache as
they reached the cañon floor running, and fired. The man
went down. But before Jesse could lever in another shell and
sight, the second Apache disappeared.

Just then the Apaches across the cañon opened up on him
again, forcing him to hunker down. For the moment, he forgot
about the second Apache. To his surprise, the rifle fire got
hotter. He emptied the magazine at them, reloaded, remembering he had seven tubes left, and shifted location again.

Firing dropped off on both sides. *Targets getting scarce now
across the cañon, heads staying down, waiting,* Jesse thought. An
old Apache game. An Apache could wait forever. He chose
his targets carefully. Off and on, he'd hear a taunting yell,
which told him he'd scored again. He loaded the fourth tube.

An uneasy silence set in. Late afternoon shadows made
dark pools in the lower reaches of the cañon. A teasing breeze
wandered through. The smallest sound seemed magnified, a
horse stamping or rattling a curb chain. A trooper's muffled
cough. Darkness would place the escort at another disadvan-
tage. *Might be wise,* Jesse figured, *to make a run for it pretty
soon, tear upcañon for the station.* Same for him. He could see
his horse from here, head turned in direction of the fighting,
ears pricked, watching, stirring nervously, as alert as ever.

He had posted himself near the corner of a boulder, looking
for fresh targets, his mind swinging back and forth about the
second Apache he'd missed, when a furious burst of firing
drove him behind the boulder. Crouching, half turned to his
right, facing across the cañon's slope on his side, he happened
to notice a little ripple of gravel sliding down from above. A

31

chill shot up his back. He whirled around, knowing at once the reason for the heaving firing: to cover the Indian working in behind him, and now leaping down at him from the brush, knife out.

The man was upon him before he could bring the Spencer around. He tried to use the carbine like a club, but the other's momentum knocked him against the boulder, making the carbine all but useless. His senses spun as he saw the knife bearing down on his chest. He drove the gun barrel upward against the forearm of the knife hand. For a split second the arm bent backward, only to slide around the barrel and bring the knife about. Jesse dropped the carbine and grabbed for the knife arm. His hands slipped on greasy sweat — caught, and there they stayed, locked. The man's strength seemed to keep growing. He groped for Jesse's throat with his free hand. Jesse tore at it with his right, but couldn't break the grip, only loosen it. His breath came short, his face only inches away from the painted features, in Jesse's nostrils the rankness of rancid sweat and the reek of wood smoke. He saw the blazing hate, the black eyes like points of fire, the teeth bared wolfishly.

They tugged and wrestled, grunting, heaving, straining, neither able to break free, the knife always there, poised to slash down. Feeling his arm there weakening, Jesse rammed his knee into the man's gut, heard him grunt with pain.

All at once they were rolling and falling, still locked in struggle, tumbling down the cañon's rough slope, the Quickloader and carbine bumping. They crashed through brush and over rocks, still locked, the Apache unyielding, the damned knife never far from Jesse's face or chest.

They fell over a ledge and hit the cañon floor, both momentarily stunned. Jesse blinked, before him, as in a haze, the wagon and the major and two troopers rushing over. He glimpsed that telescoping scene an instant before the Apache tore his knife arm loose and lunged for him.

A deafening blast shook Jesse's ears. He saw the Apache recoil, a vast astonishment widening his eyes, and drop the knife, his lower face a bloody mess, the streaks of white paint running red. Jerking away, Jesse saw the major standing over him with a smoking revolver. He and the troopers pulled Jesse to his feet, and they all ran for the wagon as bullets began digging spurts of gravel and dust around them.

A trooper shouted a new alarm and pointed.

Jesse glanced up, hearing a chorus of wild cries. Apaches were climbing over the parapet, dropping and sliding down. All along the cañon wall they were coming. He heard the major shout: "Hold your fire till they charge!" Very coolly, he reloaded his revolver and faced about downcañon.

Jesse had hardly posted himself at one end of the wagon when Apaches hit the cañon floor, jumping and whooping, their half-naked bodies like sculpted bronze in the fading light. They rushed for the wagon, screaming like fiends, firing. Absolutely fearless.

Carbines banged together.

The charge faltered — then swept on, as savage as before. When a warrior emptied his muzzleloader, he didn't stop to reload. Instead, he shifted the rifle to one hand, unsheathed a knife, and kept running a weaving, elusive course, never ceasing to yell.

Jesse focused his fire on the center. It was pointblank range now, hard to miss. He could see bodies falling. The charge was slowing, but not finished. *By God, they're brave.* He loaded another tube, just in time to see an Apache, running like a deer, leap inside the troopers' line. A trooper went at him with the butt of his carbine. The Apache dodged, drove his knife into the trooper's shoulder. Another trooper shot the warrior in the chest. The bullet knocked him backward, still slashing. Suddenly he crumpled and stayed down.

In the cañon the charge was broken and dying. Bodies lay scattered and writhing in front of the wagon, some downed warriors still yelling defiance. It was about over, Jesse saw, save for those retreating down the cañon. Now and then one would stop and fire back.

Jesse kept firing at the figures. In a short while, even they were gone, and finally, indeed, it was over.

For a suspended run of time everybody just stared down-cañon and up at the deadly parapet, the troopers with powder-blackened faces, mouths agape. The stillness was numbing. Acrid powder smoke still overhung the cañon. Jesse's ears were ringing. Of a sudden he felt the full weight of the afternoon descend upon him, the old letdown weariness of the battlefield.

He looked around to find the major regarding him in question, and Jesse nodded. "Yes, Major, I think we'd better make it back to the station while we can. I'll help."

"I believe you've already done considerable, sir." The major threw him a further look, seemed to put it away for now, and called the corporal.

Quickly, eyes on where the Apaches had vanished, they lashed one dead trooper to a saddle, gathered up two wounded, mounted them, and moved off. Jesse and the major, walking, formed the rear guard with the driver.

"My horse will ride double," Jesse offered.

"Ordinarily, I'd decline," the major said with nearly an ironic smile. "Unbecoming to a dashing cavalryman, y'know, but right now I'd ride a burro."

The driver found a like seat with the corporal.

There was still some amber light left in the sky as they plodded along the wash to the station. Not until they'd hallooed twice did the old man open the gate and wave them in.

"I'm afraid you soldier boys was all kilt," he told them, his voice still skittish. "I'll git a fire goin'. I've got plenty deer meat . . . you're welcome . . . but am plumb outta coffee."

"We have plenty coffee," the corporal said.

They laid the dead trooper inside by the station wall and covered him with a blanket. Heeding the obliging old man, a stooped, wizened, bird-like little character who hadn't stopped talking while he hopped and fluttered about them, they took the wounded to a room and removed their jackets and shirts. One had a knife wound in the left shoulder. The other had taken a bullet high in the chest on the right side. Both men were barely conscious.

Their comrades stood around, shuffling and looking at each other in a helpless way. "About all we can do is bandage 'em, tear up their shirts," the corporal said, and sent a man for water.

Thoughtfully, Jesse said: "Looks like the bullet went on through his chest. That's good. Better than a gut shot. While you boys tear up the bandages, I'll go see if I can find something we can use for a poultice."

They looked at him in puzzlement.

Without further explanation, he left the station and walked out a short way, scanning the desert in the fading light. Not finding what he sought, he went farther out. Seeing a clump of prickly pear cactus above the deep wash, he cut off three ear-shaped pieces and brought them in. While the major and the troopers watched, he carefully cut out the stickers with a knife, peeled off the outer green skin, and said: "Now let's tie these on the wounds. Front and back for the chest wound. One will do for the knife wound."

"What is it?" the major asked.

35

"Prickly pear cactus. Strange as it may seem, it helps . . . cleans and heals. Apaches and Mexicans use it for wounds. About all they have, but it works. Plenty of it around."

"Beats what the brutal butchers who called themselves surgeons did during the war. Man shot in the leg or arm . . . cut off the limb." The corporal seemed to shake his head in wonderment at the efficacy of primitive medicine.

With the corporal helping, Jesse wrapped the poultices in place, using strips of gray flannel shirt. In his mind, the knife victim would make it; the other man might, with luck.

The troopers made a fire, and presently coffee and bacon smells rose. The old man shared strips of dried deer meat and gratefully accepted coffee and hardtack.

"Why stick it out here in Apache country, old-timer?" a trooper asked.

"First place, I don't bother the 'Paches, they don't bother me. Like I told the feller that rides the purty red horse, the 'Paches think I'm crazy. Jest the same, I stay cautious. They may git me someday at that. Only reason I stay is fer the gold. There's gold around here. A big vein of it somewheres. I've found a trace of it now and then, enough to keep me lookin'. The mother lode's out there somewheres. You bet it is."

"Meantime, how d'you get by?"

"Times I'll trade a little with folks comin' through in wagon trains headed for Californy. Help 'em out, if I can. Trade fer coffee and flour, maybe ammunition, some old clothes. Maybe trade 'em a little bitty nugget or some deer meat. Oughta see their eyes light up when they see the sparkle o' that gold. They're ready to trade then! Sometimes they'll give me a sore-footed animal that can't make it on. I'll keep it up till it's sound again. Trade it to the next bunch o' hopefuls comin' through."

"Figure you'll ever find the mother lode?"

The old man's watery eyes took on a faraway expression. "Jest might tomorrow, soldier boy. Might tomorrow. I know it's out there."

Afterward, Jesse picketed the horse and mule outside the station and put down his bedroll. In the pallid light, he saw the major come to the station's entrance and look around. Jesse went over to him.

"Have a drink with me, Major."

"Why, thank you. I'd be delighted."

"If you don't mind tequila?"

"I can't think of anything better after today."

From the bedroll Jesse dug out a bottle and passed it to him. "I want to thank you," Jesse said, "for rushin' out there. I was just about finished when you fired. That Apache's strength never seemed to weaken."

"In turn, I can say that we'd still be down there, finished for certain, if you hadn't come along with the Spencer carbine. That was the most lovely of sounds when you began laying down a sustained rate of fire. It took them completely by surprise . . . by the way, it's time that we know each other. I'm Major Emory Gordon." He held out his hand.

They shook hands.

"Jesse Wilder, Major."

"More than glad to know you, Mister Wilder, and also to tender the thanks of the escort for coming to our aid. You didn't have to take part. You could have stayed out of it."

Jesse shrugged. "I know. I must say I even thought of that. I've been in some tight fixes, too. I guess I acted on impulse. Sometimes things just work out, Major."

"And when that happens, you'll find that somebody has gone out of his way and risked his own hide doing it."

"Sorry about your boys."

"There's always a price, isn't there? My orders call for me to be in Fort Bowie by tomorrow. For what reason I'm not privileged to know yet, except that, whatever it is, it's not worth today's cost of getting there in such a rush."

Jesse had a drink and passed the bottle back. Gordon took a swallow, returned it. "You're welcome to ride with us in the morning, Mister Wilder. Might think about it. I thank you again, sir." He extended a hand.

"My own again, Major. Luck both ways." He held out the bottle. "Believe there's a round of drinks left for your boys."

As Gordon nodded his thanks and turned to leave, he paused in that characteristic way he had, Jesse remembered, when something seemed to cross his mind at the last moment. "At Fort Cummings, I was told about Captain Jesse Wilder, an ex-Confederate, who recently rendered certain gallant and meritorious service. Good night, sir."

Jesse said nothing. He had enjoyed these few moments with a fellow soldier; they brought upon him the realization of what he missed traveling a solitary road. Gordon struck him as an interesting man. Very proper, but not unbending. A good officer. He'd conducted himself quite well today, showed leadership under fire. A contrast after the many posturing blunderheads and egotistical fools a man encountered in uniform along the way, ramrod straight on the parade ground, barking commands, but unfit to lead in the field.

Chapter Three

After breakfast at daybreak, they buried the trooper. Major Gordon spoke the simple words, and they covered the grave with rocks. On a large flat stone, set upright, the corporal scratched the man's name and regiment, the 4th.

Jesse rode up as they were saddling to return to the cañon for the wagon.

"How do you size up the situation this morning, Captain?" Gordon asked. "Will they be waiting for us again?"

"I don't think that's likely, though I wouldn't attempt to make an absolute prediction about what an Apache thinks. However, they got hurt bad yesterday. Unusual for them. Apaches can't stand losses like that very often. I'd say they'll lay off Doubtful Cañon for a while . . . until a fat wagon train lumbers along for easy pickin's."

Dropping down into the cañon, Gordon spaced his men at wide intervals, and they proceeded with caution, holding mounts to a walk, watching the walls and rims. They rounded the bend Jesse remembered.

The cañon was deathly still and empty save for the wagon and the dead mules in harness. Nothing moved along the parapet.

"Why, they've carried off their dead!" Gordon exclaimed.

"It's their way," Jesse said.

He helped free the mules and drag them aside and hitch two somewhat unwilling cavalry horses to the wagon. Then, turning around, they rumbled upcañon to the station.

They loaded in the wounded, and the major hurried them off, riding point with the corporal. Jesse followed, leading the mule.

In a little less than two hours, they emerged from the Peloncillos and down a gentle descent to the valley of San Simon, as Jesse recalled from the map. There, on the east side of a dry-bed creek, they came to an adobe stage station fast surrendering to the elements. A man-made earthen tank behind the station held brackish water, which tasted better than it looked.

They watered and rested for ten minutes. Restlessly, Gordon ordered the escort to mount, and they pressed on across the broadening desert, following the well-defined stage road. At this rate, Jesse reckoned, the major would arrive on time. It was evident that he followed orders to the letter, though after yesterday Jesse figured he was flexible enough to go by the spirit of an order, which allowed for changes when the unexpected arose. The miles fell away, the horses scuffing up clouds of dust that turned the troopers' blue jackets to a reddish tint.

Now it was afternoon, the sun holding them in its grip like a vise. The red horse and the mule moved tirelessly, swinging along. Jesse sensed anticipation in the mounted men and the wounded suffering in silence as they gazed off toward the cool mountains where Fort Bowie lay. Then they were climbing, going at a horse-grunting trot.

In the distance, high and clear, like voices calling in the mountains, they heard trumpeters blowing Retreat. Within the hour, they clattered into a pass, wound through a cañon, and Jesse saw the fort take orderly shape. Everything was open, arranged around the parade ground on a broad slope below the mountains.

After a short distance, a sentry called out a challenge.

"Detail from Fort Bliss, with two wounded needing immediate attention," Gordon said.

"Corporal of the guard! Corporal of the guard!"

A man came running out of the evening gloom.

"I'm Major Emory Gordon, Corporal, on special assignment, with an escort from Fort Bliss. We have two seriously wounded. Show us to the hospital."

The corporal saluted. "Yes, sir! Follow me."

He turned and started trotting, leading them across the parade and just beyond to a low building, where a light shone. The corporal hurried in. The detail helped the wounded dismount and was assisting them forward when the corporal returned with another trooper.

Gordon then asked the location of headquarters and struck off at once for a two-story building at one corner of the parade. *Duty calls,* Jesse thought, *and there is considerable hurry about this assignment.*

The corporal led the detail off to the stables. Jesse followed and unsaddled. The stable sergeant took immediate charge and obligingly led the horse and mule to water, then hung the horse gear on pegs and put down grain and hay for them in stalls with the detail's mounts. Finding himself with bedroll, canteens, carbine, and Quickloader, Jesse was thinking of going to the post trader's when the corporal took everybody to the enlisted men's mess.

After supper, Jesse was shown to an empty cot in the barracks and put down his stuff. He yawned and pulled off his boots, stretched out, and closed his eyes, shutting out the hum of voices.

"Captain," a clear, cordial voice said.

Jesse looked up.

Major Gordon stood at the foot of the cot, his expression a mix of apology and understanding. Jesse started to rise, but Gordon said: "Don't get up. Sorry to disturb you. Just want to say you're welcome to bunk in the bachelor officers' quarters."

Jesse sat up. "This is fine, Major. Thanks just the same."

"Well, I'll look for you in the morning, but not early. Meantime, don't run off on that red horse before I see you. Rest easy." He seemed extra thoughtful as he walked out.

I'll look for you in the morning. What could that mean, beyond a routine farewell? Jesse didn't ponder on that very long. In moments, he was asleep.

When stable call sounded after breakfast next morning, he took his stock to water, and groomed his horse in the stable with brush and currycomb while the troopers groomed theirs outside on picket line. As an added care, he inspected the shoes on both animals, found them secure, and cleaned their feet with a hoof hook.

"If I may say so, Captain, you didn't learn that in the infantry," a now-familiar voice spoke as Jesse finished.

Major Gordon had been there for some moments, Jesse realized as he looked around. "Yes, sir," he said, "after I left the infantry, I learned that a good, solid horse, looked after every day and fed before a man feeds himself, is the best way to keep the scalp firmly in place."

Gordon smiled.

When Jesse put the hoof hook away, Gordon said: "I take it this means you're preparing to leave?"

"Pretty soon."

"May I ask if you have anything definite in mind? I mean a particular destination?"

"Well, I understand Tucson's the next town on west." His voice came back to him vague and without purpose, almost shiftless.

Gordon looked apologetic. "You must pardon my directness, Captain. Usually, I don't nose into another person's affairs. The reason I ask is that I have a favor to beg of you."

Jesse shrugged. "Can't see that I could do much about anything, just driftin' through."

"You did a great deal back at Doubtful Cañon . . . *just drifting through,* so to speak. You demonstrated what one experienced fighting man can do in a tight situation."

"I believe it was more surprise than anything."

"That, but not all," Gordon replied crisply. "It was the Spencer and knowing to get up higher to a position that enabled you to establish a field of sustained fire. A green trooper would have started firing from the cañon floor, which wouldn't have won the day."

Jesse's suspicions were aroused. He felt his ease disappear. "What is it, Major?"

"As customary, I made an immediate verbal report to the post commander, then followed with a complete written report about what happened at Doubtful Cañon. As a result, the C.O. would like very much to talk to you."

"Talk?"

"In other words, he not only wants to thank you, but he wants to visit with you. I've filled his ear with quite a lot about you. He is Colonel W. S. Chilton. I would consider it an honor, Captain, if you could delay your departure long enough to do that."

"I reckon, Major, you could say I'm in no big hurry. Man gets few chances to visit with a colonel, does he?"

As they headed for the two-story building, Gordon said: "The colonel was a brevet brigadier. Served mostly in Virginia. An able cavalry commander. Hard-tailed. On Sheridan's staff last year of the war. Earlier, he was in the big fight at Brandy Station."

An orderly escorted them into the C.O.'s office. Colonel Chilton stood as they entered and held out a quick hand to Jesse. "I am very glad to meet you, Captain Wilder. Major

43

Gordon has pretty well filled me in about your timely rôle at Doubtful Cañon."

"Pleased to meet you, sir."

Chilton was a tall, soldierly-looking man of middle age. A grayish beard framed a lined, thoughtful face that seemed to reflect the wear of years of war. He projected a quiet air of command, a man wholly in charge of himself and events around him. His slate-gray eyes were keenly appraising on Jesse as he motioned for them to sit.

"I want to express my very personal appreciation to you," Chilton said.

"Thank you, Colonel."

"You are welcome to whatever the post might provide. Any personal needs. Blankets, rations, ammunition. Extra forage for your stock. A veterinarian. A farrier."

"Thank you, sir. I've been well cared for, and my horse and pack mule are taking to all this good Army feed."

"There is an unusual aspect leading up to all this," Chilton said, and paused. "Major Gordon tells me that, while at Fort Cummings, they were still talking about a Captain Wilder, a former Confederate, who played a leading part in a most unusual sortie into the mountains that concerned the very life of the commanding officer's little son."

"I was one of an advance detail that went into the mountains and located the gang's camp and sent word back for Colonel Taylor to bring up the command. The boy was being held for a ransom that his father couldn't possibly have met."

"You say a gang?"

"A pack of the most brutal cut-throats possible. All were killers many times over. Wanted in Texas and the South and elsewhere. Led by a madman named Fogel, who'd been drummed out of Fort Cummings for stealing several thousand dollars from the post trader's safe. A detail caught him heading for El Paso. Colonel Taylor ordered Fogel flogged fifty times, the letter D branded on each cheek, then drummed him out of the service."

Chilton's bushy eyebrows went up. "Such punishment would provide motivation. Flogging was abolished by General Order Number Fifty-Four back in August of 'Sixty-One. Branding was not, though it should've been. But in extreme cases such as this, the post commander could do just about whatever he deems necessary to set an example for the command. I knew Taylor back in Virginia. He was never one to hold back. Why he was known as Fighting Dick. Please go on."

"Well, sir, Fogel left, swearing revenge. With the proprietor of a gambling and drinking dive just off the reservation who had criminal connections back in the States, he began gathering a gang of killers . . . some thirty or more. They started preying on immigrant wagon trains traveling the old Butterfield Trail from Mesilla to Cummings. They'd wipe out an entire train and pick it clean . . . everything, stock, harness, saddles, jewelry, bedding, dishes, pots, pans, lanterns, and clothing down to babies' shoes. No one was spared. Not even women and children. I was with a detail in charge of Lieutenant Tom Ayers, escorting some wagons out of Mesilla, when we came upon the remains of a train of ambushed Arkansas folks. It was the most brutal, heart-rending sight I've ever seen . . . worse than any battlefield. The gang would haul the booty in wagons to their mountain camp. When they had enough, say, to fill a string of wagons, they'd take it under guard down to Janos in Chihuahua to sell at high prices. Everything's scarce in Mexico." Jesse checked himself. He'd been talking without letup. Neither man had scarcely moved. "I'm afraid I'm too lengthy," he said.

"On the contrary, Captain Wilder," the colonel assured

him. "Feel free to relate everything in detail. It's important that we know here what recently happened east of us involving our people. Do continue."

"Before long," Jesse said, "Fogel got rich. How much he shared with his killers we never learned. The main thing they got from him was a hideout from the law, especially the Texas Rangers. If they tired of the killing and tried to leave, he had 'em tracked down." He stopped again; they waited. He went on: "Meantime, Colonel Taylor's eight-year-old son, Jaime, liked to ride. Always with an escort, of course. But he kept wanting to ride into the mountains, which was strictly forbidden. One day he slipped out of the post alone and rode into the mountains. His pony came back riderless. We searched till darkness blotted out the tracks leading into the mountains. From the tracks it appeared that two riders had taken the little boy."

"Then you picked up the kidnappers' trail next morning at first light?" Chilton led on, his interest growing.

"No, sir. We lost the tracks on a rocky slope. Next afternoon a rider rushed up to the post with an ultimatum from Fogel . . . signed *El Comandante*. You see, Fogel fancied himself as a military man. He had the boy, and he demanded a hundred Spencer rifles or carbines and ten thousand American dollars or gold. If Taylor mounted a rescue attempt, the boy would be shot. Fogel warned that he had the post under observation." He paused again, thinking back.

"But you found the trail, after all?"

"Not that one. But by following a hitherto unnoticed trace of wagon tracks leading out of the mountains to the gambling dive near the reservation, we located the camp. To escape observation, we tracked it by a full moon . . . slow work at best . . . and sent two troopers back to the post. Colonel Taylor then brought up the command at night. At daybreak

46

our advance detail made a dash for the cabin where we thought the boy was being held. We'd seen a Mexican girl taking in food. About the same time, as planned, the command hit the camp."

"Ah, frontal attack, hell-bent . . . in Fighting Dick style," Chilton added. "Brandy Station all over again. I can see it now."

Jesse smiled. "Not quite, sir. Fogel, having served at Cummings, must've figured what Taylor would do. And he'd planned rather well. Posted men in wagons near the camp and more men across the clearing to establish an enfilading fire. But, instead of charging into camp as Fogel must have expected, the colonel slipped around through the woods below the camp . . . outflanked the wagons and surprised 'em."

"What about the boy?"

"In the detail, hidden in timber, we knew we couldn't wait past daybreak to make a surprise dash to the cabin. We heard gunfire just as Ayers led us off. Ayers and I ran to the cabin . . . broke in. The boy wasn't there . . . that stunned us. We ran to Fogel's headquarters, a big log house. Kicked the door in and searched it room by room . . . no boy. We feared the worst, then. Had Fogel murdered the boy? We heard a girl scream and ran outside. The brave Mexican girl had taken the boy near a wooded arroyo for protection. One of Fogel's crazed killers . . . the guard . . . was after the boy with a knife. We shot him. I don't think Fogel ever intended to give up the boy. He wanted to murder him in revenge. Maybe draw his father to the camp for a parley over the ransom, and kill him, too."

"What happened to Fogel?"

"Killed late in the fight . . . went down swinging a saber, shouting that he was *El Comandante*. In his white buckskins and black boots, he looked like some character you'd see parading across stage in a cheap melodrama. Whatever he was, madman or not, he was very dangerous. The worst kind, motivated further by the flogging and branding."

No one spoke for several moments. Then Chilton said: "A most gripping and unusual story, Captain, which shows the Army and the frontier draw the bad with the good." He regarded Jesse with increasing interest. "May I ask what you did before the war?"

"I was a schoolteacher in Middle Tennessee. Grew up in the country. My father farmed some and raised mules for cotton farmers in Mississippi and Alabama. He'd freed his slaves a few years before the war."

"Then into the Confederate Army."

"In General Cheatham's Division of the Army of Tennessee . . . from Shiloh on. Wounded at Franklin, I ended up, by mistake, I'm certain, in a Yankee hospital in Nashville that probably saved my life. They took good care of me, and I got well. I then had two choices . . . go to a prison camp or wear the Union blue out West as a volunteer to fight Indians and do escort and post duty. But I couldn't wear the blue. I'd have felt like a Judas."

"I can well understand that feeling, Mister Wilder, after four years in the Army of Tennessee. Please continue. Feel free to do so."

Jesse said: "I was with a bunch sent to Camp Morton, near Indianapolis. It was what you'd expect of any prison camp, North or South. Poor food and sanitation. Disease. Men dyin' like flies in the barracks. The smells a man never forgets. The graveyard detail every morning. Three of us dug an escape tunnel. But somebody told on us. A Reb, hoping for better rations. They jailed us. I'd still had a twenty-dollar gold piece a male nurse had given me in the hospital. An Irishman named Pat. I'll never forget his kindness. He just wanted to give it to me

. . . thought I might need it. I used it to bribe a guard I thought I could trust. We left our unlocked cells and ran for the gate, which also was supposed to be unlocked. They shot us down. My two friends died. I didn't have a scratch. Seemed I was always the damned survivor . . . Shiloh and Hoover's Gap, where the Spencer repeaters mowed us down . . . Atlanta, Franklin. Three days later, after much soul searching, feeling like the worst of traitors, I volunteered to serve in the Army of the West and took the oath of allegiance to the United States of America . . . with the understanding that I'd not bear arms against the South or be asked to."

He leaned back, amazed at himself. How long had it been since he'd talked at such length and never before virtual strangers? But it was a release to have let go his thoughts before veterans, who knew all about war.

Chilton and Gordon still seemed in an attitude of rapt listening, his words echoing in their minds, their soldierly eyes warm with understanding.

"What then, Captain?" the colonel asked softly.

"I understand there were several regiments of us out West, known as galvanized Yankees. About a year and a half later I was mustered out at Fort Leavenworth." He wouldn't tell them that his father had left him out of his will because he'd worn the hated blue — that was a family matter — or that old neighbors had turned their backs on him and walked away when he returned home. Only Mr. B. L. Sawyer, the family lawyer, had understood and had asked Jesse to stay in touch later, which he had, several times.

"Having served in the Union Army, I knew there was nothing for me back home in Tennessee, where I was considered a traitor. I went to El Paso. Soon after, with Cullen Floyd, another ex-Reb from Mississippi who'd served in the Army of the West, I found myself in Mexico, training Juáristas to fight

Maximilian's forces. Believe me, those peasants made good soldiers. Tough . . . they could march all day on a handful of *pinole* and some dried beef and *panoche*."

"*Pinole?*" Chilton asked.

"Ground dried corn or mesquite beans. You stir in some water and sweeten it with *panoche,* half a pound of dried beef, and half a pound of *panoche* . . . but most times they didn't have that. No cooking utensils needed . . . just a tin or earthen cup for water. They made canteens out of gourds. They never faltered in a charge and were very effective with machetes, a fearsome weapon in close and quicker than a bayonet. A true Mexican . . . I don't mean the mixed-blood *mestizos* who are part Spanish . . . is a Mexican Indian, about as tough as any Apache, and can travel for days at a swinging dog trot like an Apache. They wore the common peasant white cotton and rawhide sandals fastened with thongs. And straw sombreros, tied under their chins with straps. Might say they were a revolving volunteer army, between home and camp. From time to time, they'd go home to look after their corn and chile and bean patches. Most always came back."

He was ready to end this, but Gordon asked: "What about weapons?"

"A mixed lot. Old Enfield muzzleloaders and old carbines ranging from Sharps and Ballards, to Burnsides and Starrs, and shotguns. Anything that would shoot. Most peons we trained had never fired a rifle before. Later, we got some Spencer rifles."

"Spencers in Mexico?"

"Enough for two companies. Our main worry at first was to prevent the boys, as we called 'em, from shooting up too much ammunition. But they learned fast and were extra proud to carry the new repeaters. Time and again we stressed not to bang the rifles down hard when fully loaded with seven

50

cartridges nose to tail in the magazine. They believed us without doubt when one blew up and killed a man. After that, we instructed them to carry one cartridge in the chamber when marching, none in the magazine."

"This is surprising to hear," Chilton said. "Did you have the Blakeslee Quickloader?"

"No, sir."

"What caliber Spencers were these?"

"The Fifty-Two-Forty-Sixes."

"Reason I ask, I believe some carbines are Fifty-Six-Fifties. I wish we had them instead of the Five Ninety-Seventy Springfields."

"Yes. Mine is a Fifty-Six-Fifty."

Chilton regarded Jesse with an expression close to amusement. "A considerable number of Fifty-Two-Forty-Six Spencers were stolen from the Fort Bliss armory in El Paso a year or so ago, and the Army's still looking for 'em." He was still smiling when he said: "It would be interesting to know exactly how the Juáristas came into the Spencers."

Jesse shrugged with ease. Colonel Taylor at Cummings had asked the same question. "I grant you it would," Jesse said. "Gun runners are thick as fleas on a hound dog along the Río Grande . . . all kinds, from Americans to Spaniards, and Cubans and Mexicans. One day a pack train showed up in camp with the Spencers, and we couldn't have been happier. We asked where they came from, and all we got was a . . . *'¿quién sabe?'*" He wasn't about to reveal how he and Cullen and a band of Juáristas had overpowered a guard and broken into the armory, packed a hundred and seventeen rifles and boxes of ammunition aboard mules, and won a race to the Río Grande.

"You, then, became an effective fighting force overnight?" Chilton asked.

51

"Except for the need for more training with repeaters. The Spencers meant we could fight the French on even or better terms for the first time. Word had reached us that an enemy garrison at San Juan de Río, made up mainly of the French Foreign Legion and Hussars, was terrorizing the countryside. Captured Mexican guerrillas were being hanged in the plaza as a public warning to the cowed citizens. Peasants were shot if they protested when foragers took their produce and live-stock. Sometimes young girls were taken from their families." Jesse looked at both officers. "Afraid I'm boring you with too much detail."

"Not at all," Chilton said. "Actually little is known of what happened down there beyond Maximilian's execution. I want to hear all about it. You were there."

"So we marched to San Juan de Río. Our objective was to destroy the garrison."

"You mean you and your friend didn't act independently? If so, did President Juárez give you the order?"

"I never saw Juárez until after the war. Father Alberto Garza, a defrocked priest who had assembled our little army of peasants, gave the order to take San Juan. He was our commander, though he refused to be called general and adopted no military trappings. He remained plain Father Garza. A great leader. The people loved him."

Chilton clapped his hands. "Another revelation. A priest leading an army of peasants! Why was he defrocked?"

"Because he'd sided with Juárez against the church."

"I see. What did you find at San Juan?"

"Nothing to our liking. We'd expected an encampment of sorts or the enemy occupying the village. Instead, they were behind a three-story stone fortress. We had no artillery. We had to draw 'em out somehow." He paused to think back. "We slipped one Spencer company down into a brushy arroyo,

52

with Cullen Floyd in command. There they'd outflank any-thing coming out of the fort. The other company we posted back under cover in the timber with the reserves, armed mostly with Enfields. I was with Father Garza, who would pass on any command in Spanish. Next we positioned an Enfield company of sharpshooters at the edge of the pines. They started firing at sentries on the walls. We wanted to avoid showing our true strength, else they wouldn't come out after us. For a while nothing changed. Were they coming or not? Then a bugle sounded in the fort, and the big gate opened, and we saw infantry filing out. Clad in red trousers, flashy shell jackets, and smart kepis. They formed a column of fours and advanced on the sharpshooters in the pines at the double quick. Their one officer, a natty fellow, marched on the right flank . . . sword out. Just one company. About seventy-five men. Very professional. As they advanced, I had the impression of battle-hardened veterans who'd fought on foreign soil other than Mexico's. They struck me as arrogant. They'd teach these primitive Mexican Indians a lesson. Now, would our boys stand and fight or panic? You never know what green troops will do the first time under fire!"

Chilton nodded. "Quite so. Sometimes one man will skedaddle and that starts it. Sometimes one man will shout . . . 'Come on' . . . and they'll rally around him. Continue, Captain. I find this intriguing."

Jesse said: "Then the unexpected happened. Our sharp-shooter company, instead of falling back deeper into the timber as planned, took it on themselves to charge the Legionnaires, machetes swinging. The Spencer company in the arroyo opened up on the last half of the Legionnaire outfit with flanking fire, but had to hold up to keep from hitting our boys now fighting hand-to-hand. The Legionnaires had made the mistake of not fixing bayonets. They started to break. I told Father Garza to call our boys back. He did. Now more red-trousered infantry came pouring out of the fort . . . three companies, bayonets fixed this time. While we brought up the other Spencer company to the edge of the pines, one of the enemy formed a front and charged the arroyo. They did it in splendid style, shouting, firing, and reloading fast as they advanced. Floyd's Spencers cut them down. Another company charged the pines on a run. A volley from the Spencers slowed them. Still, they came on. The repeaters banged again. This time the red trousers halted . . . they seemed bewildered. Another volley so soon from muzzleloaders? What was wrong? When the third Spencer volley struck, they started to mill, then run." Jesse put a hand to his chin, reaching for other details.

"By this time where was the third company of Legionnaires?" Major Gordon asked.

Jesse nodded. "Yes. Where was it? We'd lost it momentarily in all the excitement and smoke. Well, it was wheeling fast on our open left flank, on the double quick. With the Spencer company busy, we brought up two muzzleloader companies in a rush. They started firing by rank . . . which doubled their rate of fire . . . the first rank kneeling . . . doing just as we'd trained them and their peasant officers. And I tell you I felt proud. I'd like to say that it ended there and our side behaved like disciplined troops. But when the Legionnaires broke, the boys gave chase, machetes out. They'd charge a bunch of red trousers like savage bulls . . . they'd cut 'em down and go on, macheting even those trying to surrender. Running amuck . . . out of control. An avenging mob. We finally got 'em back in some sort of loose order, thanks to the *padre,* but not until they'd even stood some Legionnaires against a wall and executed 'em." He was scowling, seeing and feeling it all again, the exultation of sweet victory marred by his anger and disgust at the senseless after-slaughter.

"Then what?" Chilton asked.

"It was a big victory for Mexico. Word spread fast. We started getting volunteers from as far as Sonora. Our ranks swelled. Before long, we had over a thousand men, and they kept coming. Some brought their families, which helped instead of hindered, cutting down on the going back and forth to farm. To hasten the green boys' training, we mixed them in with the veterans, instead of forming all new companies and battalions. Still short of rifles, sometimes two men would share the same old Enfield. But every man furnished his own machete."

"What about supplies?" Chilton asked. "That was a considerable number of men to feed."

"There were plenty of cattle on the big ranches, and we helped ourselves. If some high and mighty *hacendado* objected, Father Garza would pay him a visit and come back with a loaded pack train. Sometimes there was blood on the saddle packs. The *padre* was a most persuasive man, one way or another. When we moved camp, it was like a migration . . . men, women, children, dogs, burros, mules, and a herd of cattle."

Chilton shook his head in wonderment.

"Truth is," Jesse said, smiling, "I ate better with the *padre*'s army than I often did in the Army of Tennessee. Well, the French didn't try to retake San Juan. We won a series of hot skirmishes, kept after 'em. They pulled out of Chihuahua City, began a slow retreat toward Mexico City. Then they made a stand at the *Presidio Montaña*, another stone fortress with towers. We tried to draw 'em out with sharpshooter fire again, but they wouldn't take the bait a second time. A long siege was out of the question with our limited supplies." He moistened his lips, the scenes like prints in his mind. "However, there was a church tower about a hundred and fifty yards from the *Presidio*. If we could get an artillery piece up there, we could fire down into the compound. At San Juan we'd captured a twelve-pound Napoleon. So we unbolted it and muscled the pieces and the carriage up the steps to the belfry."

"Ingenious," Chilton murmured.

"After a few rounds, we got the range, and the French came out after us . . . they had to. By that time their barracks buildings were burning, and we hit them when they formed in company strength inside the compound. Meanwhile, we had the Spencer companies waiting in position. With the repeaters and the twelve-pounder firing canister when they came out, it was soon over."

"Many prisoners?"

"Several hundred, kept under close guard. Some Juáristas still wanted to execute 'em. But no more of that. We kept driving south, fighting pitched battles as we went. Our army kept growing. My friend, Cullen Floyd, died in a charge. Suddenly it was all finished at Querétaro, when Maximilian surrendered, and President Juárez ordered him shot with two Mexican generals." He sat back, finished. He would tell them no more. If he said that as a Citizen General he'd pleaded vainly with Juárez to spare the three lives, he'd sound self-glorifying, or that he was known in Mexico as *El Soldado del Pelo Blanco,* the soldier with the white hair. Neither would he tell them about Ana. That had no place here.

Colonel Chilton stepped to a cabinet. From it he took a bottle of whiskey and three small glasses. At his desk he filled the glasses and handed one to Jesse and another to Major Gordon. Lifting his own glass, he said: "To you, Captain Wilder. A most fascinating and unusual account. Your experiences are remarkable. You have my utmost respect and admiration as a fellow soldier, sir. I feel highly honored to know you."

"Yes, indeed," said Gordon, raising his glass.

For a moment, Jesse was put at a loss. "I . . . I thank you, gentlemen. I guess what it all comes down to is that I'm a survivor. Why, God only knows. I do not. I've often wondered." He'd spoken simply, without pretense.

He found the bourbon excellent, befitting the post commander. They sat in silence, the only sounds the distant commands and the jingling of horses moving on the parade ground. When the glasses were empty, Chilton looked at Jesse. "Major Gordon said he was told at Fort Cummings that you declined the offer of civilian scout."

Jesse nodded.

"May I ask why, Captain? And excuse my delving."

"It's simple, Colonel. I'm tired of fighting. I've carried a rifle since 'Sixty-One."

"Which I can truly understand. The reason I'm asking so many personal questions, which I hope you will pardon, is because a situation of unusual international importance has arisen that requires a special type of man. One of them is Major Gordon, here, whose service in the Shenandoah Valley with General Sheridan was outstanding."

Jesse was feeling uneasy. *Now it's coming.*

"About a month ago," Chilton said, frowning, "*Señorita Alicia Reyes*, only daughter of the governor of Sonora, was traveling under escort when bandits attacked. They wiped out the escort and took her and her *duenna* prisoner. They are now being held for a ransom of two million *pesos* at a stronghold in the foothills of the Sierra Madre near the village of La Gloria. That's a great deal of money even for a governor to raise in a short time." Chilton paused as if to collect his thoughts concisely. "In desperation, Don Emanuel Reyes has requested the United States, through the State Department, to help. President Johnson, who is eager to improve relations along the border, has directed that it be done. Hence, Major Gordon's sudden arrival. All this is on the q. t., of course. It can't be known publicly that American troops are going down into the Sierra Madre. It's a matter of national pride in Mexico, which is very touchy, that goes back to its war with us. We have to respect their feelings."

Jesse jogged his head in understanding. An old weariness moved through him. "Has the governor mounted a rescue effort?"

"He's been warned that his daughter and the *duenna* will be executed if he tries. So he's stalling for time while he dickers back and forth by messenger and tries to raise the money, which he isn't likely to do. He was a newspaper editor of modest means in Hermosillo before he became a Juárista leader in Sonora. As you know, Mexico is poor. Sonora is one of its poorest states, devastated for years by Apache raids and bandits. Commerce between towns is at a virtual standstill down there. The leader of the bandits calls himself *El Tigre*."

"How much time does the governor have?"

"*El Tigre* has set a deadline two weeks from yesterday to have the ransom in hand. Time is fleeting."

"What is known about this self-styled Tiger?"

"Very little, except that he's overrun the area for some years, growing stronger as the poverty worsens. The people of La Gloria are cowed and afraid to raise a hand against him. A few dared. They disappeared. He rules by fear and a few ostentatious gratuities. Yet some regard him as a benefactor, because he spends money in the *cantina* and a few stores. At rare times, he hands out a little food and cheap clothing, even throws them a few *pesos*. Makes a big show of it."

"A little can seem like a great deal in Mexico when you've been poor all your life. How many in the bandit band?"

"Reports are vague. But always a large band. It's increased

58

within the past year, Governor Reyes says."

"How would I figure in all this?" Jesse asked curiously, though he could already see the shape of things that never seemed to change.

Chilton had a manner of looking straight at a man and instilling in him confidence in what he was about to tell him. He did so now. "We are forming an unofficial rescue mission from here. Major Gordon will be in command. The detail, or detachment, necessarily will be small, unobtrusive, dressed like miners. It can't look like an expedition, in keeping with Mexico's sensitivity about Americans on Mexican soil. In short, Captain, we want you to go along as scout. Do you speak Spanish?"

"Enough."

"Fine! It's what we need . . . in addition to your invaluable experience. The United States government will deposit one thousand dollars in your name here if you agree to go. An additional five thousand will be yours if the mission is successful."

"If not?"

"You would still have your one thousand."

Even a thousand dollars was a lot of money on the Southwestern frontier, Jesse realized, but this had gone on long enough. He was being drawn into something beyond his will. He came to his feet. "Colonel, I understand the situation and know something about Mexican bandits, having fought them in Chihuahua. They're worse than Apaches, because they wear two faces and oppress their own people. I feel for the governor. I fear for the safety of the women. But I'm not your man, sir. I've . . . I've just seen too much fighting. I know you understand. You, gentlemen, please excuse me."

Nodding to both officers, he abruptly left the room.

He thought next of his horse and mule, but it was too late

to leave now. He'd need an early start for Tucson, which was about three days' ride. Let his stock rest and enjoy another day of Army feed.

Thinking of camping needs, he went to the post trader's store and purchased tinned food, coffee beans, a small sack of flour, a slab of bacon wrapped in heavy paper, pipe tobacco, a box of matches, two bottles of tequila, a hunting knife, underclothes, a gray flannel shirt, and two pairs of heavy socks.

The trader, a roundish, ruddy-faced, gregarious man, said: "I reckon you're gettin' ready to pull out?"

"Just passin' through."

"Well, if you're headin' for Tucson, be on the lookout for Apaches. Gettin' harder and harder to get merchandise in here from the west. Might be a good idea to travel at night."

"Might," Jesse agreed. Somehow yesterday's anticipation of traveling on had dulled. The situation at La Gloria bothered him. Another instance of a lawless land where often life wasn't worth more than a string of chiles or a lame burro. He could use the money. But if he took it, he'd be nothing more than a mercenary, as worthy as the mission was.

He walked to the barracks and began packing his purchases, his mind alternating between leaving and the mission. He looked up as Major Gordon came in.

"I'm not hounding you," Gordon said, "and I want you to know that I respect your decision. However, there wasn't time to tell you everything. I think you should know that some deserters from the French army have joined *El Tigre*'s band. Our information is that they belonged to a Colonel Dubray's regiment, the Sixth Hussars."

Jesse flung around, startled, aware of old emotions slamming through him. He was stunned. "Dubray . . . Colonel Dubray, you say?"

"A Colonel Jacques Dubray. You know of him? If so, Colonel Chilton thought perhaps you could provide some information that would be valuable to the mission."

"I know him, all right. He was the notorious Colonel Dubray, in command at San Juan and the *Presidio Montaña*. He got away from us at San Juan. Slipped out the rear of the fort with some of his staff. Tried the same tactic at the *Presidio*. But we were waiting. I shot the bastard out of the saddle myself. It was also a personal matter. You see, Major, he led the Sixth's raid on the Juárista camp that killed my Mexican wife, Ana, and many others. She was going to have our child."

The shock of Jesse's words left Gordon without reply for a moment. Then he spoke in a voice deep with feeling: "I'm very sorry, Wilder. Very sorry, indeed."

"That's war," Jesse said, finding his voice again. "The innocents are often caught in between, as you well know. Why I feel used up. Why I keep on the move, I guess." He paced back and forth, in a state that surprised him after all the time that had passed. Pausing, he crossed his arms and put his left hand to his face, feeling the pain rising in him as vivid and wrenching as ever. *The 6th Hussars. A brutal bunch of bastards around San Juan. A Legionnaire regiment, recruited from the dregs of Europe.* With a sudden, impulsive movement, he turned to Gordon. "Tell Colonel Chilton I'll consider going as scout. But I need some time. I'll let him know by this afternoon. I know time is critical."

Gordon looked at him searchingly. "Very well, Captain. I understand how you feel. But think about it before you decide for sure. You could wait till morning."

"I'd better decide today. Get it done with."

Time seemed to stand still. He stayed to himself in the barracks, trying to sort things out, supposing he was a damned fool even to consider going. In a thrust of painful thought, he tried to divert his mind from what had happened in Mexico, but could not. He could look back and see again, quite clearly, step by step, what had led to what was to have been his last ride with the Juáristas before he took Ana to El Paso to start their new life.

Cullen had said: "Father Alberto wants to take most of the command south tomorrow where a villager's reported a big camp of Hussars. We'll leave one company here. I'm not askin' you to go, ol' Reb. Just thought you ought to know."

Cared for by Ana, Jesse had recently recovered from a long bout of fever. Should he go or not? He need not take part in the fighting. Just go along as an advisor. Let the Juáristas know that their cause was still his, now that he was able-bodied. A farewell show of arms.

Ana had clung to him throughout the night, as if sensing what he would do, and, when morning came, he'd said: "I've decided to go with the boys. This will be the last time."

She hadn't objected, but in the fathomless black Indian eyes he could read dread and great fear. "I know you go," she had said. "I know last night. I no want you go. I afraid for you. But you go. You man. You fight for my Mexico."

And when the red horse had been saddled and he had come to the front of the tent, she regarded him a long time without speaking. He had kissed her again and again. There was nothing more to be said.

"Go with God," she had said, and he had felt her arms releasing him.

When he had joined the command and had looked back, she had been watching. He had waved. She had waved, a picture he took with him, framed in his mind. Already the morning had turned forbidding.

But the villager's report was only a ruse to draw the main command away while the Hussars had struck the camp. By the time the Juáristas had seen through the deception, they had been too late. It had hardly mattered that the villager, a French informant, later had paid with his life.

Jesse didn't know how long he'd sat there, his mind locked on the past. But much time had passed. It was afternoon now, and he could hear the sounds of troops at drill.

He seemed in the grip of a strange inertia, a sort of painful stupor, an inaction he fought against, torn this way and that. He got up and walked out. For a little while he absently watched the wheeling troops. Presently, he found himself drawn to the stables, seeing the red horse and mule busy filling up on government hay. As Jesse approached, the horse, ever wary, snuffled and turned his head. Jesse's eyes went to the red ribbon still adorning the black mane, made so by loving hands.

He froze in mid-step, his gaze fixed. He knew then that he was going. He could never even the score. But he could strike one more blow. *One more.*

Chapter Four

When he entered the C.O.'s office, Chilton and Gordon were waiting. By the colonel's desk stood a large map tacked upright on a wooden stand. Chilton waved him to a chair and said: "Major Gordon tells me you've decided to reconsider your decision. I appreciate that, Captain, particularly in view of your great personal loss, which the major told me about, and for which you have my sincere sympathy, believe me."

"Thank you, sir. I know first hand what the Hussars did around San Juan. Their brutal pillaging and terrorizing and raping and murdering. It's like a call from the past that I can't ignore. I've decided to go as scout, serve any way I can."

"Fine! It couldn't be appreciated more. We need your experience. Your pay will be as I first stated. A thousand on deposit here now. Plus five thousand on your return after a successful mission. Is that satisfactory?"

"More than satisfactory, Colonel. I really hadn't thought about the pay. My first concern is the size of the rescue party, which you said will be kept small. How many men will go?"

"As of now twenty-three . . . in addition to you and Major Gordon and the guide, Governor Reyes's son, Agustín."

"Going up against a band of well-armed bandits and Hussar thugs. Twenty-three of us armed with single-shot Springfield carbines." Jesse smiled wryly, weighing the odds, realizing he'd let old emotions override his better judgment. Once again, as in Mexico with the Juáristas, he'd let himself be drawn into another cause. Well, so be it. He was determined to go.

Chilton nodded. "I know what you're thinking, and you echo my own concern. We'll be outmanned and outgunned, which we'll offset by leadership and discipline and purpose. I wish we had Spencers, but there's no way we can requisition by courier and get any in here before you leave. California has none, and Fort Bliss' entire stock of repeaters has been transported to Fort Clark at Bracketville, way down on the lower Río Grande, to fight Comanches and Kickapoos, the latter raiding across from their haunts in Mexico. Washington wasn't thinking of ordnance when the operation was approved, only of the need to hurry."

Jesse gave a little jerk of his head. This was shaping up as one hell of a fight.

"In addition to the Springfields," the colonel stressed, "each man will be armed with two Colt Army Forty-Four revolvers. I doubt that *El Tigre*'s ruffians will carry side arms that good. Each man will carry sixty rounds for the revolvers and two hundred rounds for the carbines."

"That's good. Speaking of the men, Colonel, you said twenty-three volunteers *as of now*. Does that mean the operation will be increased soon? That's a mighty slim force."

"I'm acting under strict orders . . . no more than twenty-five cavalrymen. It takes a particular breed of man on a demanding mission of this caliber. The official thinking is that a unit this small dressed as miners will attract no unusual attention. Agustín Reyes tells me that *El Tigre* has spies in all the little villages north of La Gloria . . . San Miguel, Bavispe, Bacerac . . . to warn him of any Mexican regulars or irregulars threatening from the direction of Fronteras, northwest of La Gloria."

Gordon broke a short reflective pause when he asked: "Colonel, what if a roving Mexican command stops and demands to know what we're doing on Mexican soil?"

"I was coming to that. There are rag-tag outfits patrolling west out of Janos in Chihuahua and back and forth from Fronteras, south of us, on the lookout for Apaches. My impression is they usually aren't very effective, since Apaches aren't fools enough to fight them out in the open. However, you will carry written permission from the governor to engage in mining exploration in the general vicinity of the Sierra Madre . . . of course, in co-operation with the Sonoran government. The paper will show an official stamp. Looks very official. Young Reyes brought it late yesterday. It will be carried in a very official-looking dispatch case. There is no mention of La Gloria in the permit. Less said the better."

"I'm surprised that the governor of Sonora hasn't rooted out this *El Tigre* band," Gordon said.

"The governor tried it about a year ago without much effect. His force of two hundred was more like militia. Not regulars. There was a nasty little fight west of La Gloria. A virtual stand-off. Then the bandits just evaporated into the mountains or broke up into smaller groups heading for the neighboring villages, which shelter them out of fear. They suffered some losses. Agustín thinks his sister's kidnapping stems as revenge for those losses."

"I still think it could be done with an adequate command," Gordon insisted.

Chilton regarded him intently, his expression somewhat grim. "You're going to have to do it with far less, Major. Necessity limits us. And time is upon us. You will depart no later than day after tomorrow. That barely gives me time to complete the detachment and make all arrangements. Unfortunately, I can't spare the post's one doctor, a contract surgeon at that, to accompany you."

Gordon seemed to settle that in his mind while he rubbed his jaw and nodded.

66

"The troopers on the mission, sir," Jesse said, "I suppose they're all volunteers?"

Chilton hesitated and glanced at Gordon, as if for support. A little run of cryptic silence followed. Then he said: "Yes . . . they're all volunteers, a special group of volunteers, you might say. At the moment, they're all in the guardhouse. We're only an undermanned three-troop post out here, Captain, and, when I asked the command for volunteers for a mission into Mexico . . . not stating the exact nature of it then . . . only men in the guardhouse volunteered. They did so to the man. Partly out of boredom, perhaps . . . mainly, I think, for a chance to clear their records. If none had volunteered, we'd have had to pick the best men and treat the mission like any other operation."

Jesse sat a bit straighter, inwardly taken aback; otherwise, he showed no surprise. After all these years, he guessed he'd reached that point in life where nothing the military did, North or South, surprised him, for better or worse, logical or as senseless as General Hood's repeated massed infantry charges against entrenched Yankees at Franklin armed with repeating rifles.

"These men," Chilton continued, a terse flatness entering his voice, "face charges ranging from desertion to insubordination, from destroying government property to trying to sell mounts and weapons to civilians, from attempted murder over a woman, to striking an officer."

"I suppose they can be trusted?" Jesse said, not without some doubt. He'd served with many types of men through the war years, a mix of brawlers and gentlemen, sneak thieves and liars, the greedy and the sharing, cowards and color-bearers. Tough soldiers, for the most part. Poor pay, hardships, the same food day after day, long hours of guard duty, manual labor around the post, and lack of amusements made frontier

67

duty monotonous and sometimes intolerable. The only thing that counted was how a man stood up in battle, and it wasn't always the loud ones who did, nor the quiet ones who didn't.

"Major Gordon has asked the same question," Chilton replied, "and with good reason. If the mission is successful, their records will be cleared of all charges. As you know from the charges, some of these men have felonies hanging over their heads. If convicted, they'd be transported immediately to Leavenworth prison. So, for them, the mission is well worth the chance to better themselves. Also beats being bound and gagged, spread-eagled on a wagon wheel, and carrying a forty-pound log around the parade ground for days."

"What happens to them if the mission fails?"

"The old saying about crossing the bridge when you get to it fits this situation. Just volunteering to go on the mission would constitute a mitigating factor." His face hardened. He made a sweeping motion. "This has to succeed, coming from the highest directive, the President himself." He turned to Gordon. "Major, I'm sure you have questions other than what we discussed earlier?"

"Yes, Colonel. I have gone over all the volunteers' records. Most are what you'd call habitual offenders, not averse to just about anything from stealing a comrade's last dollar to outright murder. And most are continually in fights."

"Exactly one reason why they volunteered . . . they're fighters. In general, most have been damned tough horse soldiers in the field campaigning against Apaches . . . better than the average trooper." A tiny glint of self-mockery crossed his face. "Perhaps I should say the few times we've caught up with Apaches and fought 'em on our terms. To put it another way, some of these prisoners are among our best men, when not in the guardhouse for brawling and getting drunk, not uncommon offenses these days in the frontier cavalry. In view of getting their records cleared, especially those charged with felonies, I believe these men will have the incentive to bring this mission to a successful conclusion."

He was, Jesse saw, being wholly blunt and determined to stick to his view about the worthiness of the volunteers, not unlike a man trying hard to believe what he wanted to believe.

Gordon, as if not to be sidetracked, said: "One man in particular held my attention. Former Sergeant Bickford . . . Rufe Bickford. Been busted so many times for getting drunk and fighting that he must put his chevrons on with hooks and eyes. I found that he's in for severely beating one Private Elias Lane over a Mexican girl at that saloon and gambling dive just off the military reservation commonly referred to as a hog ranch."

"If Lane dies before you leave, Bickford will not go," Chilton assured. "He'll remain here to face a general court-martial and very likely will be found guilty, judging from the evidence. Too bad. His short-lived promotions have come from exemplary duty in the field. He served three years in the Army of the Potomac, Pleasanton's First Division . . . was mustered out as a sergeant. Apparently got bored and reënlisted. It's back at the post where he gets into trouble. Whiskey and women, plus a cantankerous nature. Might say, a typical horse soldier."

"What is Lane's condition, sir?"

"Right now he's hanging on. Semi-conscious."

"If he's near death when we leave, and Bickford is permitted to go," Gordon said, "I should think that would prompt him to go over the hill at the first chance on the march, figuring that Lane would be dead when he got back."

"It might. But, based on his record in the field, I'm gambling that he wouldn't desert under those circumstances."

"I guess what I'm coming around to, Colonel, is if a man

tries to desert, shall I shoot him, if I can? There'd hardly be time to track him down."

"You also will be traveling under my verbal orders, Major, which, as you know, will not appear in the official order and are quite flexible. In other words, use your own judgment as determined by what you're up against. If a man tries to desert, shoot him at once. However, I can't see a lone trooper deserting in Apache country, if he wants to stay alive very long. I should think they'll stick with the detachment."

"The records show several others as potential trouble-makers," Gordon said, looking at cards taken from a jacket pocket. "Former Private First Class Hugh Kaufman, in for desertion and stealing government equipment. To wit, one six-year-old bay horse, and all the horse furniture, and all the issued arms. A bold devil. Sneaked off from the post in broad daylight after drill. Caught ten miles on the road to Tucson, going at a gallop. Made no resistance when captured. In Tucson, he probably could've sold the mount and horse furniture and carbine and revolver for a fat price, enough to get him to the California gold fields with some to spare. Brought back lashed face down across the saddle as an object lesson. During the war, he would've been shot on the spot. I see he's been up and down, but no higher than P.F.C. Usually on report."

He looked at another card. "And there is Private Isaac Cramer, in for insubordination. Never been promoted. Likes to fight and gamble and get drunk. Refused to go on a wood-cutting detail into the mountains. Played sick. After examination by the contract surgeon and refusing to take the usual cure of quinine and Epsom salts, was declared fit for duty. Still refused to go. So far his most serious offense, which is bad enough. Spends about as much time in the brig as he does on duty. And there is Private John Webb, in for cursing and striking Second Lieutenant Ben Myles. Made corporal

70

once . . . just once. Busted and never promoted again." He looked up at the colonel. "No further information. Sir, I wonder what the circumstances were?"

Chilton said: "The lieutenant, who was fresh from West Point, took a detail out on scout. Webb was on a mount that was particularly hard to handle. He kept jerking the animal, which the lieutenant thought was excessive. The lieutenant reprimanded Webb. Then the cursing and striking. Webb returned to the post under guard. Likely what led to that was the whiskey Webb had in his canteen. I regret to say it, but drunkenness is the bane of the frontier cavalry. On payday we've had as many as twenty per cent of the post's enlisted personnel in the guardhouse for being drunk and disorderly. Even spread-eagling a man doesn't seem to reduce rate of the offenses, nor does burying the bottle, which is no trifling chore out here in this flinty soil . . . digging a hole ten feet square by ten feet deep, burying the bottle, and filling in the hole again. It helps to sweat out the whiskey. Those men in for minor offenses have already started serving their sentences. Those facing felonies still face trial. The mission must sound like a pretty good gamble to them."

"Also there is Private Patrick Connelly," Gordon resumed. "Evidently a true son of the Old Sod. In the last three months, he has been in the brig six times for fighting. Last payday he took on two at once."

"And whipped 'em both," Chilton said, with satisfaction.

"In target-range training I see that he's rated first class as a marksman."

"Which means he hit the target six out of ten shots at four hundred yards or less."

Gordon grinned dryly. "Guess we can use him."

Other troopers were discussed briefly, and then Jesse, thinking more details needed to be gone over, asked about

71

the distance to La Gloria.

"Approximately a hundred and forty miles as a crow flies," Chilton said. "Add thirty or forty to that by winding trails. You should be able to make it in a week or less."

"I would suggest, Colonel," Jesse responded, "that we not push the mounts faster than twenty-five or thirty miles a day . . . that the march be made at a walk to save the horses. That horses and pack mules should be reshod before we leave, and that each animal carry an extra set of shoes and a supply of nails."

Chilton and Gordon both nodded. "Basic needs," Chilton said, "often overlooked in a hurry. That will be done."

"Also, Colonel, that we lead two extra saddled mounts. Going down they can carry something."

"Yes. Mounts for the women. Good. I hadn't come to that." Chilton stepped to the map and pointed. "For one thing, water won't be a problem. A rare advantage in the Southwest. You'll depart from San Bernardino Springs, here on the border, two days' ride or more from Bowie. I will post a troop at the springs soon after you depart, in a state of twenty-four hour readiness, under orders to cross the border if necessary. From the springs you'll strike southeast down the San Bernardino River, which is the most northerly branch of the Yaqui." He traced a slanting course with a forefinger. "Down here, you'll follow the Bavispe River. La Gloria sits at the foot of the Sierra Madre, and the Bavispe River flows nearby. I'll see that you get a map to take along, Major."

The conversation switched to other specifics. Chilton said the detachment would take thirty pounds of grain for each horse and pack mule, which he called "short rations." And hatchets for firewood, a dog tent for every two men, and eight days' rations. "Carry nothing you can do without. Any good cavalryman should be able to stretch one day's rations into

72

three. Any further questions or suggestions, Major?"

"Not at the moment, sir."

"Captain Wilder?"

"This may seem like a small thing, sir, and perhaps needless on a fast march. But I suggest that each man carry two blankets. It gets cold in the Sierra Madre."

"The extra blanket will be included."

"And in the rations I would include some extra coffee."

"Spoken like a true cavalryman, Mister Wilder. Coffee alone will keep a man going long after rations play out."

For some minutes the three discussed the terrain and what to expect.

"You will find much devastation below the border," Chilton said, making a sweeping gesture across the lower section of the map. "Northern Sonora is like an economic vassal for the Chiricahua Apaches. A virtually defenseless land where they raid at will, take what they please, but leave enough so there will be something to come back for next time. The villages are like beleaguered outposts. Sometimes the Apaches come in and trade for mescal. Then all hell breaks loose, and the villagers fort up in their homes. A tough life down there. Not that the Mexicans don't fight back. When the people go into the fields, they travel in groups and post guards around while they till their corn and bean and chile patches. If the Apaches are threatened by Mexican regulars, they merely fade into the Sierra Madre, knowing the soldiers aren't foolhardy enough to follow and march into an ambush."

"Apaches," Gordon said slowly. "I'd almost overlooked them except as a distant threat. Any suggestions, Colonel?"

"Put out flankers. Post pickets at night. Hobble your mounts."

"Captain?" Gordon asked.

73

"Be up and ready before dawn, which is their favorite time to attack. Or at sundown, when the light is bad, which makes the shooting bad, and they come jumping. Another favorite tactic is to set up an ambush where an outfit will cross a deep wash, posting warriors in the brush and rocks on the far side. Not firing until the lead riders reach the middle of the wash. The situation can get very confused. Riders going down. Horses bolting. Then the Apaches charge, yelling like demons as only an Apache can yell. I learned that in a telling way with some Juáristas in Chihuahua. A fearful experience you never forget. To this day, I never cross a wash without first scanning the other side with great care."

He didn't tell them that in the initial charge he'd killed at least five Apaches, probably more, with the Spencer, and was on his third seven-shot tube when the Apaches broke. The repeater had saved the little escort. *Now,* he thought grimly, *approximately the same number of us are heading back into Mexico, and like before, only one repeater in the outfit.* He still questioned his judgment in going, but he had given his word and so wouldn't back out.

"The only reported Apache activity in recent weeks has been west of the springs along the border," Chilton said. "They hit a trader's outfit bound for Tucson. Chief Loco's band. That places them well off your course. Now, gentlemen, I want you to meet Agustín Reyes, who's been resting after his long ride." He called for an orderly to bring Reyes.

He was there in moments, as if he'd been nearby, waiting impatiently to be called, a slim, proud young man in linen shirt under a short buckskin jacket, gray sombrero, leather breeches, and sharp-toed boots. There were silver spurs at his heels and a revolver on his right hip. The black eyes and quick smile in the high-boned, mustached face of classical features expressed instant cordiality. He swept off his hat and smiled graciously. Jesse guessed him no older than twenty-one or -two.

Colonel Chilton made the introductions, Gordon first, and referred to Jesse as "Captain Wilder, late of the Confederate Army of Tennessee."

Reyes shook hands eagerly, visibly impressed.

"Major Gordon has just arrived from the East," Chilton said, "and will command the La Gloria mission. Among other duties, he served with distinction under General Sheridan. Captain Wilder will go as scout. He more recently trained and fought with Juáristas in Chihuahua. He was at Querétaro when Maximilian surrendered."

Reyes shook hands again. "*Señor* Captain, you have my utmost gratitude for your services to my Mexico."

"It was a worthwhile cause," Jesse said.

"My father and I heard many stories about your army."

"Father Alberto Garza was in command. I hope you heard of him? A great leader. A fine man."

"Yes! The unfrocked priest who assembled an army of peasants. You must tell me more about him, *Señor* Captain."

"There is much to tell."

When all were seated, the colonel went over the details again for Reyes, and the departure was set for day after to-morrow.

"*Señor* Colonel," Reyes said, his voice rising with emotion, right hand over his heart, "I extend to you and the major and the captain and to His Excellency, your *Presidente* Johnson, the heartfelt gratefulness of my family. Alicia, my little sister . . . my only sister . . . is the flower of our family. We Reyeses will never forget your efforts. These *bandidos* are another sorrow of my Mexico, and we have many. They're like wild beasts preying on innocent people."

75

"It's going to be a very difficult mission," Chilton said, "but it can be carried out. Have you ever been to La Gloria?"

"I was there a few months ago, planning to buy cattle. It didn't work out. There were so few cattle to buy."

"Did you hear much of this *El Tigre?*"

"Only in whispers. The people live in great fear. Those who do speak out in public are probably his spies, hoping to draw out those against him."

"Where is his stronghold in relation to La Gloria?"

"He has taken over the headquarters of what was once a small ranch or hacienda, abandoned some years ago because of Apache raids, and built a wall around the main buildings, the house and stables and storerooms, and added a barracks for his men. It's a virtual *presidio, Señor* Colonel. It overlooks the Bavispe River and La Gloria. The villagers call it La Hacienda. You can see sentries on the parapet. He's built towers at the corners of the wall and one by the huge wooden gate."

"So you did get a close look at the place?"

"I rode past it and back, on the river road, out of curiosity. I could feel eyes. I felt I was being watched every step my horse took. It gave me a cold feeling. It is an evil place. Now a prison for our Alicia and Rosa, her *duenna*. I worry constantly how they are being treated. As you say, it will be difficult getting them out."

"By chance, did you learn anything about this *El Tigre?* His background? His habits?"

"I was told, in whispers, that he started out as a mule driver in Chihuahua, known as one Juan Silva. Next he turned cattle rustler, and then bandit, with a small gang. When the chase got close in Chihuahua, he'd slip over into the Sierra Madre around La Gloria. When chased hard in Sonora, he'd slip back into Chihuahua. But he'd always return to around

76

La Gloria. My father came very close to catching him once. We think that is why he took Alicia." Reyes paused. "Habits? Once a week he rides into the plaza at La Gloria and gets drunk in the *cantina*, and throws a handful of *pesos* around for public effect, with him always his bodyguards. He goes nowhere without them."

"Something to remember," Gordon said. "How many bodyguards?"

Reyes studied a moment. "Twenty or more . . . at least twenty. He rides a beautiful white Arabian stallion, stolen in Chihuahua, always surrounded by his bodyguards."

"About a platoon," Gordon observed.

"These bodyguards," Jesse asked. "Are there Hussars among them?"

"Some. How many I don't know. It's my impression that he trusts them more than his own men. I was told that his lieutenant is a huge Hussar also known for his cruelty. He had a red beard of which he is most proud. A vain man. He is called *El Hombre Grande* . . . the big man. I gathered that most of *El Tigre*'s men fear and hate him. If they try to desert, they are shot."

"No doubt the bodyguards go well armed."

"To the teeth, *Señor* Captain. Rifles and carbines and huge pistols at their belts and beeg knives, which they like to brandish to intimidate further the poor people of La Gloria. Two bandoleers across each bodyguard's chest. Very impressive!" His voice shook. "Brutes, they are! Parents have sent their young daughters away. Only a few whores remain."

"What does *El Tigre* look like?"

"A short, thickset man, they say, with bushy brows. A broad mustache and piercing black eyes which are constantly moving. He always dresses in a suit of white linen. The villagers say it is the eyes you remember. They try not to look

77

at him directly when he rides by or dismounts . . . because the eyes frighten them. He seems to see right through a person."

"You learned much in the short time you were there, Mister Reyes," Gordon complimented him. "All this will be helpful in some way."

"*Gracias, Señor* Major."

Chilton glanced about, waiting. When no one spoke, he said: "Tomorrow morning I'll muster the volunteers and you can look them over. Some may back out, after thinking about it. Thank you, gentlemen."

Dismissed, Jesse went to his quarters. Now that he had decided to go, he found himself in a thoughtful mood, his mind oddly on home, when he had no home. He would write his one friend back in Petersburg, Tennessee, Mr. Sawyer, who had suggested that Jesse contest his father's will, which left everything to Jesse's sister, Mary Elizabeth Somerville, now living in Lexington, Kentucky, and Jesse's brother, Claiborne, now of Corinth, Mississippi. Jesse was the youngest of the three. He had refused to fight the will's provisions, saying it was his father's right to dispose of his holdings as he wished. What hurt most was loss of family, loss of the past, which had been a happy one when his dear mother lived. Mary Elizabeth, married young, was gone from home when Jesse was growing up, and he and Claiborne, the spoiled first son, had never been close. Jesse was always the tag-along, always left out and ignored, often teased to his despair. When the war broke out, Claiborne had obtained a government post with a major's commission in Atlanta and fled to New Orleans before the city fell. Claiborne, who with the sister wouldn't agree to sharing the estate with Jesse at Mr. Sawyer's suggestion, thinking as their father had about Jesse's wearing a Yankee uniform out West, which they regarded as a family dishonor . . . never to be forgiven, suh! Never!

Fire-eating Claiborne, Jesse recalled, shaking his head, who had never fired a shot in the war. Claiborne, always so high on honor, but had never served in the field in any capacity.

Sighing, he crossed to the post trader's for paper and pen and on a counter there began writing:

Dear Mr. Sawyer:

Instead of going on farther west, as I expected when I last wrote you from Fort Cummings, I find myself in southern Arizona at Fort Bowie about to embark on a special mission into the Mexican state of Sonora, the details and purpose of which I cannot divulge at this time. I will go as a U.S. cavalry scout with a small detachment of special volunteers.

Much has happened since my last letter. I took part with cavalry in the submission of a gang of cut-throats preying on immigrant trains on the old Butterfield Trail from Mesilla, New Mexico, to Cummings. There was also the rescue of the commanding officer's little son, held captive in the nearby mountains.

I am fortunate that my health remains good, and I still ride the once-wild red mustang I told you about, a true battlefield horse, endowed with wary intelligence and endurance suited for this arid land.

I trust this will find you in good health and enjoying your worthy profession.

Once again, sir, I wish to thank you for standing up for me in the settling of my father's estate and

**for being my one steadfast friend at home, when
no one else did, which I shall never forget.**

Sincerely,

Jesse Alden Wilder

He always felt a sense of peace with his past, after writing
Mr. Sawyer, and it was more so now. Although he could never
go back again, because there was nothing to go back to, even
old neighbors having turned their backs on him when he returned after being mustered out of the Union Army of the
West, he could not forget what once had been rich with love
and lasting friendships. Starting with bloody Shiloh and ending with equally bloody Franklin, all his boyhood friends had
died in the war. As the only survivor of that group of carefree
young men who feared the fighting would be over before they
could enlist, Jesse could not escape feeling guilty. Sometimes,
when his nightmares haunted him, he'd glimpse their upturned
faces — not only in the smoky hell of battle, but forever young
and fair, forever marching, marching on.

He paused, the letter evoking all the old hurts. He hoped
time eventually would heal the bitterness back there, and
someday understanding and forgiveness would prevail. There
had to be a beginning somewhere. He paused again, then
quickly added this postscript:

**Should you have occasion to write Claiborne or
Mary Elizabeth, please tell them that I wish them
well.**

There! He'd said it. Got it out of him at last. A first step.

Chapter Five

A sergeant called the volunteers to attention, the most slovenly troopers in Jesse's memory. Instead of at least an attempt at military erectness, they stood slouched and indifferent, a kind of reckless defiance in their manner and eyes, as if they held a grudge against the world and didn't give a damn who knew it.

"At ease," Colonel Chilton barked.

They seemed to slouch even an extra notch.

Chilton looked them over. "Aren't we short some men, Sergeant?"

"Yes, sir. Two. Private Douglas is down with a pain in the belly, which the surgeon thinks is appendicitis. Private Henderson got his jaw broke. Seems there was a little scuffle in a card game."

"A scuffle with whom?"

The sergeant cleared his throat. "With Sergeant . . . er . . . Private Bickford, sir."

Jesse frowned. *Already down to twenty-one.*

"I see. Now all you men understand the nature of the mission for which you've volunteered. And, as stated before, you understand this is a chance to clear your records? If it isn't understood, speak up."

A trooper with an Irish brogue said: "Sir, I have to drop out. I got to thinkin' about me wife and two kids, an' the old woman's raisin' hell with me."

"Very well," Chilton said. "Sergeant, have this man escorted back to the guardhouse."

Jesse frowned again. *Twenty.* But realized he wasn't including the major, Reyes, or himself.

As the two marched off, Chilton said: "I now turn you men over to your commander, Major Emory Gordon." He returned Gordon's salute and left for headquarters.

A C.O. could do that, Jesse thought ruefully.

Gordon eyed the troopers one by one. Jesse stood behind him to one side. Suddenly Gordon barked: "Atten-shun!" The command startled them. They straightened.

"Going with the detachment as scout is Captain Jesse Wilder," Gordon told them and turned to Jesse, who nodded at the men. "We'll depart at daybreak tomorrow," Gordon said. "This afternoon you will be issued carbines, revolvers, and a hatchet for firewood, though there may be times when fires are out of the question. You will be issued sixty rounds for the revolvers and two hundred for the carbines. Rations for eight days. Two blankets for each man instead of the customary one. A dog tent for every two men. Thirty pounds of grain for each horse and each pack mule. From the post trader you will draw rough civilian clothing and hats. The idea is we want everybody to look like miners, or close to it. Therefore, we'll take along some shovels and picks, which also might come in handy for various purposes. Now, the first order of the day will be drill. I want to see how we'll look mounted up. On the march, whenever possible, horses will be groomed every day."

So saying, he marched them to the stables where the stable sergeant issued them mounts. Gordon then ordered the horses groomed on picket line before saddling, which produced some muttered grumbling. Jesse followed the same procedure with the red horse, saddled, and, when Gordon ordered the volunteers to mount, Jesse joined them, riding to the major's left as he led them in a column of twos across the parade ground. Not halting at the end, he continued off toward the mountains. The volunteers looked soft and out of condition for the saddle, Jesse noted, and in poor order. Gordon had the same observation, because he halted the column, faced about, and said: "Who among you is Private Bickford . . . Rufe Bickford?"

"Here, sir."

The speaker, holding up his right hand, was a muscular trooper with thick shoulders and a thick neck, riding near the front of the column. His burly body appeared about to envelop the McClellan saddle. He wore a bristly, sandy beard, and his broad, pitted face, from the punished nose to the scars around his eyes, bore the marks of a brawling man, indicating an odyssey through numerous barroom and barracks fights and projecting the bold image of an aggressive individual who never backed down but was ever ready to add fuel to a situation leading up to a good fight. Hair hung from his forage cap to his neck like a yellow mane. His pale eyes, washed out and cynical, were those of a veteran campaigner wise to all the ups and downs of soldiering, let come what may: fists, clubs, bottles, and beware the trooper who underestimated him, figuring he was all bluff. Energy seemed to flow out of him. Jesse fixed him in his thirties.

These impressions Jesse caught as Bickford faced the major. In fairness to Bickford, Jesse remembered that a noncommissioned officer needed more than stripes to hold his rank among rough horse soldiers. He had to whip any man who challenged him, which could be often on payday, when the raw whiskey flowed and old resentments surfaced. If he couldn't and allowed himself to be pushed around, thus losing control of the men, the troop commander would have to replace him before long. First sergeants had to be the toughest of all the noncoms, with little capacity for remorse or pity. Tough. Extra tough.

"Henceforth," Gordon said, "you will be acting first sergeant for the duration of the mission . . . if all goes well. Among your duties, you will compile a roll of the detachment, muster the men each morning, and call the roll."

Bickford seemed to grow even larger in the saddle as he saluted and said: "Yes, sir!"

"Now, who is Patrick Connelly?" the major asked.

A trooper at the rear of the column said — "Here, sir!" — and held up a hand.

"Come forward," Gordon ordered.

Promptly, Connelly did so and halted. Gordon returned his salute with a snap. "Henceforth," he said, "you will be acting corporal during the mission . . . if all goes well. Among your duties, you will pay special attention to the pack train and see that the packs are properly placed for the comfort of the mules and that the mules are cared for . . . at all times."

"Yes, sir!"

"Dismissed," Gordon said.

Jesse grinned. *He's picking the best fighters. Also warning them that their temporary promotions depend on how they conduct themselves and things go.*

Connelly was a wiry little chunk of a man who looked several years younger than Bickford. He had a ruddy Irish face and a somewhat puckish grin, accented by a broken front tooth, no doubt incurred in a payday fight, quick brown eyes, and a ginger beard. He held himself straight, like an old trooper. He had a fighter's hands, big knuckled and scarred, which went with his stout chest. In all, he created the effect of a man primed for either a fight or frolic; it made no difference, he was ready.

Oh, for the Irish, Jesse mused, *the backbone of the U. S. cavalry, but steeped in superstitions from the old country. Good with horses. Good men to have at your side.* He'd experienced that not long ago in the savage little fight in the mountains above Fort Cummings to save the Taylor boy.

Connelly dropped back in the column as Gordon led them to the post and across to the stables. As they dismounted, a horse whirled and lashed out with a hind hoof and his unaware rider fell to the ground with a cry of great pain.

"It's Myers," Jesse heard Connelly say.

Several troopers gathered around to help. They lifted him to his feet, but he collapsed. "He's got a busted leg," one said.

"Take him to the hospital," Gordon ordered, and two men grasped Myers between them and gingerly started him for the hospital.

Jesse watched them go with a silent groan. *Nineteen now*.

Afterward, told that rations would be issued last, the volunteers drew weapons and ammunition at the armory. Jesse, who had over two hundred rounds for the Spencer in his packs, drew only for the Colt Navy. Of all the goings forth to battle, he thought, one would always stand foremost in his mind. The Army of Tennessee in a column of fours, some of the boys singing because they were back on home soil, hurrying northward on a cool November day toward its ill-fated destiny, shot to pieces at bloody Franklin, which was the beginning of its end as an army, Nashville the finishing blow. General Hood, pained by old wounds, in a terrible mood after his order to close the pike at Spring Hill wasn't carried out. Who was to blame? But there were whispers of a general who'd gone off to see a pretty lady at a nearby plantation. Thus, the Yankee Army slipped through to Franklin and entrenched, and six thousand Johnny Rebs died for the oversight.

Jesse broke off the thought, aware about him of the first signs of early tension among the volunteers by a few words and gestures, their getting ready to the accompaniment of ringing sounds coming from the farriers' shed. Besides a trooper,

Jesse remembered, a mount had to carry about one hundred pounds of saddle, saddle blanket, weapons, ammunition, rations, the trooper's personal gear, a picket pin and lariat, horseshoes, bridle and halter, and saddlebags. And, so loaded, was expected to march thirty miles a day or more, maybe fifty on a forced march.

As the day wore on, Jesse was in the barracks going over his gear and supplies, when the volunteers trooped in with clothing from the post trader's, joking about the change in uniform.

"Ye'll be a handsome cuss in yer new duds, Tim Moriarty, a pleasin' sight, indeed, when them Mexican girls down south lay eyes on ye," Connelly joked.

"Why else do ye think I volunteered, Actin' Corporal Connelly?" Moriarty replied, strutting a little. "That an' fer the gold we'll be minin'."

"There'll be no time for foolin' around with Mexican girls," Bickford broke in sourly. By that, Jesse knew him to be irascible and without humor. "And what church-raised Mexican girl would get close to an ugly Paddy that smells like a horse?"

Connelly only rolled his eyes at the squelch. "But, Actin' First Sergeant, sir," he said, laying extra emphasis on the rank, "what's Moriarty to do if the girls bunch up around him as usual? Take cover? Him that's said to be the foinest-lookin' lad in the outfit."

"Yeah, Actin' First Sarge," Moriarty chimed in, evidently enjoying the attention, "what am I supposed to do? Fight 'em off with a club, Sir Sarge?" He was a strapping, black-haired, young man with reckless eyes and a droll mouth.

Bickford drilled a menacing look at both men. "You wouldn't be makin' light of my promotion, would you?"

"Oh, no, sir. We's just addressin' ye in the proper manner, is all," Connelly said, at stiff attention, and overdoing it, which

Bickford couldn't miss. "Showin' our respect for yer rank. Just hope it ain't brevet. Same as I expect to be addressed for me own promotion as actin' corporal, Actin' First Sergeant, sir."

"Like hell," Bickford said and started on. A step and he wheeled around, fixing his eyes only on Connelly. "You better keep in mind what happened between us once before, *Acting Corporal*. It can happen again. Remember that."

Bickford took the cot next to Jesse's and began sorting out the heavy civilian clothing: one blue flannel shirt, one checkered shirt, two brown denim pants, and a brown denim jacket, a slouch hat, durable leather gloves, and a pair of heavy work shoes.

Looking up, Bickford seemed to see Jesse for the first time. "Captain," he said curiously, "what are you doing in the enlisted men's barracks? You should be over in the bachelor officers' quarters."

"Although I have that rank, I'm not a captain in the U. S. Army," Jesse said, aware that the hum of voices in the barracks had suddenly ceased and the volunteers were faced his way, watching.

"Might I ask, then, Captain, what army you served in?"

"The Army of Tennessee, Confederate States of America. Later on, I was a noncommissioned officer in the U. S. Army of the West, out on the plains after the War Between the States."

"You mean the Civil War?"

"Call it what you like. To Southerners, it will always be the War Between the States. But the war is over as far as I'm concerned."

"I was at Gettysburg," Bickford said, stressing it.

"I wasn't," Jesse said. "But the Army of Tennessee had its own Gettysburg at Franklin, Tennessee."

"I helped fight the Secesh for nigh onto four years. The

87

South had no right to pull out of the Union."

"I believe the war settled that pretty well," Jesse said, trying to put an end to the conversation.

"I lost my brother at Kennesaw Mountain, fightin' the Army of Tennessee."

"I'm sorry to hear that, Sergeant. The war cost the lives of many fine young men on both sides." He would not add fuel to Bickford's bitterness by telling he had stood in a trench that scorching June day, firing at the lines of blue coats charging up the hill in brigade strength. How impressive they looked, how absolutely brave they were, General Cheatham's Tennesseans holding their fire until the Yankees were only sixty yards away. Then horrendous slaughter. How the Yankees kept coming, a few breaking through to plant colors on the works. A fierce struggle over the flags. When it was over, the wounded in front of the trench were crying for water. How utterly stupid and unfeeling it all was, equal to Hood's charge at Franklin, as if General Sherman, with his huge army, could afford to throw away the lives of several thousand men.

"That it did . . . all because of the Secesh."

This, Jesse saw, was about to leap beyond the bounds of a calm discussion on the war, instead, into the swirling rapids of emotion leading to possible violence. But he wasn't going to back down before this contentious, single-minded man who insisted on raking up old coals of the past.

Striving for a reasonable tone, Jesse said: "Among those factors that helped bring on the war, two stick in my mind. The bullheaded Abolitionists in the North, who made no effort to understand the South and its problems. In the South, we had the hotheaded planters and fire-eating editors like Robert Barnwell Rhett of the Charleston *Mercury*, and politicians like Yancey of Alabama raving for secession. Rhett and Yancey never fired a shot. But they and others like 'em led the South on and on until it was too late. To a lot of Johnny Rebs, who never owned a single slave, it was a rich man's war and a poor man's fight."

Instead of oil on the waters, Jesse's words seemed only to goad Bickford as he hardened visibly and said: "I got no use for Southern gents and their lordly ways. Ridin' around on a gaited horse, tellin' niggers what to do, livin' off nigger sweat."

Jesse shrugged. "You might have to look a long way to find a Southerner that fits that definition now."

"Oh, I don't know. I wonder if you didn't used to fit the part?"

Jesse felt his anger surge, but he tight-reined it. Hell, this was ridiculous, a man who not only insisted on fighting the war over again, but, laughably, was calling him a gentleman, of all things. "I was a schoolteacher before the war. My father farmed a little and raised and sold cotton mules."

"Did he own slaves?"

"He did once. He'd freed them several years before the war."

"When he had slaves, did he whip 'em?"

"Not that I ever saw or heard. Besides, my mother wouldn't have allowed him to do that. Most slave owners weren't cruel to slaves."

"I think *they all* used the whip."

"I'm afraid you're just echoing Abolitionist propaganda."

It was coming, it was unavoidable, Jesse sensed. So did the volunteers. They were tensely watching and waiting.

"Like hell," Bickford said. "It's the truth."

"Far from it."

"You callin' me a liar?"

"I'm telling you you've been misinformed."

"I said, you callin' me a liar?"

"If that's what you want to hear . . . yes! You're a liar . . .

and a god-damned blind one at that!"

Bickford was already advancing toward him at a crouch, a kind of raw anticipation filling his battered features. "Come on, Secesh," he snarled. "Let's see if you can back up that fancy Southern talk."

Jesse raised his arms and squared himself. Bickford rushed, apparently hoping to catch Jesse by surprise. Jesse sidestepped him and drove a right fist to the sergeant's left jaw. It was like hitting stone.

Jesse backed off, set for another bull-like rush. It came swiftly, the other punching with both hands, landing short, powerful blows to Jesse's ribs. Bickford left his face open, as if daring Jesse to hit him. Jesse punished the nose and mouth and eyes. Blood squirted. Bickford wiped his mouth with the back of his left hand. But he never faltered, coming on doggedly, coming on.

Suddenly Jesse felt a cot against the back of his legs. At the same time Bickford rushed again. A fist to Jesse's throat sent him reeling backward over the cot to the barracks floor. He landed hard on the flat of his back, unhurt, the wind momentarily knocked out of him. He was getting up when Bickford leaped on him, punching Jesse's face. Jesse rammed his right knee into the man's crotch. When Bickford yelled and fell aside, Jesse reared up and smashed the pitted face again and again.

But he was gaining nothing there. Bickford seemed unfazed, still advancing at a crouch. "You can't hurt me there, Secesh. I can take everything you've got all day long."

By now the volunteers were yelling and crowding around closer, Connelly's Irish face in the fore. Gradually it registered on Jesse that they were yelling for him, that they must hate Bickford to show such open favoritism.

Although Jesse was beginning to handle the rushes better,

feinting and stepping aside and getting in some hard licks, the sergeant was slowly and methodically wearing him down, his short arms flailing away with windmill body punches, while seemingly unhurt himself. Jesse had to do something, change tactics. His long-armed punches to the face and body, though keeping the sergeant off him, showed no telling effect. Meanwhile, Bickford, working on Jesse's ribs and now and then on Jesse's face, seemed content to take whatever Jesse threw at him. All this time, Jesse began to see, the sergeant carefully guarded his ample midsection.

"Come on, Secesh," Bickford taunted. "Let's see what you've got. I think you're yellow, like all Southern gents livin' off nigger sweat. Show me some guts."

The volunteers yelled in alarm when Bickford wobbled Jesse with a right to the jaw. As if sensing victory, the sergeant charged in for the knockout. Jesse shook his head, clearing it, and pulled back, watching, still retreating, watching for the one opening. Bickford rushed faster, impatiently, getting reckless as he raised thick, windmill arms for the finish.

Abruptly, Jesse stopped and crouched, causing Bickford to miss with two wild swings to the head. Then Jesse sank a right hand to Bickford's open belly. It was soft and pulpy. He followed with a left and another right to the same place. Bickford grunted, hesitated, muttered something. Suddenly, he had to check, hacking for wind, his pale eyes bulging. He was hurt, but he wasn't about to quit. He seemed to pull himself together. Guarding his belly this time, he charged in a wild, heavy-bodied, flailing rush. Jesse's blows to the bloody face and chest had no visible effect, in his ears the din of the troopers yelling encouragement. In the next flurry of punches, the sergeant broke through Jesse's guard and threw him to the floor.

Jesse rolled away, expecting Bickford to jump on him. But

before he could get up, Bickford was close upon him, one foot coming in high, primed to stomp. Jesse, flat on his back, kicked upward suddenly with both booted feet. They took Bickford by surprise, fully in the pulpy belly, lifting him off his feet. Bickford yelled and fell to the floor, clutching his lower body with both hands, his face twisted in pain. Jesse hacked for wind and pushed up, unable to do so quickly. That slowness gave Bickford the little respite he needed. Because just as Jesse found his footing, Bickford spun around with desperate effort and staggered to his feet and stood swaying there, blood streaking his sandy beard, arms working, muttering through frothy-red lips: "Come on, Secesh. Come on. Show me."

It was now or never, Jesse knew, because his own strength was ebbing fast. Gathering himself, he feinted for Bickford's face with his left. When Bickford instinctively, wearily, raised his hands, Jesse drove a right first to the melon belly, then mustered all his power and sank a left and another right there.

Bickford let out a great high-pitched — "Ah!" — and another — "Ah!" — and collapsed, pitching forward in pain. This time he was finished.

Jesse stood over him, his breath coming in ragged gasps. "Get up," Jesse said. "Get up, god damn you!" He could barely stand. The room and the faces were spinning weirdly in many colors, constantly changing. He found his voice again, looking down at Bickford, grinding out the words. "For your further information . . . I helped train Benito Juárez's army in northern Chihuahua . . . fighting the French. One war we Johnny Rebs sure as hell won. I was a Citizen General. I also fought Apaches."

Bickford's response was to turn on his side and vomit.

Jesse turned away, glad it was over. Inside his head a giant drum was beating away. His chest was pounding wildly. His body felt like one great bruise. Bickford had come near finishing him. It was all so senseless, over a war now ended except for the carry-over emotions, which wouldn't go away for a long, long time.

The volunteers crowded around him. He flinched when somebody slapped him on the back. Connelly followed him out to a water trough.

Suddenly everything went black. Jesse started to go down. He reached for the trough for support, missed, and would have fallen if Connelly hadn't grabbed his arm. Bit by bit, like light breaking through a murky dawn, the world righted itself: the spinning buildings, the barren mountains, the blue bowl of the sky. Jesse doused his head, then stripped to the waist and washed up.

"That was a foine fight, Cap'n," Connelly said admiringly. "No Irishman could've done better. Ye're the first man to stay the course with Bull Bickford and lay him out. It's long been needed. I fought with him meself once and was doin' all right. Started workin' on that big gut, just like you did. Ye saw how he guarded it. But when I hurt him, he bulled in close and knocked me out. I got a glass jaw, the worst thing that can happen to an Irishman. Must be me sainted mother bequeathed it to me, the way she hated fightin'. Even so, I might've won if I'd had on me fightin' joolry."

"Your fightin' jewelry?"

"Yes, sir. Worn special for payday brawls. Some call 'em drinkin' joolry. Ye take a horseshoe nail and bend it into a ring, with the head of the ring worn on top of the fist. One for each hand. I tell ye they will cut a swath."

It hurt to laugh, but Jesse did a little. He shook his head, swaying, feeling his jaw. "Helluva way to start off on a campaign. A fight with the first sergeant."

"Nothin' better, Cap'n. A good fight clears the air. We'll

all march better now with the Bull in his proper place. No extra lordin' it over us. Ye'll see how we get along."

"Tell me something. Besides wanting to clear your record, why did you volunteer? All you men?"

"For a variety of reasons, Cap'n. Prisoners don't just stay in the guardhouse . . . they work. Volunteerin' beats fillin' water barrels, handlin' the sprinklin' cart, cleanin' up privies, haulin' off manure and garbage, an' buildin' brick walls. A cavalryman's proper place is in the saddle."

"You're a good man, Corporal. I'm glad you're going along. Good luck to you."

"Thank ye, Cap'n. Same to ye. As fer me rank, I know it's only brevet. I'll never make sergeant with this glass jaw."

Chapter Six

They formed in the muddy first light, horses snuffling, troopers coughing, the cool desert night still lingering over the parade ground. Acting First Sergeant Bickford called the volunteers to attention and ran through the roll, the answering voices clear and prompt. Gone was yesterday's slack indifference.

Bickford about-faced, snapped a very proper salute to Major Gordon, and reported: "All present and accounted for, sir. Detail formed." His battered face showed one black eye and a puffed cheekbone. Not much damage, it seemed to Jesse, considering the savagery of their encounter. The man had a jaw like rock. But he bet Bickford's gut ached.

Gordon returned the salute, sized up the detachment, and barked: "Prepare to mount." Another moment, then: "Mount!"

They hit the saddles, leather squealing.

"Left by twos . . . march!"

Gordon led them at a trot across the parade and onto the trail. Agustín Reyes rode on his left, astride a proud black Arabian. Jesse, at Gordon's motion, moved up to the major's right, leading his mule. The prancing Arabian would attract keen Apache eyes, Jesse figured, as would his blood-red horse with the blaze . . . as would any good horse.

As sergeant, Bickford was the lead rider in the following little column of troopers. In the rear, Acting Corporal Connelly rode in charge of the nine-mule pack train and the two extra saddled mounts.

Glancing back at the column, feeling for these few men,

Jesse saw Connelly wave. They looked a bit strange, civilians in military formation. *Orders.* Why did the rump-sprung geniuses in Washington, ignorant of actual conditions in the West, send a paltry few on such missions that called for more? Missions complicated by great distances, uncertain forage and water, exhausting heat and bitter cold — logistical problems not faced before. To his knowledge, no U.S. cavalry unit had ever penetrated the rugged and mysterious Sierra Madre before. One answer, naturally, was that no more men could be spared from the always undermanned remote posts. In this case, however, it was a matter of ticklish international relations. Relations, hell! Ten or fifteen more men could make a big difference. *Sorry, orders.* And if you're going to send so few, why not at least equip them with Spencers! *Sorry. They're all down on the lower Río Grande border fighting Indians.*

He was thinking too much again. He faced front and settled down for the lengthy day, in the accustomed familiarity of the march.

Before long they left the mountains and came out on the desert floor and struck south, trailing banners of reddish dust that announced their coming.

Gordon, leading the point at a walk, said to Jesse: "We may have to make dry camp tonight, but San Bernardino Springs will make up for it. A good look at the map tells me it's a three-day march to the border." He looked startled. "What happened to your face, Captain? Did you fall down? Don't tell me you've been in a fight?"

Jesse tried not to look discomfited. "Yes, sir. A fight."

"What!" Gordon couldn't believe it.

"About the war, if you can believe that. Sergeant Bickford challenged me after he asked where I'd served as captain and I told him in the Army of Tennessee. There were some verbal exchanges. One thing led to another. He lost a brother at

Kennesaw Mountain, where my division fought."

Gordon was dumbfounded. "Who won?"

"I did. But we both took a beating."

Anger began to replace Gordon's surprise. "We can't have this. If we weren't already started and didn't need him, I'd send him back under arrest. I'll speak to him at once."

Jesse said quickly: "Let it rest, Major."

"But challenging an officer!"

"But not a U.S. officer."

"Just the same. . . ."

"I think maybe it did some good. Settled matters down in the ranks. Corporal Connelly says so, says it's the first time Bull Bickford's ever been licked. Says it was needed. The men actually cheered me."

"You must be one hell of a fighter, Captain."

"I wouldn't say that. A man fights harder when he gets jumped. I've had to fight before, but not often. Maybe I got in a lucky blow. It's over as far as I'm concerned. I thought the war was over, too, but obviously it's not for everybody. Too many memories."

Gordon still hesitated, still angry.

"I'd appreciate it, Major, if we just drop it for now."

"All right. For the moment, at least. But I've seen men shot for less. He will have to conduct himself properly or else." He threw up his hands, a gesture of futility. "Whatever happened to military discipline?"

They rode on. Gordon posted flankers. The morning coolness soon gave way. By ten o'clock it was hot. By noon the sun was a molten eye, glaring down at them. Dust coated faces and clothing. There was scant talk in the column. The Chiricahua Mountains, massive and forbidding, flanked them on the right. The lesser Peloncillos, barren and craggy, began to shape up on their left as the valley broadened.

Reyes pointed southwest into the Chiricahuas. "See that face up there on top, Major?"

Gordon looked, searching. Soon, he exclaimed: "By George, it is! A magnificent Indian face. Even has a Roman nose."

"It is called Cochise Head, after the Chiricahua chief."

"He looks formidable. Are you superstitious, Mister Reyes?"

Reyes smiled. "No, *Señor* Major, but I am respectful. The farther we ride, the deeper we go into Apache territory."

The three repeatedly scanned the foothills and glaring stretches with field glasses, Jesse now in possession of Army binoculars. By this time he found himself in a familiar practice developed long ago, nearly routine, as if he'd done this most of his life. The war years had sharpened his senses to a keen edge. Not only instincts of survival, but his sense of smell and eyesight and what to look for, and, even beyond that, sometimes the odd sensation of being watched or observed. Fighting Apaches did that. A man always sat an uneasy saddle in Apache country, suspicious of changes. A ravel of dust. A rustle of gravel while scouting a cañon on foot. Just a *tink* of metal. In Chihuahua, he remembered hearing an owl's call one night. Another owl seemed to answer. He heard that twice. At daybreak next morning the Apaches hit the camp.

He had expected Gordon to follow a "book" march today, resting ten minutes every hour and nooning forty-five; but he did not, though mindful of the horses, holding to a walk and resting briefly each hour. At noon he stopped for twenty minutes, while the men ate cold rations, then resumed the march. Instead of camping early, he continued until half an hour before dark. Dry camp. They had covered about thirty miles or more, Jesse judged. Enough.

At the start of the mission he'd wondered if the battle-hardened major would command in exaggerated West Point style, which Jesse had seen demonstrated by a few officers, both North and South — stiffly aloof from the enlisted men, overpunctilious, issuing orders as if they came down from the deities on Mount Olympus, patronizing toward those of lower rank. Quite the contrary today. Gordon had issued orders without pomp, and easily conversed with the acting noncoms. Both Bickford and Connelly seemed to like being under his command. Which caused Jesse to muse. *A campaign is a great equalizer. It brings out the best or worst in a man.*

"Any suggestions for tonight, Captain?" Gordon asked, looking off at the mesquite and greasewood dotting the flat.

"The usual, Major. Hobble and picket the stock inside camp. Change sentries every few hours. Be up and ready before daylight."

"Think we were observed today?"

"Probably. Be hard not to see the dust we kicked up."

"If so, I wonder if we looked curious to Indian eyes. White men riding in column, flankers out, but not dressed like soldiers."

"They know only fools would ride strung out."

"I'll tell Sergeant Bickford to pass the word to the men to make cooking fires. I see no need not to. A useless precaution, since our presence is known."

"Nothing cheers a cavalryman like coffee, hard bread, and bacon."

"You're welcome to mess with Reyes and me."

"Thank you, Major. I will. But I'll do my own cooking. It's too old a habit to break."

While Jesse picketed and hobbled his stock and made camp, Bickford reported to Gordon, listened attentively to the orders, saluted again, about-faced, and started on his duties. As he passed Jesse, his washed-out eyes struck hard once at

Jesse's face, a remembering look. Only that. Jesse didn't speak or nod. It would be a mistake, a sign of weakness, to defer the slightest to this tough-twisted man. Better to maintain a military distance for now.

Jesse poured water from one canteen into his hat to share the contents equally between the horse and the mule. Some nights they'd had less than that, some nights nothing on the long ride out of Chihuahua.

Corporal Connelly was leading a mule by. In his blue flannel shirt and rough pants and jacket and wide-brimmed slouch hat, which was much too large, pulled down around his ears, he reminded Jesse of a country bumpkin come to town on Saturday.

"How'd the march go, Corporal?"

"Foine, Cap'n. Never better."

"I understand you're a top marksman."

"I'm blessed with good eyes, is all. I never fired a shot till I joined the cavalry. In the Old Sod, we couldn't afford a gun or shot. Among me duties, there's two I look ahead to. Handlin' the hawrses and target shootin' me Springfield."

"And," Jesse said, smiling, "maybe a round or two of fisticuffs now and then."

"That, too, I might say." Connelly rolled his eyes. "Ye see, it breaks the monotony. Well, I best be gettin' on, Cap'n. Glad to visit with ye."

"Same to you."

Soon Jesse heard the corporal's amiable voice down the line of busy troopers. *There*, he thought, *goes a damned good horse soldier.*

After he fed the red horse and the mule grain, he joined Gordon's orderly hustling wood for the supper fire. Presently other fires sprang up, like yellow tapers struggling fitfully against the light wind whimpering out of the cooling desert

100

darkness. There would be a full moon tonight, which was good. In a short while, a mingling of smells drifted over the bivouac: wood smoke, coffee boiling, and bacon frying, interlaced with the closeness of horse and mule sweat. Troopers' voices made a pleasant hum.

Jesse felt a deep-rooted contentment stealing over him; all this, these bits, had been a part of him for so long now. Later, the sentries would stand like a shield around the camp. On a long march a man took his brief rest and simple food when he could, savoring each to the fullest, wasting nothing.

"Mister Reyes," Gordon said as they ate, "do you think you can find water for us by tomorrow evening?"

"Yes, *Señor* Major. There's a little creek that flows out of the mountains. A good place to camp. From there it will be an easy march next day to San Bernardino Springs."

"That's soon enough, keeping in mind our deadline. Let's see. Eleven days from today. We should make La Gloria three days from the Springs. The worst mistake we can make is to hurry too fast. We want to reach La Gloria with horses in good condition, with still a lot of bottom left in 'em . . . ourselves as well."

"Have you arrived at a rescue plan yet, *Señor* Major?" Reyes asked hopefully.

"I've been mulling over what we might do. We can't just rush in there pell-mell first thing, though we might, later, depending on what we find. You've said the hacienda is well guarded. But guard duty can be monotonous. There could be a laxness, say at *siesta* time, say when this *El Tigre* and his bodyguards ride into La Gloria for entertainment. How many men does that leave at the hacienda? And in what part of the hacienda are your sister and her *duenna* being held? And could there be more than one entrance to the stronghold? Perhaps some of the villagers work at the hacienda. If so, they could

101

furnish much information."

Reyes thanked him with his dark eyes. "You are considering many things, *Señor* Major. I know that. I'm just anxious."

"I fully understand. In addition, we must act like miners and camp away from the village. *El Tigre* will hear of our arrival almost immediately. We can be assured of that. You said he has spies everywhere. We can't hide and don't want to try to hide, which would arouse suspicion. So we'll go into town. Buy some things. Trade a little and listen much. Money loosens tongues, particularly when the people are poor." Gordon stopped, frowning. "For our needs, in my saddlebags, are *pesos* and American silver dollars, mostly *pesos*. Will the dollars spend in La Gloria as readily as the *pesos?*"

"They will welcome the dollars, which are as good as *pesos,* but not American greenbacks."

"Good. I'll pass some to the men, but not enough to get drunk on." He turned to Jesse. "How do you see the mission from here, Captain?"

Jesse reflected a moment before he spoke. "So far as arms are concerned, I believe we have an edge through organization and discipline. At close quarters, if it comes to that, we'd not be outgunned with our side arms, even though we'd be outnumbered. What we find probably won't be the same as we see it from here. There will be surprises. As you and I know, Major, war is like that. We'll have to expect the unexpected. Be ready at all times."

"Quite true. We, in turn, will have the advantage of being a surprise for *El Tigre*. The poor villagers will have to be our main source of information. Mister Reyes, I don't believe we've ever nailed down what you could ascertain was *El Tigre*'s full strength. His bodyguards, you said, number twenty or so, counting the Hussars."

"Yes, *Señor* Major, that much is accurate. The bodyguards

are his best men. As for his entire band, I should say at least fifty, even seventy. But no more than that."

"The worst mistake we can make, from the standpoint of strategy, is to underestimate the enemy's strength, without, however, becoming too conservative and losing our dash . . . our own ability to surprise. One of the first pieces of information I'd like for us to pick up is in what part of the hacienda your sister and her *duenna* are being held. That is most vital. We can act from that."

Reyes nodded gravely.

"There must be villagers who work at the hacienda as cooks or servants, or as woodcutters. The stronghold has to have wood."

Reyes's expression was doubtful. "I talked to only a few who said they'd even been inside the hacienda. That was bringing in supplies bought in town. They said they were closely followed, a guard with them every step. They weren't invited to have a drink or visit. In fact, they hardly had time to look around before they were escorted to the gate. As for wood, they must cut their own." He made a sudden recalling motion. "One did tell me he saw a low building where men went in and out. Others sat on the verandah . . . that would be the barracks. There is also a main building . . . the house. I'd think that would be *El Tigre*'s headquarters, and where Alicia and Rosa are prisoners." He became downcast. "But who knows where this terrible man is holding them and under what conditions?"

"These villagers," Gordon asked, "did they see the gate to a back entrance?"

"They didn't mention one. They did see that the wall encloses all the buildings."

Gordon turned to Jesse again. "How would you say, based on your experience, we prepare for the unexpected?"

"I'm a fine one to advise a major of cavalry with your record," Jesse said. "You don't really prepare, except to stay alert, try to look ahead. Among other things, we can keep the hacienda under observation at all times. See what goes in and out. Somehow we'll have to get in there. If not through the gate, over the wall. How high would you estimate the wall to be, Agustín?"

"About ten feet."

"Then we can scale if we have to."

"Have you ever scaled a wall?" Gordon asked dubiously.

"No, sir."

"Neither have I."

"Back at Fort Cummings," Jesse said, "I was told that Apaches had slipped inside by simply throwing a rope over the wall and climbing up after it. There would be a rock tied on the end of the rope to hold it against the wall. For that reason, they kept the armory locked at night."

"Very interesting, except we're not Apaches."

Further discussion fell away after supper. Gordon instructed Bickford to post sentries, each man to stand two hours. The fires shrank to pools of ruby light, and the bivouac gradually became quiet. Jesse checked his stock on picket. Afterward, from his bedroll, he watched the great golden ball of the moon glide out of the eastern sky bathed in haze. The night grew chill about him, the stillness broken only by the stamp of a hoof or the rattle of a halter or a sentry's boot crunching gravel. An owl hooted off in the mesquites, but there was no answering hoot. That told him it wasn't an Apache, or likely was not, or maybe was not. You could never feel positive about an Apache until you saw him. In Chihuahua the Mexicans said that Apaches never attacked at night because rattlesnakes came out when it was cooler, and there was danger of being bitten. Common sense. Yet you couldn't afford not to post sentries in case they did attack. That one time could be fatal. He fell asleep thinking that he had made a complete reversal of his intentions after leaving Fort Cummings. He had firmly planned to continue on west to Tucson, perhaps to California. But a man couldn't ignore his past, and his past was drawing him back to Mexico and what had happened there.

Chapter Seven

Major Gordon had the volunteers up and ready before dawn, prepared if an attack came hurtling and screeching out of the east, with the creeping first rays in the fooling grayish light that made shooting bad.

But nothing happened.

They waited some more, until the sky turned pink, some more until the sun burst through, clearing out, sweeping clean, and the desert floor stood stark and silent. *Anyway,* Jesse thought, *it was a good simulation of preparedness for an attack.*

Then Bickford barked the muster roll in his blunt fashion. They fed the horses and mules from the forage sacks and quickly started breakfast fires.

Not many minutes had passed when they were in motion again, going at a walk, flankers ranging in advance, left and right. An hour slipped by. Another burning day set in. The detail traveled like a moving dust cloud. The volunteers' faces became reddish masks. Time seemed to loiter.

Once Jesse glanced back at the pack train, now, in a sense, the outfit's rear guard. Connelly rode on a flank, where he no doubt could see better how his charges were doing. Catching Jesse's attention, he waved cheerfully. When a pack slipped, he called out a halt and, with another trooper, shifted the bundle back into position, retied it, and they went on.

When the sun stood at midday, Gordon ordered a twenty-minute halt.

Jesse dismounted, eased the saddle cinch on the red horse, issued him and the mule each a ration of water from the second of the three canteens. He was cinching up again, when

106

he heard Bickford say: "Kaufman, your saddle blanket has slipped. Better resaddle."

"Aw, it looks all right, Sarge."

"The hell it does. Unsaddle!"

"Aw, Sarge."

"I said unsaddle and fix that god-damned blanket. You want a sore-backed horse? Fix it or start walkin'!"

Grumbling, while Bickford stood by watching, arms folded, the trooper unsaddled and set the blanket evenly and smoothly on the sweaty back and resaddled. He was a long-faced man, tall and stooped, with bloodhound eyes and a careless manner. His eyes kept wandering off to the unchanging landscape.

Kaufman. Jesse ran the name through his mind. That was Kaufman, in for desertion and stealing issue arms and a horse and all the equipment that went with the mount. Slipped off in broad daylight, after drill. A surprise way to desert. Apprehended on the road to Tucson. Jesse could only wonder why he'd volunteered when he seemed unfit or unwilling as compared to the others. When they mounted up and struck out again at a walk, Kaufman took his usual place in the center of the column.

At this walking rate by a good cavalry mount, which amounted to about four miles an hour, the afternoon began to wear away. But as yet, the creek Reyes had promised wasn't in sight.

It happened, then, nearly in unison, as Gordon, Reyes, and Jesse pulled up and looked off toward a brushy rise below the Chiricahuas — at a single Apache on a gray horse outlined there. He seemed to linger unnecessarily as he observed the column. In another moment, he vanished.

"Well," said the major, matter-of-factly, "so we have been discovered, though I thought we would be long before this."

"Probably a scout," Jesse said. "Yet I'm surprised he'd show himself."

"He is very bold," Reyes observed. "Boldness could mean a big war party."

"At least we've been forewarned," Gordon said, riding on.

A flanker clattered up on the run. "See that Injun horseman, sir? Right out there in plain sight?"

"Couldn't miss him, could we? Continue on as before, but at the first sign of trouble, swing back immediately to the column."

"Yes, sir!"

They didn't see the horseman again.

It was close on five o'clock when they reached a noisy little creek lined with dwarf oaks and junipers. There was a rush as the horses and mules smelled water.

An abundance of water and wood made for a cheerful bivouac. Troopers joked around the supper fires. Connelly bantered Moriarty about "all them Mexican girls waitin' for ye south of the border," and "yer not as ugly as Actin' First Sergeant Bickford says ye are."

"He's uglier," a voice broke in.

"Aw," Moriarty replied, "Sir Sarge is just jealous of me good looks. However, me natural modesty prompts me to say that at times I do smell just a little like a horse."

"A modest lad ye are, Tim Moriarty," Connelly continued. "A model for all us foine sons of the Old Sod to try'n follow, impossible as that be."

Moriarty bowed from the waist. "I feel even more humble to be so honored, Actin' Corporal Connelly, sir. But there's nothin' I can do about me horse smell. A bath would bring only temporary good. Next day I'd smell the same. So why take a bath?"

Bickford, who had made his own cooking fire and ate alone, didn't respond, but it was evident to Jesse that he wasn't fooled by the thinly disguised sallies in his direction. After supper, he reported immediately to Gordon for further orders.

He first inspected how the horses and mules were picketed. There was no straight line as such, the winding contour of the creek determining the rather loose order.

That done with few changes, he strode back to the center of the camp and said: "Actin' Corporal Connelly, you and Private Moriarty will have the honor of standin' the last watch with Private Kaufman and Private Webb. You two will walk your posts back and forth on the south and west, which I will so designate. Kaufman will take the north side, Webb the east, which I will so designate."

Jesse smiled. Bickford had them in a mild way, but he had them. The last watch was the least preferred.

Moriarty merely shrugged.

"Yes, sir, Sergeant," Connelly said, revealing no hint of surprise.

Bickford glared at him. "Don't try to soft-soap me, Actin' Corporal Connelly. You left out the actin' part of my brevet promotion. I want no unearned promotion stated by you."

"Oh, no, sir, Actin' First Sergeant," Connelly said sweetly. " 'Twas a slip of me memory. Ye see, I be so used to thinkin' of ye as first sergeant without the actin'."

Bickford threw him another glare and named the others for the other watches, barking out their names, and showed them exactly where they would walk their posts. Striding back, he saluted and reported to Gordon. "All posts established for the night, sir. Does the major have any further orders?"

"Nothing further, Sergeant. Of course, you will have the

entire detail alerted and on guard before daybreak."

"As usual, sir."

"Very good, Sergeant."

Bickford saluted and walked back to his dwindling fire, a look of pure satisfaction on his wrecked face, plainly delighting in the power of his station. He sat by the fire, smoking a smelly pipe, alone and liking it, no doubt aware that the eyes of the detail were upon him. In no more than ten minutes, he was in his tent, snoring.

Jesse nodded to himself. No trooper ever bested a tough first sergeant for long. Not that they wouldn't try again.

Little by little the sounds of the bivouac lessened. Tired voices faded to murmurs and ceased. A trooper coughed. Now just an occasional jangle from the picket line.

Somehow Jesse found sleep elusive tonight. An hour must have passed, though it seemed much longer, when he heard a coyote wail in song from the Chiricahuas. Another coyote answered. The red horse, picketed within a few yards of Jesse, stirred. He also seemed restless tonight. By the last of the ruddy glow from his supper fire, Jesse saw the horse face in the direction of the mountains, his blaze a milky blur. He held that position for a while, then went back to grazing, only, warily, to turn and face the mountains again.

An owl's *hoom-hoom* rose from the woods up the creek. Some minutes dragged by. Jesse heard an owl call again; this time it seemed farther away, off toward the north in the mesquites. Could it be the same owl, or was it another owl? The question nagged at his consciousness until he heard it no more and slept.

Later, briefly, he heard the muffled movements and voices of the sentries changing, and slept again.

Deeper in the night a slight noise on the north side of the bivouac broke his light sleep. He sat up, listening. The red horse had heard it, too, and was faced that way.

Jesse waited. But whatever had disturbed him didn't sound again, and no sentry gave the alarm. He lay down and went back to sleep.

Before the first suggestion of daylight, Bickford had the volunteers up and posted here and there, crouched, watching the eastern sky, carbines at the ready, alert for any movement toward the camp.

The sky changed from slate gray to a rose color. Heads turned, eyes straining. As yet, nothing moved in the mesquites and brush beyond the creek's timber. Time crawled. The light grew stronger. There was nothing out there. Nothing was coming.

Troopers began to stand up and turn around.

Suddenly, Bickford's blunt voice shattered the quiet. "Where the hell's Private Kaufman? Where is he? He'd better not be dogging it again!"

As the detail moved back to the picket line, a man said: "I believe his mount's gone, Sarge."

"What!"

Bickford rushed back there, looking and jerking as he hurriedly scanned the horses and mules. "So it is. That big bay with the star." He strode over to Major Gordon, who had observed everything from his camp, which sat back a short way from the others.

"Sir, Private Kaufman has gone over the hill. He was on the last watch, north side of the bivouac. Shall we go after 'im? He can't have more'n an hour's start."

Gordon didn't answer at once. "In view of the short time Kaufman's been gone," he said, speaking deliberately, "we can do that. Otherwise, we couldn't spare the time. Take two men. If you haven't found him by around ten o'clock, say . . . no later . . . head back. We have to make San Bernardino Springs by evening."

111

"Shall we shoot him, sir?"

"If Kaufman resists, yes. If not, tie him across his saddle and bring him in."

"Yes, sir!"

"Too bad we don't have enough men to send him back to the post under arrest. And keep an eye out for Apaches, Sergeant."

"You bet we will, sir."

Bickford quickly singled out Privates James Ryan and Sam Tate for the purpose. Gordon's voice rose above the hurrying sounds. "Captain Wilder, I'd like for you to go with the detail."

Jesse acknowledged the order and started saddling. When he looped the Quickloader over his shoulder, he was ready.

Other than one quick, straight-on glance, devoid of any expression, as if he welcomed no more help and Jesse didn't exist, Bickford ignored him as they formed. In less than five minutes, they were riding north, the four of them side by side, the sergeant on one end of the foursome, Jesse on the other. Hardtack in their saddlebags would do in lieu of the hot breakfast they were missing.

The tracks lay as an open book before them.

"Here, he's leadin' his horse out," Bickford said, looking down at the clutter of horse and boot prints. "Here he mounts." It was all obvious to a trained eye.

These careful movements, Jesse realized, leading a gentle horse off the picket line and out into the desert, saddling there, had waked him and his own horse in the night.

"He's headed for Tucson again, sure as hell," Bickford said disgustedly to no one in particular.

"Where else would he go?" Ryan asked. He was older than most of the volunteers, probably in his forties, a quiet Irishman compared to the rollicking Connelly and Moriarty, an unpretending man with sensitive features, his large dark eyes set in the hollow-cheeked, short-bearded face remindful of an ascetic. Jesse wondered what his offense was and decided it couldn't be a felony. Not this quiet-seeming man.

"Only a damned fool would desert in the heart of Apache country," Bickford snorted. "On top of that, there's no water between here and the post, and he wouldn't dare stop there. He don't make sense."

"Kaufman is from Chicago," drawled Tate, a short, plump-bodied man with an open, impressionable face, as if coming from Chicago was something. He struck Jesse as maybe a Midwestern farm boy. Weary of the drudgery of clearing and planting and harvesting, he'd joined the cavalry, looking for adventure. Instead, he'd found trouble. He went on in that slow, recalling tone. "Worked in a butcher shop for his old man 'fore he joined up. Told me he got plumb sick of that. Cuttin' up carcasses. Stuffin' sausages. All that muck and stink. Pretty soon he got just as sick of horse soldierin'. Never satisfied."

"What did he think he was made out to be, anyway?" Ryan asked. "A Chicago lawyer?"

"Maybe a poet. I know I saw him readin' a book once. Sometimes I'd see 'im sittin' in the barracks with a dreamy look on his face. Sometimes he'd write somethin' down in a little notebook he carried. I asked him to let me look at it, but he never would. Said it was too personal. For his eyes only. Sounds like a poet to me."

"A poet, hell," Bickford scoffed. "All he had on his mind is gettin' to Tucson and peddlin' a good horse with all the furniture and arms for three hundred dollars. Plenty of civilians will pay that. He's just a common thief. What's more, he's let his own outfit down. He don't give a damn about us. Whether we catch up with him or not, dead or alive, he's left

113

us another man short at a time when we need every man we can muster and more. I despise deserters. He ain't the first one we've had."

Jesse was aware that Bickford expressed a general view shared by officers and enlisted men. Not only did a deserter bring burdens to others, he was always considered a traitor.

They trotted on, mostly in silence, the early morning passing without change, the coolness gone, the tracks leading always to the north. They found where Kaufman had halted and, apparently, debated within himself — the turning point of the hoofs, this way and that, telling of the rider's indecision.

"Why would he hesitate here?" Bickford questioned. "There's no particular place to go, as far as he is from everything."

"Maybe he's thinkin' we're after him," Ryan reasoned.

"Could be . . . or we don't figure he's worth the trouble to capture, which is about the truth." Then, to Jesse's surprise, Bickford asked him: "What do you think, Captain?" Was the sergeant, being in command, feeling the pressure of what he must do, keeping within the range of his orders, and time a pressing factor?

"Well, Sergeant, he could be having second thoughts about deserting. He's beginning to see how hard the going is alone, and how far he is from civilization. What about water? He knows there's none till the post. He can't go there. And Tucson's still a hell of a long way. There's nothing for him east but more desert and mountains . . . west, the Chiricahuas and Apaches. We might look pretty good to him right now. But he's afraid, if we do catch up, we'll shoot him. He may be about to panic by now."

They continued at a steady walk, against a wind whipping grit off the sandy waste.

"I keep thinkin' we'll see his dust," Bickford said.

114

But they saw no dust, the limitless distance ahead bright and clear, and the sun beginning to burn.

It was getting close to around ten o'clock by the sun when they noticed a change in the way Kaufman was riding. His mount was digging in, the tracks deeper, his stride lengthening. Now galloping, now running.

Now ahead of them, against the climbing sun, they saw black dots circling, diving, rising.

"Buzzards!" Bickford said. "God damn!"

A short distance and they saw where horse tracks, also on the run, had swept in from the Chiricahuas. A bunch of tracks. Some yards on and more tracks from the west.

Bickford halted. He looked at the others. They looked at him.

"A big war party," Bickford said. "They saw Kaufman's dust and took after 'im. Easy pickin's." He bit off a chew from a plug of brown tobacco. On second thought, he offered it around.

"Makes me sick," Ryan said.

"Got my own," Tate said.

Jesse declined with a shake of his head.

They proceeded at a much slower, dreading walk. No need to hurry now. They knew what they would find.

About a mile onward, they pulled up when they saw Kaufman spread-eagled, the sockets of his gouged-out eyes staring at the turquoise sky, his white body seemingly an alien intrusion on the reddish sand.

"Funny, we didn't hear any shots," Ryan said.

"Maybe he figured he could outrun 'em," Bickford said. "When they closed in, he froze. They didn't need to fire. Why waste bullets?"

They looked a little while longer, reluctant to dismount, heads lowered, frowning, faces grim, dreading and putting off what they had to do. Dismounting, they saw that the body had been stripped of all vestiges of white man's attire, including socks. Besides much needless slashing and hacking, the Apaches had cut off Kaufman's private parts and stuffed them into his gaping mouth, the ultimate dishonor in their eyes for the hated white race.

Tate turned away and gagged.

Still, they stood around, until Jesse looked at Bickford, who nodded and said: "Yeah. We've got to bury him here. Can't take him back to the bivouac."

"We can mark the grave with rocks and brush," Jesse said. "Maybe a stone marker when the detail returns this way."

"Ain't you the hopeful one," Bickford said and drowned a lizard's head with a torrent of tobacco juice.

"Have to be to make it in this game, Sergeant."

Bickford looked up at the sun. "It's past ten o'clock. Let's get busy."

They dug a grave with pocketknives and pieces of flat, thin, reddish rock, a shallow grave at best, and stared critically at their makeshift work. Still, it was the best they could do under the circumstances and, they hoped, deep enough to keep varmints out. As if of the same mind, they all removed their hats for a moment, each man holding his thoughts within, and then they mounted and rode south, their eyes on the Chiricahuas, where the many horse tracks had disappeared.

Chapter Eight

"Mister Reyes assures me that we'll reach San Bernardino Springs before dark," Major Gordon told Jesse. "Our long march yesterday made up for what we lost today."

Despite the morning's delay, the volunteers were now making good time. The column, better organized after two days of travel, moved at a steady rate as it scoured up a low-hanging cloud of the reddish dust. Connelly kept the pack train up tight.

Sergeant Bickford's report had been concise and accurate, including the objective facts without undue emphasis on the gory details. The mark of a veteran noncom, Jesse noted, who could be counted on in the field. Gordon had picked the right man to serve as first sergeant. But by the time Ryan and Tate had passed on to others particulars of the gory mutilation, it had been a sober detail of horse soldiers that pulled out of camp. What had happened to Kaufman could happen to them.

While he rode along, Jesse played the morning over in his mind. Mutilation not only planted fear in an outfit; it was worse than battle deaths. Any man would fear torture, the unbearable pain. Death in battle a man could expect. If that was his fate, he hoped it was over fast, without the lingering pain of wounds from which he couldn't recover. Savage mutilation would be death by degrees. Was Kaufman still alive when his final degradation took place? Probably. That would go with Apache cruelty. The thought sickened Jesse. He could feel only compassion for the man.

There was no early afternoon halt, no need for one. The major headed them on. Jesse heard no grumbling, sensing everyone was thinking of the bounty of the springs that awaited them, same as he was.

An hour or more crept by.

Jesse, looking far off, glanced casually to the west and froze, staring hard. "Major," he said, pointing. "Look!"

It was the gray horseman again, boldly watching. He seemed to mock the column with his disdain for cover. Instead of vanishing suddenly as before, horse and rider remained sculpted against the sky, unmoving, yet wisely beyond rifle or carbine range. Jesse uncased his field glasses and brought them to bear. He couldn't tell much about specifics at this distance. The horse looked rangy and big, likely some luckless immigrant's mount taken in a wagon train massacre. The Apache made a small, indistinct shape. Jesse filled in the rest: usual headband around coal-black hair hanging to his shoulders, naked to the waist, breechcloth, moccasins, and leggings. Apaches didn't go for bandoleers, like Mexican bandits.

"Why does he keep parading himself?" Gordon wanted to know, frankly puzzled.

"Even based on what little I know about Apaches," Jesse replied, "it strikes me as most unusual, even self-defeating. This way they lose their way of fighting. Too costly. They see our flankers. A small wagon train might be another matter . . . easy to ride over. But they see what we have, and they'd like the pleasure of killing more White Eyes, which they relish equally with killing Mexicans. Getting Kaufman and that good horse and equipment made 'em hungry for more. So . . . ?"

"I think they'll hit us early in the morning at the springs."

"I'm afraid you're right."

"Another way to look at it, Major. They're watching in case another man leaves. They might think Kaufman was a messenger. Maybe we'll send another man north."

"They're a big war party, judging from the tracks reported.

They must feel rather confident."

"We can take extra precautions tonight. Not that we haven't before. By the way, I thought Sergeant Bickford conducted himself well today."

Gordon eyed him in surprise. "You say that after the trouble between you?"

"In the field, everything shakes down, levels out. We're all in the same boat. Past differences seem pretty damned unimportant."

Gordon let a little smile hover around his mouth before he spoke. "Since you're being honest, so will I. I deliberately directed you to accompany Bickford to see how you'd get along, hoping you would. A breaking in, you might say."

"Well, it had to come sooner or later. But don't get the idea we'd sleep in the same tent. He hates my guts, blames the South for everything, and his Abolitionist views make me see the Stars and Bars all over again."

When they looked westward again, the gray horseman had vanished.

Not long after that, they noticed glints of light in the lower reaches of the Chiricahuas. Farther to the south more flashes.

"They're signaling with hand mirrors," Jesse said, still watching. "If a man didn't know better, he might think that's sunlight on a crow's wings."

"Which tells us they're on our flank, headed south as we are," the major said.

Short of sundown, they reached San Bernardino Springs.

After watering and while the horses and mules were feeding, Gordon walked over the area with Reyes and Jesse in the fading light. The ground here was fairly level and cleared of brush, evidently long used as a favorite campsite near the springs over the countless years. Beyond it grew a tangle of thorny desert growth.

"I want a field of fire," the major said, "and I don't want the bivouac strung out as much as last night."

They stopped before a nearby mesa, looming over them.

"The *Mesa de la Avansada* . . . the Mesa of the Advance Guard," Reyes explained.

"Of the Advance Guard?" Gordon asked. "What's the meaning?"

"In the days when Spain ruled Mexico, *Señor* Major, a *presidio* garrisoned with soldiers stood here to guard this section of the northern frontier against savage tribes. I've been told that *padres* also established a mission near the *presidio*." He pointed south. "Those crumbling adobe walls are said to mark the site."

"Can't say the situation has changed much in a coupla hundred years," Gordon said, with a dry smile. He kept looking at the mesa.

"We could put our backs to the mesa," Jesse said, "and the picket line at the base of the mesa."

"Hmm. Yes . . . get 'em behind us, out of the way. Establish a defensive perimeter in the shape of a half moon around the bivouac." He clapped his hands. "I believe that's it, gentlemen. Now let's get after some supper."

Tongues of fire licked the bracing night air. Wood smoke laid down a pleasant scent, blending with the cooking smells.

After supper, Bickford called out the men to stand the night watches.

"I don't want anybody gettin' nervous and firin' at coyotes and keepin' us awake," he warned them.

"How can ye tell the difference in the dark, Sarge?" Of course, Jesse knew, it was Private Moriarty, affecting a tremulous voice.

120

"Only an Irishman would ask such a dumb-John question. Easy enough. You can tell it's an Apache when a shadow yells and jumps out at you with a knife. Then you can fire, Moriarty."

"Thank ye, Sarge," Moriarty replied, mockingly humble. "I feel much relieved now, knowin' what to do."

"You'll never know what to do, Moriarty," Bickford shot back, squaring around at him, sarcasm shaping his mouth, the campfires lighting up old battle scars around his eyes and chin. "Maybe we'd better fix you some tea and toast before we tuck you in and make you comfy for the night in your feather bed." His voice dropped to a syrupy tone. "And maybe you could use another blanket? Gets chilly at night on the desert. Could one of you boys spare sonny boy a blanket?" Swiftly all that changed, his face in the customary scowl as he barked: "You're on the last watch, Moriarty . . . you and Connelly, and Cramer and Webb, and you'd better be on time! No doggin' it."

"Ye know me, Sarge."

"Too well!"

"Have I ever failed in me duty when called?"

"You'd better not start!"

Jesse enjoyed the banter, knowing the troopers did, too, even Bickford, to some extent, because he always had the last word. Banter kept an outfit loose and in good humor. He would've offered to stand a watch, but knew Bickford would say he wasn't needed.

Major Gordon crossed over. "Sergeant, before we settle down, let's build some fires farther out . . . past the mule packs and saddles. Keep them going through the night. Post the sentries well back. It will extend the perimeter and give us elbow room, if we have trouble before dawn."

"Yes, sir!"

Afterward, Jesse stretched out and smoked, his back against

his bedroll, letting his thoughts drift, watching the fires marking the bivouac's extended perimeter. A picture sprang unexpectedly to his mind: the fires like footlights on a stage, the volunteers the actors in pantomime as their voices slacked off, hushed, died. The only camp sounds were the restless stirrings along the picket line. Tonight *El Soldado* and Chico, the mule, were picketed with the others. Jesse usually thought of his mount simply as the red horse, seldom using his given name. *Why was that? Was that because it was special, which it was?*

He finished the pipe and sought his blankets, fully clothed, the Spencer and Quickloader by his side. On nights like this he slept in short snatches, his conscious self always near the surface of wakefulness. Over the years, that had become fixed, part of him. He was always awake before first light, his senses like a clock.

He watched the changing sky. Bands of roving dark clouds screened off all but slim threads of filmy light — *just when we need light*. A cool wind rose, straight out of Sonora, making soft whimpering sounds; by three o'clock the desert night would be cold.

He thought: *Down to eighteen volunteers*. It was unreasonable for officials in Washington even to consider that an outfit this small — "I'm acting under strict orders . . . no more than twenty-five men," he could hear Colonel Chilton saying — could achieve so much . . . their numbers already thinned before they left Bowie. Yet Chilton apparently had made no effort to refill the ranks to twenty-five. Was that for lack of volunteers? No doubt Major Gordon was a highly qualified officer, proven so in battle. But the weight of this mission on one good man was onerous, and unfair, when handed so few to command.

Looking back, he thought that his young years in the war had been spent often following, and surviving, unreasonable

122

orders that bordered on imbecility. Only by the grace of God had he survived. Thus, in time, the South had, literally, run out of cannon fodder. It wasn't war — it was murder. The North had been just as wasteful, but it could always replenish its ranks, while the South could not.

Enough of this looking back, he thought, pulling up a blanket. If he was going to sleep, it had to be during these early hours. Upon that, he lay back and slept.

It seemed only a short while until he opened his eyes, instantly awake, but he sensed that he had slept several hours. He lay there, listening and looking at the loose cloud formations still in passage, still allowing only miserly light from the full moon. On his right a trooper snored without letup, the volume alternately rising and falling. Scattered stamps and rattles sounded along the crowded picket line.

He sat up. The perimeter fires had burned low. Against that shallow light, he could see the silhouetted figures of the sentries slowly pacing back and forth . . . halting for a time . . . staring off into the night . . . pacing again . . . halting.

He continued to watch, unable to go back to sleep.

The sentries changed.

About then he heard an owl hoot. It seemed to rise not far from the lower end of the picket line. A sort of high-pitched *hoo-hoo-oo*. He waited, expecting another, hoping it wouldn't come.

Some minutes straggled by. He heard a sentry's boots scuffing gravel. Something, some sense, told him another hoot was coming, told him because the first hoot had been quite close, not out in the desert.

He tensed, waiting, knowing it was coming.

Next time it seemed to be moving around toward the front of the bivouac, a low, quavering *hoo-hoo,* different from the first call. He thought he knew the meaning of that subtle difference.

The picket line stirred nervously, which told him even more. *They sense something.* He could picture the red horse warily watching.

The sentries continued their pacing, halting, and looking. They didn't seem alarmed. Well, it didn't matter yet.

By now the outlying fires were down to dull coals.

The third hoot brought him to his feet. It was even different from the first two, a kind of drawn-out, moaning *hoooo-hooo.*

He knew for certain now as he drew the Quickloader's strap over his shoulder and slipped a shell from his jacket in the chamber, making it an eight-shooter. Each hoot was different; each hoot meant a different Apache. *They're getting into position now, waiting for the light to be behind them, in the eyes of the White Eyes. Then they'll come jumping.*

He was faced that way when Major Gordon and Sergeant Bickford came over.

"What do you think, Captain?" Gordon asked, low. "I couldn't sleep. Heard you get up."

"They've worked around the perimeter, Major. From the lower picket line on."

"How can you tell?"

"By the hoot owl signals. The calls aren't the same, so more than one Apache is makin' 'em."

"How much time do we have?"

"Till daybreak . . . or less."

"Which will come in about an hour or less. I believe it's best that we get the men up."

"I'm for it."

"Sergeant, get the men up quietly. I'll post them."

"Yes, sir!"

There followed the shuffling sounds of men getting up and

their restrained voices, and, when they were assembled, the major directed Bickford to post Connelly on the lower flank nearest the picket line with two men because he was a crack shot, and three men on the other flank. He ordered others spaced around the perimeter at close intervals, crouched behind the low barricade of packs and saddles, leaving a reserve of three troopers, counting Bickford, near the center, with the major, Reyes, and Jesse.

"Remember, there's nothing more effective at close quarters than your Colt Army Forty-Fours," Gordon told them in a low, but heartening, voice before turning them over to Bickford. And to Jesse he said: "Captain, I want you at my elbow with that Spencer repeater if we need some concentrated fire mighty quick."

"I understand, Major."

"Mister Reyes, you stick with us."

"I am here, *Señor* Major."

As an afterthought, Gordon had Bickford issue hardtack all around from the packs.

Now they waited.

Time seemed stuck. The night filled with foreboding.

A hoot owl's ominous call broke the taut silence. It sounded like the first signal, Jesse thought, that high, distinctive *hoo-hoo-oo*, except its location had changed from the lower picket line to in front of the bivouac. *So they're forming there.* That was his guess, his feeling, his sense — if you could outguess an Apache at night.

But minutes afterward the same call sounded from the left flank. What did that mean? Another hoot rose near the center, a moaning *hoooo-hooo*, a ghostly call, enough to make a man's skin crawl on a night like this.

"What do you make of the calls now, Captain?" Gordon whispered.

125

"They seem to be shifting around."

"Where do you ascertain they'll attack?"

"Anywhere, Major. That's not telling you much."

"It's always best not to be too set on what you think the other side will do, Captain," Gordon said, speaking reflectively, as one might from battlefield experience. "Otherwise, you can't react effectively."

"I believe we're as ready as we can be, Major. We're all right."

The night seemed to hang as the air grew colder. The clouds stubbornly continued to release only stringers of hazy light, which created an eerie, formless glow over the bivouac.

The waiting grew tedious as the tension built. Jesse could hear troopers shifting about now and then. He and others in the so-called "reserve" would crouch a while, then stand. There was nothing to be seen beyond the bivouac. Out there it was a dark void of mesquites and catclaw, greasewood and prickly pear cactus and yucca, where only an Apache could crawl and hide.

Jesse looked at the sky. It couldn't be long till the first light.

"What do you think now, Captain?"

"They have to be in position by this time, Major. We haven't heard any more hoots. They're waiting for daybreak, same as we are."

The sky began to alter ever so subtly. Jesse kept shifting his eyes from the sky to the dark mass of brush, back and forth. He figured the Apaches would time their charge when the first bold stroke of blazing, blinding light enveloped the camp. Not before.

The sky took on a gray tone.

For a fleetness it stayed that shade. The silence was gripping.

Now, like a light brush stroke, a blush pinked the sky.

"Get ready, Major."

They were all standing, eyes intent on the curve of the bivouac.

The clouds began to break up. The blushing sky turned red.

Still nothing happened.

But all at once sunlight blazed down hard upon the bivouac. A pause. No more than a pause, and out of the blinding east charged a wave of jumping, half-naked shapes, screeching and firing. The entire front seemed to be bobbing with bronze bodies.

Carbines banged. Troopers yelled.

Jesse fired at the dodging wraiths.

The major was coolly shooting, holding a Colt revolver straight out, in the accepted target-range stance. Young Reyes was beside him, taking aim with a rifle.

An Apache dropped with a cry in front of the barricade. Still screaming hate, he started crawling forward, knife in hand. A trooper shot him dead.

Powder smoke bloomed everywhere. Jesse got its bitter taste. In the fog of grayish-white smoke, and with the Apaches jumping, it was difficult to tell how effective the defenders' fire was. A trooper on the line dropped his carbine and slumped over a pack.

The frightful screeching and yelling never ceased.

After some moments of this, Jesse sensed a change. In an unusual turn of fighting, the Apaches had inexplicably fallen back after their initial charge against the center. Fading into the brush, they kept up firing.

Jesse stopped shooting. So did Gordon.

To Jesse, there was a puzzle about this tactic. It wasn't Apache style to charge briefly and pull back. Their first charge was usually a determined one. If they failed to overrun the enemy, only then did they fade away.

He had just loaded a second tube of shells when gunfire erupted on the lower end of the picket line. He jerked that way.

At the same instant, Gordon shouted: "Captain Wilder . . . Sergeant Bickford! The lower picket line . . . they're flanking us!"

Jesse glimpsed Apaches bunching there. It was threateningly clear now. The brief frontal attack was only a feint. Through the drifting smoke, he saw Connelly standing his ground and firing. A trooper with him staggered and fell.

The Spencer's barrel grew hot in Jesse's left hand as he worked the loading lever. Half-naked bodies seemed to be everywhere before him. Some went down or spun away, hit, but more came on, a surprising number of them. The Spencer snapped empty. No time to reload. He jerked the Colt Navy. Gordon and Reyes, on his left, were getting off shots.

Now everything became more confused amid the rolls of acrid smoke, with Apaches screeching and troopers shouting, and horses and mules rearing and lunging on picket ropes, the horses neighing wildly, the braying mules making as much noise as a brass band.

A trooper and an Apache swayed in struggle. The Apache broke free, his broad-bladed knife flashing. The Apache rushed the trooper. Jesse shot the Apache once, but that didn't stop him. A second bullet to the head knocked him down. The trooper flung about in slack-mouthed surprise. It was Bickford, who quickly reloaded.

As suddenly as the Apaches had struck, they seemed to waver and fade, raising piercing cries. As if on signal, they withdrew and melted into the tangle of mesquites and brush.

Jesse saw that it was finished. Apaches weren't ones to

hang around once a fight was lost.

The detail's shooting dribbled off. Some of the volunteers quit and stood about uncertainly.

But the major's cool voice caught at them. "Sergeant Bickford, let's maintain a slow but steady rate of fire into the brush for a few minutes. Raise your sights a little, men. Let's keep them occupied till we're certain they're gone."

"Yes, sir!"

"And Corporal Connelly," Gordon said, "bring the wounded over here."

Bickford barked: "Prepare to resume firing. Fire!"

As the firing picked up, Jesse reloaded the carbine and started spacing his shots, lifting the angle of fire. He could see nothing. The Apaches were gone.

When the cease-fire came, they found one dead trooper. He was Private Cramer, in for insubordination, Jesse recalled.

"Isaac won't have to worry no more about quinine and salts," a trooper said sadly, shaking his head.

Danny Maguire, his back against a pack, was clutching his middle. It didn't look good for him when they stretched him out. His face was pale, and, when they opened his jacket and shirt, Jesse saw that he was bleeding heavily.

"Me sainted mother said I'd come to no good, if I left the Old Sod," said Maguire, a stocky, brown-haired young man with devilish dark eyes. He grimaced, trying to grin. "I told her I'd go to America and come back rich. She said I was chasin' false idols, like the Good Book says. Me mother was right."

"Buck up, you Mick," Connelly said roughly. "You're gonna be all right." Only words, they all knew, including Maguire.

Connelly tore up a shirt from a pack and bandaged him, and they did the best they could for him, which was little, and the major told Bickford to keep guards posted while they cooked breakfast. Above all, he said, they had to have plenty of coffee.

Gordon, hands clasped behind him, his concerned eyes on Maguire, turned to Jesse. "A gut shot. Poor fellow. I hate to see this happen to a man. Maguire can't ride. I'm wondering about a sort of blanket litter for him. However, I question whether blankets would hold between mules fore and aft. At best, it'd be an awkward getup, further complicated by how the mules would tolerate it."

Jesse studied a moment. A thought deepened, formed. "I've heard of taking yucca stalks or poles and making a crude travois. Tying a blanket between the poles, and laying grass over it for a bed."

"A travois? You mean a mule would drag the poles?"

"Yes. You'd tie the poles to the sides of the mule's pack, then tie the trailing poles together."

"How would you hold everything together?"

"Cut up some blankets."

"Hmm. That . . . and there should be some light rope in the packs. Let's try it. Be more comfortable for him. About all we can do. I'll see that he gets some whiskey I have in my pack. I'll send a man with you to cut the poles."

Walking beyond the perimeter with a trooper, Jesse saw a scattering of Apache bodies. A costly attack for them, he knew, because the little command was prepared. In the brush, he found a few more. His estimate of Major Gordon continued to grow. Besides being a good officer, he looked out for his men.

With axes, they cut yucca stalks and carried them back. After breakfast, they would assemble the crude, primitive thing. They might have to lay shorter poles across the trailing poles for support. It wasn't going to be as easy as Jesse had first thought.

Gordon's orderly had built a fire, and Jesse was boiling coffee there when Bickford walked by. He stopped and said: "I owe you."

"You don't," Jesse said.

Bickford took a step back, in instant affront. "What do you mean I don't owe you? Ain't my life worth something?"

"I don't mean that at all, Sergeant." *What did he exactly mean?* His next words came awkwardly. "I mean, you're not obliged to me in any way. You'd do the same for me or any man. So would I. The chance of battle."

Bickford stared hard, taking that in. "Always the uppity Southern gent with your fancy talk."

He strode on.

Jesse watched him go over to his own small fire, shared with no one, feeling annoyed with himself and an irretrievable regret. He glanced around and knew that the major had heard.

Jesse sighed. "Guess I said the wrong thing. I just meant. . . ."

"I know what you meant. You were damned glad to do it. Sometimes it's hard to put into words and sometimes just as hard to understand, yet both persons mean the right thing."

"Maybe, as the poet said, it's not so much what you say, but how you say it. He thought I sounded uppity. God forbid! What he meant was he'd like to return the favor, and I didn't give him the chance. Why didn't I get up and offer my hand?"

"Why didn't he offer his hand to thank you?" Gordon said reasonably.

The coffee was ready. By mutual consent, they let the matter rest there.

131

Chapter Nine

After burying Private Cramer and marking the grave with his name and regiment on a stone, the little command rode solemnly south down the sandy valley of the San Bernardino River in a tight column of twos, trailing streamers of coppery dust, the travois bearing Maguire pulled by a gentle mule. At times Maguire would wave a bottle and say something self-mocking, his venturesome Irish heart forbidding him to be otherwise. He was half drunk and growing weaker, but it didn't matter. When a solicitous trooper asked if he wanted a drink of water, he laughed and said — "Water . . . when a man's got whiskey?" — and waved him aside.

Jesse rode close by in case the contraption broke down. If it did, there was plenty of replacement yucca about.

Before midday, following a road paralleling the river, they began to see signs of devastation, which Reyes pointed out as evidence of relentless Apache raids: the country deserted and gloomy, fields grown up in weeds and cane and mesquite, adobe houses standing empty, their windows like dark, melancholy eyes staring hopelessly at the column. Jesse could feel the haunting silence, the mocking emptiness, the vanished hopes. Talk among the volunteers fell away.

They saw no one. The only sign of life appeared in the great dome of the turquoise sky where red-tailed hawks, ever restless, ever searching, sailed and dived.

They came upon little mounds of rocks beside the road with pitiable crude wooden crosses marking the graves. The yucca travois required repairs only once, and they camped before dark at the junction of the San Bernardino and an easterly tributary, in the shade of graceful walnut and ash trees.

After watering and feeding, Gordon ordered the horses groomed for the first time since departing Fort Bowie. "We may not get this chance again soon," he said. "Our mounts need it."

They marched to the picket line with currycomb, brush, and hoof hook, and Bickford took charge, displaying obvious relish as he pulled out a watch the size of a turnip.

When he barked — "Commence grooming!" — the men fell to the job with a will.

Jesse, joining in with the red horse, remembered the usual time spent on the lower front legs was two minutes.

"Change!" Bickford barked next, and everybody switched to the lower rear legs. Two minutes there.

"Change! You're lagging, Moriarty!" Bickford was enjoying making them hump.

Then they moved quickly to the near side — neck, shoulder, arm, elbow, back, side, flank, loins, croup, and the hind leg to the hock. Four minutes.

"Change!" Bickford's bark was getting louder as his eyes followed every move.

Then the chest between the forelegs, the belly, and between the hind legs.

"Change! Keep up, Moriarty!"

Then the offside neck, shoulder, arm, elbow, back, side, flank, loins, croup, and the hind leg to the hock. Four minutes.

"Change!"

Then the head, ears, and throat. With the hand, rub the throat between the forks of the lower jaw. One minute.

"Change!"

Then brush and lay forelock and mane. Two minutes.

"Change!"

Then brush out the tail. Two minutes.

"Change!"

Then, using a bandanna, wipe out the eyes and nostrils and muzzle. Two minutes.

"Change!"

Then clean out the feet. Two minutes.

"Cease grooming."

The troopers stopped, finished.

Bickford about-faced and accorded the major a swift salute. "Grooming completed, sir."

"Very good, Sergeant," Gordon said, returning the salute. "Dismiss the detail."

Bickford about-faced. "Grooming detail dismissed."

There was an abundance of dry wood and water, and the command soon had supper fires blazing, with one flank of the bivouac against the creek. As evening drew on, Gordon ordered sentries posted and scheduled for the night, and the detail to be up before daylight in a position of readiness.

"What about tomorrow, Mister Reyes?" Gordon asked while they sat around the fire after supper. "What lies ahead of us?"

"Tomorrow, *Señor* Major, we will reach the Bavispe River and make camp there. Progress will be slow, but again there will be wood and water, and again we shall see much devastation caused by the heathen Apaches." His voice was sad and resigned.

"How often do they raid?"

"At their will. But mainly in the spring and fall, when there is plenty of water. They like to wait for a full moon before they capture Mexican stock so they can drive them at night. We passed the ruins of two small villages today, wiped out long ago. Only a few people escaped. I'm told that after they killed the men, or the handful of soldiers stationed there, they

134

dragged the women out by the hair, then killed them and the children, sparing only the few little ones they took back to raise as Apaches in the mountains. My country is poor and weak, *Señor* Major, too weak to defend itself."

"Do you think the Apaches will jump us again?"

Reyes shrugged philosophically and looked at Jesse. "*¿Quién sabe?* But I think not. Certainly not the same war party. Perhaps Captain Wilder can answer that better than I can."

"I agree with Agustín," Jesse said. "We hurt them badly at the springs. But be up and ready as usual before daybreak. The farther south we go, the more distance we put between us and the Chiricahuas. But others could come at us out of the Sierra Madre, where they have camps."

"You never take anything in war for granted out here, do you, Captain?" Gordon observed.

"It's wise not to, Major. A man will lose some sleep, but that's better than his hair."

Gordon chuckled. He asked Reyes: "About how far do you figure we are from La Gloria?"

"About seventy or eighty miles. We'll be entering some broken country, and the march will be slower."

"We're well within our time limit. Beginning tomorrow, we have eight days left. I've looked at the map Colonel Chilton had drawn for us. It's helpful, though very general. Your personal knowledge of the land and villages is what we need most."

With such plentiful wood at hand, Gordon directed Bickford to build up the supper fires to last well into the night. With that light and a clearing sky under the big moon, the bivouac swam in a soft glow.

Jesse looked about his stock and went to his bedroll, thinking by tomorrow they would be deep into Sonora. After this time, he had no qualms about the volunteers as a fighting unit. They were damned good horse soldiers, tough and full of banter. They'd fought well at the springs. It was terrifying to fight Apaches up close, particularly the first time. Their hideous yelling and screeching as they charged could rend a man trembling and fumbling, unable to fight effectively. You felt the grip of numbing fear, which Jesse had, even if you'd fought them before. The volunteers had stood up to it.

He slept on that solid thought.

It must have been late when he heard a commotion, a cursing voice, and hoofs stamping. He sat up, carbine in hand. The fires still burned. By their dingy light and the sallow moonlight filtering through the timber, he saw Bickford emerge from his dog tent.

And, at the rear of the tent, he was startled to see none other than Chico, the mule, chewing voraciously at the top of the sergeant's tent. Chico had pulled his picket pin. Now he stood there, picket rope dangling from his halter, while he enjoyed Bickford's shelter.

Putting down the carbine, Jesse dashed over fast and grabbed Chico's halter.

Bickford saw him at once. "Your god-damned Mexican mule's chewed a hole in my tent big enough for a buzzard to fly through. At first, I thought it was a bear nosin' around camp for food. Get him back on the picket line."

Jesse did just that, with alacrity. Coming back, he was all apology. "Sergeant, I'm mighty sorry. First time he's ever pulled his picket. I'm very sorry."

"Sorry, hell!" Bickford exploded, and crawled into the ruin of tent.

Jesse went back to his camp. Glancing at the sky, he saw the moon was three quarters down. Everybody was awake by now. He could hear voices and muffled laughter that was more than a few chuckles.

As he slipped into his bedroll, he heard an Irish voice that had to be Moriarty's, overly correct, lifted in mocking concern: "Sure sorry about yer tent, Actin' First Sergeant, sir. Hope it don't rain. Would ye like some tea and toast to make ye nice and comfy fer the rest of the night, sir?"

"Shut up, Moriarty!"

Moriarty, doubtless knowing his limits, said no more.

Daybreak passed without alarm, and they were cooking breakfast when Corporal Connelly hurried over to Major Gordon.

"Sir, I regret to report that Private Maguire just died. When I took his coffee to him, he was gone."

"Oh . . . too bad, too bad." Gordon sat there in silence for a bit. "You men go ahead with breakfast. Thank you, Corporal."

He then put down his coffee cup, punched the palm of his left hand, and said to Reyes and Jesse: "We're losing too many good men, and we're not even there." He punched his hand again. "God-damn thick-headed Washington officialdom, I say, for limiting us to such a small force. More concerned with international relations than their own men. How much do they think a mere handful of hard-assed horse soldiers can do? As good as these men are? It's the same old story. People back there never know what they're asking of good men."

Lifting his arm in an unfinished gesture of disgust, he went quietly over to where Maguire lay face up to the morning sky and Connelly stood by morosely. Gordon removed his hat. Looking down, he said: "I never heard him complain once, and he knew he wasn't going to make it."

"No, sir," Connelly said. "He never did. Wasn't brought up that way. He was a good Irish lad."

Gordon continued to gaze at the young, marbled face, his

137

own infinitely sad and unusually gentle. He closed his eyes and seemed to nod to himself in understanding, his lips compressed. Another moment and he put his hat back on, saluted the dead trooper, faced left, and walked off, calling Sergeant Bickford.

The sun was high in the sky before they laid Danny Maguire to rest and formed and rode south in a column of twos, following the meandering, swift-running San Bernardino. Soon the way roughed up to broken country. After more than an hour of this, slowed by the jungle of coarse grass, cane, willow, and ash, Reyes led them away from the river to toil up and down the bluffs on the right side of the stream.

There seemed no end to the lonely land, so barren of human life. They passed more abandoned adobes, gradually melting down to mud hovels, the adjacent fields long ago taken back by nature. They passed a deserted ranch house where a bold gray wolf stood possessively in the courtyard entrance, his yellow eyes assessing the riders, and they passed an orchard of gnarled dead fruit trees and the tangled ruin of a vineyard, and more rock-covered mounds with wooden crosses.

Jesse was glad when someone spoke up and relieved the solemn air of the gloomy column.

"Where are all the gurls ye promised, Actin' Corporal Connelly?" the irrepressible Moriarty wanted to know, his deep voice carrying the length of the column. At the start of the march Bickford had ordered him to ride at the rear with the pack train.

"Ye've been spoiled, Private Moriarty," Connelly took it up. "Ye must learn patience such as practiced by meself, waitin' fer me promotion to come through, actin' though it may be."

"Yer a fine model of a man, Actin' Corporal Connelly, I know. I'm honored to ride in the same column with ye, sir."

"That 'tis not fer me to say," Connelly replied loftily. "But all things come to him who has patience. Remember that."

"Why, ye sound like a bard of the Old Sod, ye do, Actin' Corporal Connelly, sir."

"Me modesty prevents me from answerin' that, Private Moriarty. But think what ye like."

That afternoon, with the rambling river still on their left, they were following the dim traces of an old road grown up with weeds and grass and yucca and the ever-present prickly pear, when a fast-moving line of dust took shape. It was approaching from their right and soon would cross their line of march.

"We have company coming," Gordon said, gazing through binoculars.

Reyes looked and said: "Mexican irregulars."

Jesse's field glasses revealed fifty or sixty riders, some on mules, trailed by a straggling pack train. They had the earmarks of a rag-tag outfit. They could mean only one thing — trouble.

Gordon halted the command and posted men in a tight front to protect the pack train, himself in the center, with Reyes on his left, Jesse on his right, and Bickford and Connelly as anchors on each flank. Then he ordered carbines drawn, and waited. Jesse laid the repeater across his lap.

The irregulars also changed formation, from their strung-out loose column of twos to fours. They approached at a dust-raising gallop. About fifty yards away, the leader threw up a dramatic halting hand and rode forward on a fine bay, flanked by two riders on each side. *What you might call aides,* Jesse thought. The closer he looked at them, the more they looked like bandits.

The major didn't move until the Mexican party halted within parley distance. At that point, Gordon raised his right hand, waiting for the other to speak.

To Jesse's surprise, the Mexican officer spoke in heavily accented, yet precise, English. "By what right are you *Americanos* in Mexico? I demand to know." He was a short, puffy man clad in a high-necked gray jacket of military cut with silver buttons the size of dollars, of which two were missing, and a flat-crowned cap. He wore greasy leather pants and high-topped black boots that showed much wear. An enormous pistol in a hand-tooled leather holster and belt wobbled on his hip. His black mustache quivered indignantly as he spoke in bursts, his glistening white teeth like piano keys. "I am Colonel Santa Ana Blanco, of the Sonoran Auxiliary," he added haughtily, a gloved hand brushing at his mustache. "I await your answer to this unwarranted invasion of Mexican territory."

"We are a party of mining engineers from Tucson, and we have papers of permission from the highest authority in Sonora, His Excellency, Governor Emanuel Reyes," Gordon replied, folding his arms while speaking in an even tone.

"Papers," the colonel sneered. "I have not been informed of any such papers issued to *Americanos*."

"I dare say, Colonel, you are not privy to *all* business Don Emanuel conducts for the benefit of the great state of Sonora. He is a very busy executive. The gentleman on my left is *Señor* Agustín Reyes, His Excellency's son. Show him the papers, *Señor* Reyes."

Blanco sneered again. "Let me see them. They are probably forgeries. If so, I shall be forced to repel this intrusion."

Young Reyes sat quite straight in his saddle and leveled a contemptuous look on Blanco. "*Señor* Colonel," he said coldly, letting his eyes stay fixed, "my father is not in the habit

140

of issuing forgeries." Deliberately, importantly, he opened a saddlebag and drew out a beautiful leather dispatch case, and from it two sheets of heavy white paper, the top one bearing a gold seal that caught the rays of the sun. Then he rode out and, with great ceremony, handed the papers to Blanco.

Jesse watched closely, approving. *That's the way to do it. Be as arrogant as Blanco, but don't overdo it, Agustín. The bastard is looking for a chance to jump us, if he can get the advantage.*

Blanco, his mouth warped, held the papers at arm's length. While he read, Jesse sized up the irregulars massed behind the colonel and his aides, his wariness mounting. They wore broad-brimmed white straw sombreros with chin straps, white cotton pants, and ragged white shirts. There was scarcely a pair of shoes among them. Some wore rawhide sandals, and some went barefoot. But every man carried a full belt of ammunition. Among their arms, Jesse recognized some old Enfield muzzleloaders, such as the South had used, a few Springfield muzzleloaders, and a mix of worn-looking carbines, ranging from Sharps and Ballards and Starrs to Maynards and Joslyns. These they held across their high-pommeled saddles, while they hungrily eyed the volunteers' good horses and loaded mules. Their own mounts looked poor and hard used, their pack mules even poorer.

Now Blanco finished reading the papers, but made no effort to return them. "I find this most unusual," he said. "*Americano* miners in Sonora."

"You saw the seal of the state of Sonora granting permission, *Señor* Colonel," Reyes insisted. "Nothing can be more official."

"But there is much lacking in the papers. There is no location set forth where you will do your mining or what you will mine. That is most unusual."

Blanco glanced obliquely at an aide, who raised a hand to

141

his sombrero. Although no word was spoken, it must have been a prearranged signal, because all the irregulars closed in threateningly, halting a few paces from the parley.

"The permission speaks for itself, *Señor* Colonel," Reyes said. "There is no higher authority in Sonora than my father, the governor."

Blanco raised his head even higher. "It states no location. It is unacceptable. I cannot let you pass."

When Reyes hesitated, Gordon moved forward, and his motion drew the entire line with him, Jesse deciding: *If they come at us, I'll get Blanco first.* The hammer of the Spencer made a distinct *click* when he eared it back, and Blanco seemed to stiffen at the sound.

"Colonel," Gordon said, his voice like a slap across the wind burning off the desert, "your authority, high as it is, cannot exceed that of His Excellency, Governor Reyes, who has given us permission to prospect in the Sierra Madre . . . that is a general location. There can be no exact location until we find favorable traces."

"Traces of what?"

"Gold, silver, copper. And if a mine is developed, most of the profits will go to the state of Sonora. Many of your people will be hired. His Excellency has employed us to do this survey in hopes it will help the poor."

Blanco appeared to take all that in with deep consideration. Then his black eyes snapped, and he said: "As a soldier who has served Mexico and Sonora for many years fighting the godless Apaches, I could not miss the military manner in which you march. Perhaps you are not miners, instead *Americano* soldiers in disguise?"

Gordon pointed. "Do soldiers carry picks and shovels? Look at them sticking out of our packs. We march like this to defend ourselves. Because we have to. The Apaches jumped us at San Bernardino Springs. We fought them off, but lost two men. Only fools would march in loose order." His gaze on Blanco contained ridicule. "Too bad your command didn't find the Apaches first. After this, perhaps you should patrol farther north where the Chiricahua Apaches range."

Blanco's head snapped up. His eyes burned. "We fight the godless Apaches where we can find them, on the desert or in the mountains. When we catch them, we kill them like flies. Their bones bleach in the sun. The rest run from us like slinking coyotes." As if that should impress the *Americanos*, he tilted his head higher and warped his mouth in his disdainful way.

Jesse was almost amused. *He's putting on a big show to bluff us, when the truth is Mexicans seldom follow Apaches into the mountains, and, when they do, seldom do you hear of a victory.*

"You say that you are not soldiers," Blanco said, his black eyes keenly observing, "but I see US brands on your horses."

"On some of them, yes," Gordon readily acknowledged. "Those are surplus Army animals purchased in Tucson, too old for fighting."

Blanco swept his gaze over the entire detail. "Your mules also carry the US brand."

"Likewise purchased in Tucson. Now, Colonel, we ask you to step aside so we may continue our journey and do this work for His Excellency, Don Emanuel Reyes. Be assured that your courteous co-operation as a field commander of the Auxiliary will be passed on to the governor."

Jesse set himself for instant imperious refusal. Instead, Blanco broke into a grandiose smile and removed his cap with a sweeping motion. "You may pass," he said, returning the papers to Reyes. "You have nothing to fear from us . . . we are friends. It's an honor to know men who fought the Apaches and won. We have been following a hostile trail for days. Once we surprised the heathens' camp. There was a bloody fight. They scattered like quail when we charged. *Vah!* After this hard time, we are worn out. Our horses and mules are in poor flesh, as you can see. Our supplies are low. Could you spare some, *Señor* Engineer?" His smile widened even more, wheedling, fawning.

Jesse's immediate reaction was to doubt Blanco's claim of surprising an Apache camp. He sensed the colonel was mostly pretense and not to be trusted. He was not surprised when Gordon, evidently reasoning that to share supplies was one way to avoid a fight, told Connelly — not giving away the command by addressing him as corporal — to cut out one pack mule, but to keep the shovels and picks.

That was done, and the column marched on, keeping close order. As they passed, the irregulars wolfishly eyed the horses and mules.

"Let us camp with you tonight," Blanco called out. "We're short of coffee. We know you have plenty."

Gordon didn't slow up. "We must decline your gracious invitation, Colonel. There is coffee on the pack mule we gave you, and bacon. Good day, sir."

Camp with robbers and murderers, Jesse thought, sensing the outfit hadn't seen the last of them.

When they were beyond earshot, Gordon said: "He was sharp to pick that up about the brands. How do you see the situation now?"

Jesse looked back before he answered. "They're palavering on what to do next. It's plain they want our horses and mules and packs."

"And . . . ?"

"My gut instinct tells me they'll try to take 'em pretty quick. They have us outnumbered three or four to one, and we're out in the open."

"I feel the same way. Mister Reyes, have you ever heard of a Colonel Blanco in the Sonora Auxiliary?"

"No, *Señor* Major. But there are officers posted here and there. The irregulars are like what you call in your country, the . . . ?" He hesitated.

"Militia," Gordon suggested.

"Yes."

They had marched on no more than a two hundred yards when Jesse, looking back again, said: "They've quit the palaver and are following us, Major."

Gordon took a quick look. "Coming at a trot, too. At this rate they'll soon overrun us." He whipped around to look ahead. There the land rolled in swells. "That rocky rise," he said, pointing. "Let's take position there and see what they do."

He shouted at Bickford and Connelly and gestured toward the rise and led away from the road at a fast trot. They had about a mile to go.

At once the irregulars started riding faster.

"They're coming at a gallop now, Major," Jesse said.

"Their intent is clear," Gordon said. "It's going to be close. We can't gallop the pack train." He looked straight at Jesse. "Captain, fire a few shots to warn them off. I want to avoid a fight if we can."

Jesse reined out of the line and looked back. They were coming at a hard gallop now, angling off the road to intercept the detail. He sent a bullet over the heads of the lead riders, then another. The red horse merely flinched at the first bang of the carbine, ears twitching.

Blanco's men charged on, never slowing. A puff of white smoke rose as one fired, and a bullet whined as Jesse heard the familiar *crack* of an Enfield.

He placed his next shot into the column and saw a rider

145

slump. After that, firing rapidly, he aimed for the clump of leading horsemen. They swept on, low in their saddles. Once he thought he sighted Blanco's jacket in the mass of dirty white riders, hoping a bullet would find him. A horse broke down, throwing its rider. Another went jerking out of the line, a foreleg dangling, its rider hauling on the reins. He hit another rider, and another. This was excellent range for the Spencer.

Suddenly, to his relief, Blanco's bunch pulled up, but more of them were beginning to fire and yell at him. But they had stopped, milling in confusion. It was time to go. No need to reload now. Everything had happened in a very short interval. Jesse whirled the red horse and tore away, bullets *humming* about him as he bent low and kept his mount in a zigzagging run. Ahead, he could see the outfit forming on the low hump of ground. The major had his field of fire again.

When he rushed up, Connelly and others were holding the mounts and mules behind the rise. Jesse handed his reins to a horse holder and joined Gordon, who was watching the pursuit.

"You checked them long enough, Captain," Gordon said. "Good. And they've quit firing. Now, damned if they're not sending a party with a white flag! What's left to parley about?"

"Whatever they say, don't believe it," Jesse said, taking a tube from the Quickloader.

"I know one thing . . . I'd like to have that pack mule back."

"It got us clear of them. A small price, Major."

Three riders, two in front, one waving a white flag, approached the rise. They rode slowly with care until within shouting distance. Then the one behind the two showed himself.

"Hell!" Jesse flashed. "It's Blanco . . . hiding behind his

146

men till he's sure we won't fire!"

"Why did you fire on us?" Blanco shouted in a hurt voice.

"You were in pursuit," Gordon yelled back.

"We were only continuing on our patrol for godless Apaches, riding fast."

"Of course, that's a lie. And when we fired warning shots, you continued to pursue us. Why didn't you halt your men?"

"My men . . . they are very young. Not used to fighting. Very difficult to control. Very impulse, as you *Americanos* say."

"Nothing's more plain than a bullet, Colonel."

"Meanwhile, your fire killed two of my men and wounded three. You also killed two of our horses."

Blanco, Jesse could tell, amused, was getting very indignant. Very dramatic. Putting on a show for effect. Making gestures, his outraged voice rising.

Gordon said: "Your men fired at our man when he tried to warn you off."

"It was a misunderstanding, *Señor* Engineer. I have explained everything. I say that on my honor as an officer of many years in the Sonoran Auxiliary."

"I don't believe you," Gordon said loudly.

"I'm tired of this shouting, *Señor* Engineer. Will you come out here so we can talk face to face, like men of high honor?"

Jesse touched Gordon's arm. "Don't go. They want to kill you. Little by little, I can see his men closing up behind him. They may charge us. Don't go and don't stand up. Everybody should stay down."

Gordon glanced left and right, and motioned for the men to stay low. Then he shouted at Blanco: "I won't come out to talk to you. There's nothing more to be said. Move your men on."

"I have one last request to make of you, *Señor* Engineer. Can you give us medical supplies for our wounded? They're

147

in great suffering. It is very sad. I think of their families. Their gray-haired mothers at home."

Jesse couldn't restrain a laugh. "Ever hear anything like this bastard? He should be strutting around on a stage in velvet drawers."

"We have no medical supplies to give you," Gordon shouted back. "We gave you a good mule with coffee, bread, and bacon."

"You refuse, then?" A most indignant question, replete without outrage.

"I said we have none to give you."

Blanco seemed to fly into a rage, beating the air with his gloved fists. "You lie . . . all *Americanos* are liars! You will pay with your blood for invading Mexico. I, Colonel Santa Ana Blanco of the Sonoran Auxiliary, will see to that. I won't let you pass. You will see. Your blood will stain the sacred soil of Mexico!"

He jerked his horse around, and the three rode back to the main band. There ensued much pointing and apparently much palavering. After some minutes, they rode off to the south.

"We should've shot the son of a bitch," Jesse said flatly. "Because he'll come at us again."

Gordon slanted him a look. "As much as I'd like to, in this case I couldn't shoot a man in cold blood. Neither could you."

"I haven't yet. Sometimes we pay a high price for observing a code of honor. You know what he'd do to us to get his bloody hands on everything we have."

Reyes regarded them both with apology. "I must apologize for this so-called Colonel Blanco. He doesn't represent the true officers of my country."

"You don't have to, Agustín," Jesse said, with understanding. "He's just a common bandit chief, posing as an Auxiliary officer, while he preys on *conductas* headed for Tucson or coming back. This is his territory."

"We're getting out of here, one way or another, when it gets dark," Gordon said emphatically. "We're losing valuable time . . . half a day. I'm trying to avoid another costly fight. Think you can lead us out of here, Mister Reyes?"

"I will do my best, *Señor* Major."

"We could follow the river. But it was running chest deep to a horse this morning. We'd be floundering around in the dark. The river banks are a jungle. More floundering. The country west of us is broken. Do you know it?"

Reyes looked penitent. "I regret I do not. It's off the main trail."

"We'd risk getting lost in that, and more floundering in the dark, and what it would cost us in time. Time and duty rule us, gentlemen, leaving us little choice."

They ceased talking to observe the bandit column, now approaching a thin line of scattered timber about two miles distant.

"I remember there's a big spring there, and it overflows and forms a small stream. A pleasant place for a picnic."

While they watched through field glasses, the bandits reached the trees and broke formation. They watered the horses and pack animals and unsaddled. Some gathered wood. Others stretched out under the trees. After a while ravels of smoke rose.

"So they're making camp," Gordon said. "This close they can keep an eye on us. Blanco will expect us to stick here all night. Tomorrow he'll lope over with some more demands. Any suggestions, Captain Wilder?"

Jesse's thoughts kept looping back to Blanco, whom he despised for preying on his own people, and whose brutal

149

counterparts he'd fought in Chihuahua. His mind played momentarily with one incident in particular — bandits attacking a little bunch of Juáristas, and the bandit leader, shot dead in the attack, turning out to be the "friendly" police chief, the *jefe*, of the town through which the Juáristas had passed the day before. He felt the rooted weariness coming over him. His voice sounded tired. "Like you said, Major, we have but one choice, and it's a tough one. We have to get by them tonight, somehow."

Gordon's roughhewn face, by now the color of saddle leather, cracked into a grin. "I'm open to anything that's guaranteed to work."

Jesse offered him the trace of a smile, his low moment fading, dispelled by this true soldier, this veteran Yankee officer. He said — "Let's see what they do with their horses." — and turned to watch the camp.

He expected the bandits to tether their horses on picket and feed them. They did neither. There seemed little or no order in the camp. A tent was erected for Blanco, evidently for him alone. Blanco entered the tent and didn't come out. *Ah*, siesta *time*, Jesse thought. He'd like some of that himself. The wounded bandits were placed under the trees and left to themselves with no care of any kind. He saw horses tied in the timber, with the pack mules distributed at random. An argument seemed to be going on. After some time, two riders drove the remaining horses out to graze the short desert grass between the camp and the rocky rise. Jesse guessed the argument had been over who was to guard the horses.

"I can see why they have no picket line, because they have no grain, but the lack of order proves they're not part of any military organization," Gordon summed up the situation. "Without grain, they're forced to graze away from camp."

150

"Be wiser to hobble nearer camp than to loose-herd like that," Jesse observed.

"That tells us they don't expect any trouble from us. They think they can rest until tomorrow, when they take us."

The afternoon wore on tediously, while the outfit lay baking in the scorching sun on the low ridge. The sky was a great molten dome. A hot wind punished them from the west.

They watched the horse guards change. Still only two herders.

They watched the sprawling camp. Once Blanco left his tent and strolled about, gazing off toward the *Americanos,* and returned to the tent, visibly satisfied with what he saw.

Jesse went down to his stock and fed them grain from nose bags. They were used to long stretches without water, so water wasn't urgent yet; by late tomorrow it would be.

Connelly drifted over. "What're we gonna do, Cap'n?"

"The major will do something before long. Don't worry."

"I don't worry. It ain't the fightin', it's the in between . . . the waitin' that drags on a man."

"I'll nod to that," Jesse said. "Better rest." He removed the nose bags and rejoined Reyes and Gordon.

"I feel as if we're being held captive by imaginary chains," Gordon said impatiently, "when all we have to do is rise up and break free." He turned to Jesse, his blue eyes alight with challenge. "The only question is how." A wordless conversation seemed to pass between them, and then he said: "I wonder if we aren't coming around to the same decision?"

"You mean the horses?"

"Yes. We might run 'em off, though the guards would resist and that would arouse the camp. Trouble with that, we might take losses, and we have to avoid another costly fight."

"I believe you're talking about doing it in daylight. If they night graze the horses . . . and from their scrawny looks they need the feed . . . I believe we can put Blanco's outfit afoot. Spook the horses right through camp, while the pack train slips by in the dark."

"Captain," Gordon exclaimed, "you speak the language of my tribe. However, there will be the two guards."

"We'd have to see about them. But, say they bring their mounts in at dusk? What then?"

Gordon rubbed his chin with the knuckle of a forefinger. "That limits us to making a night march, slipping around their camp. They'd hear us. They'd pursue."

"That'd be better than waitin' for tomorrow, the advantage all theirs. Let's do something, Major."

"We will . . . tonight. You bet. I feel much better about this now."

Gordon called Bickford and Connelly and with Jesse talked over their options. If the bandits held their horses in camp, the detail would wait until late, then move out at a walk to angle around the camp, the troopers riding between the enemy and the pack train. If the bandits left the horses on night herd, Captain Wilder, Sergeant Bickford, and four others would spread out and dispose of the guards and yell and fire revolvers to stampede the horses straight into the camp. By that time, the pack train, which had left earlier, would be well on its way.

That settled, they ate dry rations and settled down to wait.

At last, the sun strode on and sank like a bloodshot eye, and the cruel wind relented, letting up, turning cooler as the haze of dusk crept in. The horse herd was still grazing out there, now just a dark mass in the dwindling light.

An hour or so crawled by. Night was closing down.

Fires marked the extent of the bandits' camp. Sometimes, when the whimsical wind changed directions, Jesse said he thought he heard shouts. Gordon said the same. "I hope they're deep in their cups by the time we leave."

For a while no one spoke. At length, Jesse said: "Moon's fixin' to light up, Major."

"It's time to start the pack train," Gordon said.

Connelly left at once and Bickford went to fetch the four troopers.

"We'll hold up till the train's out a way before we leave," Jesse reminded Gordon.

"Right. Damn it, I don't know why I can't ride with you men. Leave Bickford and Connelly in charge of the train and the rest of the outfit."

"There's just one thing, Major," Jesse said quietly. "You're in command, and you should be with the command. That's how I see it, sir. How it used to be."

"The burden of command," Gordon answered, outright derision in his voice. "You're right, of course. That's how it used to be and still is. But it cuts out a lot of things. Mister Reyes, I'm glad you'll be with me."

Jesse walked down to the red horse, and he and the others led their mounts back. An orderly brought Gordon's horse.

When the first mules in the pack train bobbed up the rise, Gordon directed Connelly to form below on the flat. As the last mule and the extra mounts trotted by, now four with Cramer and Maguire gone, Jesse and the five troopers followed down to the assembly point and held up.

"We're all formed," Gordon said shortly. "Give us a few minutes before you start. Perhaps it would be advisable, Captain, for you to take the left flank, Sergeant Bickford the other. Once you spook the herd good, get 'em going hard . . . break away. Try to stay reasonably close together. Charge with a yell. Watch for the guards. Above all, no extra heroics. Good luck!"

Once again, time seemed fixed. The jangling sounds of the

153

pack train and the shuffling of hoofs faded bit by bit, muffled, until there was only the drone of the night wind.

"You about ready, Sergeant?" Jesse asked.

"I'm ready, Captain."

"Let's go."

They swung away into the filmy darkness, relieved now by the climbing moon. First at a walk, then at a slow trot, eyes straining to pierce the gloom. The night was much like when they'd waited for the Apaches to attack at the springs, streaked and murky, moon wash dripping from a changing sky. The drumming of the trotting horses, though light, seemed unusually loud to Jesse in the stillness.

A few minutes slipped by.

As they trotted on, the low bulk of the horse herd took sudden shape. Where were the guards? The herd loomed quite close now. There was an audible rustling of nervous hoofs, and snorts, and snuffles.

Jesse heard a startled Spanish voice call out: *"¿Quién es?"* Who is it? And again: *"¿Quién es?"*

Now, Jesse knew, *now!*

The six spread out and charged, yelling, and the falsetto of the rebel yell tore through Jesse's throat. *"Yee . . . haaa! Yee . . . haaa . . . haaa . . . haa!"* They all kept yelling. Before them the horse herd folded back like a dark wave breaking, snorting and colliding, amid thuds and screams. At the same time a bullet whined from Jesse's left, and he swerved the red horse, hearing the *crack* of a rifle. Instantly, on that one crash of sound, the herd ceased its uncertain milling, whirled together, and fled in terror. Glimpsing the blur of a white hat, Jesse fired the Spencer and saw the white hat no more. *The other guards? Where were they?*

Bickford's high-pitched warning shout on the right jerked at him. In the confusion over there, Jesse saw not one white

154

hat but three. Meaning flashed over him. Blanco had posted extra horse guards. Jesse reined that way, but a milling horse barred the way. He heard Army sidearms popping, and saw gun flashes, and then he lost sight of the troopers on his right in the scattering of horses.

He dashed on, yelling at the horses, letting the red horse run, seeing no more white hats on his side. Then he pulled up hard, his mind on the troopers. But the firing had dropped off. As he checked, he heard the mounting rumble of horses running wild, and seconds later, like music in his ears, the sudden shock and clatter of hoofs trampling pots and tinware, and voices shouting alarm and cursing. *The camp!*

Enough!

As he reined up, hollering — "This way . . . come on!" — a little knot of riders swept toward him on the run. For a breath he wasn't sure, seeing no white hats . . . yet. Then he heard Bickford's hoarse voice — "Let's get the hell outta here, Captain!" — as he rode past.

They rushed away, in their wake the bedlam of the camp.

Jesse was beginning to wonder where the pack train was when a line of horsemen bulked abruptly. Somebody shouted: "Halt!"

He heard Gordon's quieting voice and Bickford quickly reporting: "Detail's all accounted for, sir. We stampeded their horses."

"Very well executed. Extraordinary. I commend you all. Now you men form a rear guard, and we'll get along."

Jesse fell in behind the rest and looked back. Other than the tiny blink of a few campfires, he saw nothing. In the distance, he could still hear horses running. There would be no pursuit tonight or in the morning.

Chapter Ten

They kept marching hard even after daybreak with no pursuit in sight, the pack train swinging along in ground-eating style, the volunteers back again exchanging light talk. Bickford seemed more at ease than any day since they'd left Fort Bowie. Had he and Connelly buried the hatchet? On second thought, Jesse decided it was only a temporary truce, if so. They halted only to water the thirsty horses and mules at the river and munch hardtack and uncooked bacon.

"That was excellent work the command did, getting around Colonel Blanco's irregulars, or, I should say, regular bandits," Major Gordon commented while they rested. "I hope we've dismounted the colonel for some time. Every man will be named in my field report."

During the day, Jesse noticed himself beset by an odd depression; its reason puzzled him. He didn't think it akin to what he'd suffered with the Juáristas, which had led to a long bout of fever, probably from drinking bad water. It had laid him low after the battle at San Juan de Río and had left him unfit for duty many days. Yet, it had brought him sweet Ana, who had cared for him and nursed him back to health, and to find love. This feeling was different; it wasn't fever, thank God. It was more like a subtle weariness, a kind of burden he couldn't measure, a wearing out, perhaps, for having gone down one road too long, more of the mind than the body. He said nothing and would not. Hell, he was lucky to be alive. They all were, for that matter, after what had happened at the springs and likely faced even a tougher fight at La Gloria, without the defensive advantage. *El Tigre*'s cut-throats would be better armed and forged by iron Hussar discipline. He tried to close his mind to the feeling, but it still persisted as the day progressed.

They bivouacked that night still on the wandering San Bernardino. Tomorrow, Reyes said, he would lead them on a beaten trail southeast to the Bavispe River, which they would follow to San Miguel, Bavispe, Bacerac, then La Gloria.

By early evening sentries were posted, and the camp settled in for the night. There was scant talk. Even Gordon, who seemed to have an endless supply of energy, conversed only briefly with Reyes about what tomorrow's trail would be like before he turned in.

It had to have been late when his demons returned to haunt him, the worn scenes seeming more savage and bloody than ever before. Jesse was feeling the high excitement of victory that first morning in the dew-wet woods of Shiloh, loading, firing, his face blackened by gunpowder, as the surprised Yankees fell back. And then the shock of seeing his comrades falling in windrows and hearing their death shrieks as the tide of battle shifted. . . . The grievous horror of Kennesaw Mountain under the broiling Georgia sun. The blue waves of Yankees marching into certain death toward the Confederate position, every shot Jesse fired striking a man at that murderously close range. It was their faces that got him, the young, wooden-like faces, that left him sickened and spent. . . . And always there was bloody, fateful Franklin. Ever charging the Yankee trenches. Ever breaking through. Ever the brutal milling and killing around the Carter House. Boyhood friends dying around him. And, always, the Johnny Rebs unable to drive the Union troops to the river. And then, as always, the pain and blackness enveloping him as the bullet slashed his skull. . . . And always now, his nightmare of rushing up to

157

the shattered Juárista camp, the red horse flying at a dead run, and finding Ana, and grief seizing him. . . .

A distant voice reached him. "Captain Wilder."

Where was he? Who was that calling? Was that Jim Lacey? Was it Todd Drake? Couldn't be . . . they'd both died at Franklin, around the Carter House. Was it another boyhood friend, John Hoover? Couldn't be. He'd died that first day at Shiloh.

"Captain Wilder, sir," was spoken in a hushed tone.

Jesse seemed to be fighting his way up through greenish water, struggling toward surface light, his breath coming in ragged gasps. He broke through, thankful for clarity. He was in a cold sweat. His head quit whirling and cleared.

He felt a hand lightly on his shoulder. "You all right, Captain?" It was Major Gordon. "You were struggling and yelling."

Jesse ran a hand through his hair and scrubbed his face. "Sorry. Bad dreams, Major. Old dreams that go 'way back."

"Old battle dreams. I understand. It's all right. Try to get some sleep now."

Jesse lay back and looked up at the star-sprinkled sky, grateful for reality and sanity. He felt exhausted in mind and body, but much better. He was going to be all right. Letting his mind backtrack, he thought he understood what had plagued him all day. A kind of elusive forewarning. He should've known what was coming. And they would come again and again, throughout his life they would come, bringing the doomed young faces and the unforgettable scenes. He supposed that was part of the price of his having survived and to remind him of the guilt he sometimes felt. But he was all right. He fell into a deep sleep.

On the fourth day from San Bernardino Springs, they entered the cañon of the Bavispe River, which was low enough to allow them to cross back and forth for easier travel.

Past mid-afternoon they rode into the dusty little settlement of San Miguel, which Reyes called San Miguelito. It was a wretched place of squalid adobes and an ancient church whose white bell tower seemed to stand bravely and hopefully above its poor surroundings. Reyes said the village and countryside were often the targets of Apache raids. Chickens ran here and there. Burros watched placidly from wooden pens. It looked like a one-*cantina* town.

The column's clattering arrival became an immediate attraction for the inhabitants. Men, women, and children gathered in the narrow streets or on the flat roofs of the adobes to observe the riders. The women, mostly in white, dark *rebozos* worn over their heads, the men in peasant white and the inevitable straw sombreros with conical crowns. The bright-eyed Mexican children were dirty and very cute. When Jesse smiled at them, they smiled back. When he gave them a little wave, they waved back. He wished that he had something to give them, because the young ones discernibly had so little. He could hear them chattering about *los caballos,* especially his red horse and Reyes's prancing black Arabian, as they pointed and ran along to keep up with these strange *gringos* on the big horses.

As the column passed the *cantina* and its apparent proprietor, aproned and portly, among the watchers, Jesse didn't miss the volunteers' longing glances cast in that direction.

Gordon noticed as well. He halted the command and called Bickford over. "Mister Reyes says there's a nice place to bivouac beyond town. When we get there, I want you and Mister Reyes and Captain Wilder to go back and get something to drink for the boys. Two bottles of beer for each man. If beer isn't available, get some tequila or mescal. I realize this is a bit unusual, but they've been through a great deal. Get enough for everybody to have a few drinks, but not enough to get drunk on. If the British Navy can pass out rum to its sailors, why can't the U. S. cavalry, after hard marches and engagements that cost lives, pass out beer or liquor as part of its rations? I'll give you the necessary money." Gordon chewed his lower lip, reconsidering. "Do you think we can do this without any breach of discipline?"

"Yes, sir! I know the men will appreciate a drink or two."

"I'll have no fights."

"Sir, if anybody wants to fight, I'll whip 'im myself!"

"Very well, Sergeant," Gordon said, masking a smile.

When they rode back to San Miguel, a leggy bay saddler was tied in front of the *cantina* that wasn't there when the volunteers had passed through. It was agreed that Reyes, with his perfect Spanish, would conduct negotiations. Inside, at the battered-looking bar, they learned that the proprietor had only seventeen bottles of beer, but plenty of tequila and mescal and *aguardiente,* which he assured them with a bow was the best in all of northern Sonora. They decided to take all the beer and sample the rest before buying.

"You gentlemen are my guests," Reyes said graciously at a table. "Your preference is mine."

Jesse and Bickford agreed to try the tequila first; it was passable. The mescal was not, in any sense of desperation, and they came to the brandy, which was equal to liquid fire. They were sipping it with care, facing the bar, when Jesse murmured: "I believe we have a watcher and an eavesdropper . . . the man leaning on the far end of the bar."

He was a short, round man, noticeably proud of his heavy mustache. Under the gray sombrero, his face looked broad and solid, the black eyes small and keen. He was dressed, not in the usual peasant white, but in a dark green shirt and gray trousers and brown boots, which marked him as above the ordinary Mexican villager.

"All he'll learn is how bad the mescal is, if he ain't tried it," Bickford said, glancing that way. "Brandy's no better. I think we'd better take the boys some tequila to go with the beer. What do you men think?"

"I'll vote for tequila," Jesse said.

Reyes agreed with a nod.

"I figure there's about twelve shots to a bottle," Bickford said, reminiscently. "Let's see. There's nineteen of us. To give every man two shots, besides a beer, we'll need a little more than three bottles. If we get four, what's left over can go for medical supplies, all nice and proper, seein' as we're plumb outta such."

"You have a remarkable talent for mathematics, Sergeant," Jesse said, warmed by the drinks.

Bickford's expression said he didn't quite know how to take that. He said: "We're short two bottles of beer. Somebody will have to do without."

"Count me out," Jesse said. "Probably the major, too."

Up to that point, enjoying the rough drinks, Bickford had been affable, for a change. "You're such a noble soul, Captain," he mocked. "So givin' it does me heart good to see it, as the Micks would say. If you had the Good Book handy, you could hold a prayer meetin' right here and now."

"You could be even more noble, Sergeant," Jesse flung back, "by passin' up a shot so another man could have a drink."

Bickford flushed. The room grew still. For a tick of time, Jesse thought the sergeant was coming over the table after him. The naked impulse was there, as strong as ever. But Reyes, always the gentleman, broke the tension with his calming voice. "Gentlemen, let's finish our drinks and return to camp. Our thirsty friends are awaiting us. Tomorrow we can get on down the trail toward La Gloria."

After Bickford paid for the beer and liquor, they put the bottles in two canvas bags and headed for the door to the drooling inducements of the proprietor urging them to return. Bickford took one sack, Jesse the other. The horses didn't like the clinking bottles. A delay ensued. They mounted with the horses still dancing. As they rode off, the sombreroed man came out and stood under the portico watching them. He was still watching the last they saw of him.

"That man back there," Jesse said to Reyes. "What do you make of him? He's not a farmer. Could he be a state official? He showed more than passing interest in the three of us just coming in for drinks."

"But we are strangers, and strangers always attract much interest in a village like San Miguelito. Evidently, he lives here."

"He looks like a *hacendado*."

Reyes gave a *¿quién sabe?* shrug.

Every volunteer was looking expectantly toward San Miguel when the beer and liquor detail arrived, whereupon they snapped to stiff attention and saluted. Bickford ignored them. And every volunteer tried to assist with the unloading, and to the man showed extra respect for the sergeant.

"Can't we help ye, Sergeant, sir?"

"Be careful of yer back, Sarge. Take it easy."

One non-Irish voice chirruped: "They say beer bottles are prone to breakage when dropped, Sergeant. Let me help."

"Let me hold yer horse, Sarge, while ye unload. He's a little bit skittish, sir."

Finally, Bickford barked: "Stand back! You're gettin' in the way. I have to report before we can issue any of this. You know that."

162

Dismounting with the sack, which he carefully placed on the ground, and handing his mount's reins to a groveling trooper, he marched over to Major Gordon, saluted, and said: "Sergeant Bickford reporting for the detail, sir, with seventeen bottles of beer and four bottles of just fair tequila. It was the best we could do, sir."

"Very good, Sergeant. I suppose you should issue the beer first."

"Yes, sir."

"How do you suggest we issue the tequila, Sergeant?"

"I've thought of that, sir. Form a line, as with the beer, and pour approximately a shot in each man's coffee cup. There's enough for each man to have two shots, and a little left over, which could go for medical supplies."

"Splendid, Sergeant. Too bad we don't have a shot glass. I commend you and Captain Wilder and Mister Reyes for the highly proper manner in which you've carried out such a difficult mission, and without delay."

"Thank you, sir."

Jesse deposited his sack beside the other and led the red horse to the picket line. When he came back, the volunteers were lining up, and Bickford began issuing the beer, reminding them: "Be guard duty as usual tonight."

Silence descended over the bivouac as they sampled the beer, some sipping, some taking long hauls at the bottle with drawn-out "Ahs." Maybe fifteen minutes later, because the beer didn't last long, Bickford broke open a bottle of tequila, and the men filed by again, their voices rising a little higher now, their deportment impeccable. He had issued the first bottle when he suddenly stopped and took a bottle over to where Gordon and Reyes and Jesse were standing.

"Wasn't about to forget you, sir, and the others," Bickford said, sounding very correct, and each man received his share in his blackened coffee cup.

"We three may have to stand guard tonight," the major joked. "These men won't get drunk, but having gone so long without even a beer, they'll get on a small high and sleep like babies." He took a sip. "I don't have to wonder what stiff-necked Washington would think of a cavalry officer issuing beer and tequila to his men on the Apache frontier. I would be court-martialed, found guilty, and dishonorably discharged for the old catch-all . . . conduct unbecoming an officer and a gentleman . . . besides the liquid issue, the specific charge of an officer drinking with enlisted men, or in their presence. Well, I learned long ago in the field that you do what is best for your men, if it calls for raiding a farmer's henhouse in the dead of night."

"Major," Jesse said, toasting with his tin cup, "you speak the language of my tribe, if I may borrow the expression."

All three laughed together.

Light was fading and the volunteers, laughing and jesting, were gathering and chopping wood for the supper fires, when a horseman, headed south, passed within a hundred yards of the bivouac.

Reyes turned in question to Jesse, who nodded and said: "I believe that's the man we saw in the *cantina* . . . the eaves-dropper. He's riding a good horse."

"He's looking us over."

"No doubt we *gringos* are somewhat of a curiosity down here to anybody," Gordon remarked.

Reyes smiled. "Tomorrow, *Señor* Major, we will bivouac outside La Gloria."

Manuel Luis Diego rode steadily southward through the dimming light, keeping his saddler to a fast trot, his mind shifting from the *gringos* to the long ride to La Gloria. He had preferred not to start this late, but reports should be relayed swiftly, a rule on which he prided himself, and for which he was well paid. He would stay overnight in Bavispe, then go on in the morning.

His thoughts swung back to the beginning of this. He had happened to be riding into San Miguel when he had seen the column of *gringos* halted in front of the *cantina*. He had reined up to look. Miners' picks and shovels stuck out of the heavy mule packs. He had ridden nearer, his keen eyes busy. Some of the horses had U S brands, which did not fit, for these were not *soldados*. All the mules bore U S brands. Little bits of information like that often proved important. He had carefully counted nineteen *gringos*, had counted twice to make certain. Preciseness was another of Diego's strong points. He had watched the *gringos* depart, having been annoyed that the entire village should turn out to see mere *gringos*, virtually welcoming them as a relief from their hard existence.

He had tied his horse in front of the *cantina* and had entered. Old Felipe, addled as usual by his cheap liquor, had noticed nothing unusual about the strangers other than they were *gringos*. In fact, he had found them friendly, which again annoyed Diego.

He had ordered tequila and was sipping it, pondering the meaning of the well-mounted *gringos*, when two *gringos* and a young Mexican of perceptible class had entered the *cantina*.

The Mexican had told Felipe he wanted many bottles of beer, obviously intended for the main body of *gringos*. Felipe had agreed to sell what he had. The Mexican and the two *gringos* then had sampled the mescal and tequila and brandy. All they had talked about was the bad mescal and, therefore, buying a few bottles of tequila. How dull. The despised *gringos* had the minds of posts! But what were they doing there?

Where were they going? Although he had learned nothing from their empty talk, two facts had stood out in his suspicious mind: the picks and shovels and the U S brands. A third fact also had surfaced: all the *gringos* were extremely well armed, from carbines to revolvers, though you would expect travelers in an Apache-ravaged land to go armed. Manuel Luis Diego was no fool! He would report these interesting facts, which could mean nothing or a possible threat. It was always important to know what came down from the north — more importantly, from Fronteras.

Now, riding into Bavispe at this evening hour, he found the cramped streets deserted. A breeze off the river spun up little spirals of dust. The even hoofbeats of his gaited saddler beat a cadence across the stillness. A dog ran out, barking at his horse. At a familiar house near the end of the street, he saw that a light burned. Good. So she was alone. But he must let her know he was coming. Manuel Luis Diego had manners, learned as the only son of once-rich *hacendado*, reduced to ruin by repeated Apache raids. After that, the son had roamed up and down the Bavispe River villages looking for a means of living, and had found it. It was his superior air, he thought. His undoubted class. Why men of standing deferred to him. Why *peones* looked up to him. Why he impressed women. He had style.

Riding up to the adobe, which was only a few feet from the street, he rapped six times — one-two, one-two, one-two, his old signal — on the heavy wooden door with the butt of his revolver, and rode around to the rear of the house. Dismounting, he opened the gate of a small shed and led his mount in. There he watered his horse from a barrel, unsaddled, and tied the horse to a halter at the feed trough under the shed. From a pile of corn in the corner, he took six yellow ears and left them for the horse. Then, picking up his saddlebags, rifle, and pack, he went out, shutting the gate behind him, and strolled to the gate in the wall that enclosed the rear of the adobe. Opening it, he entered and paused.

As he expected, she was waiting on the patio, which was ablaze with flowers. A parrot squawked nonsense from a cage under the low-hanging *ramada*. Her one pet. That god-damned parrot! He couldn't stand it. She had it trained to say: "Forgive me, Holy Father," and "Jesus loves you."

He crossed over, and she said: "Don Manuel," — she was always respectful — "you are back sooner than I expected. Why is that?"

"My work," he replied vaguely, mysteriously, a little irritated that she should ask about matters that didn't concern her. That was a woman for you: always prying. He'd told her nothing; that way, he took on importance in her credulous eyes. "I'm going on to La Gloria early in the morning," he said.

"Good. The night is young. I will feed you, and then. . . ."

She kissed him on his bearded cheek without passion and led him inside. Her name was Josefa; despite the wear of her profession, she had managed to look years younger than she was. Possibly, he'd thought many times, because she was a devout Roman Catholic and confessed regularly and was thus forgiven. She often spoke of the "heavenly Father" and the "blessed saints," talk that always left him uncomfortable. She wasn't a good-looking woman, her features were too flat and plain for beauty; but her voice was soft, and she was dark-haired, with the blackest of eyes and a clean, sturdy body, and she knew how to take a man in her arms and make him forget the rigors of a long ride across the desert with the rhythm of her tireless strength. Her passion was steady and endless and workmanlike, of even more duration than his own.

Josefa was also pure Tarahumari Indian, which showed in

the way she endured life without complaint in a harsh land dominated by those of haughty Spanish blood. He'd never heard her laugh, but she was always evenly pleasant. He prided himself on his macho image around women. To that in late years, he had built on the rather mysterious air he'd adopted, which further intrigued them. One time a drunken whore in La Gloria, going beyond the bounds of manners with her upper-class customers, had asked him: "What do you do? Are you a government official?"

He'd knocked her clear across the crib. "Don't ever ask me what I do. I cannot say. It's forbidden." Which it was, in a way; in another, it was all pose. Well, let them think whatever they wished, it helped the image he fancied.

Now, Josefa took him into her bedroom, past a tiny altar in the corner with a statue of the Virgin Mary, and laid out his belongings with care. Somehow the mere sight of the altar bothered him. He stepped past it fast and didn't look again. When in bed with her, he studiously avoided it, as if the Virgin Mary were watching him and questioning his faithless way of life.

"I have some warm supper left," she told him. "Come on."

He took a bottle of tequila from his pack and followed her to the little kitchen. There she poured water into a pan on a bench by the door and handed him a bar of soap that smelled of roses and a towel. He washed his face and hands, dried, and opened the tequila, placing it on the small table, already neatly set, waiting for her to pour the drinks, which she did, handing him his glass.

"My house is your house," she said, and downed the hot tequila like a drink of spring water, her Indian face showing not the slightest reaction.

He blinked at the fiery stuff and swallowed hard, forcing it down, somewhat amused at her. He'd never seen her drunk.

168

He wondered if she had an iron stomach, in contrast to most Indians he'd seen, who sloshed down the vilest mescal until dead drunk, falling as mounds of flesh outside the *cantina* and in the streets. Was that because Josefa had only one purpose in life, which was to survive? She was, he admitted, a strong woman.

They drank some more, Josefa never changing expression. Now and then they would talk of mundane things: whether the river was up or down, and would the Apaches come again when the moon was full, and would the poor people of Bavispe have good corn and bean and chile crops this year? Otherwise, they just sat there and drank.

Afterward, she put food before him and, in her gentle way, urged him to eat. If he didn't, she said, he'd be sick in the morning and facing a long ride to La Gloria. He ate to please her, the beans, the tortillas, and the odd-looking, bland-tasting squash. The food was plentiful, but not as tasty as he was accustomed to. She cooked like an Indian, he thought, and Indians were not good cooks. In the mind of a Spanish-blooded *hacendado*, which he still thought himself to be, the owner of land as far as he could see, an Indian would eat or drink anything. Yet the Indians were still here; they had survived Spanish torture, rape, and disease. They would be here forever because they were part of the cauterized earth, and they were the color of the earth.

After dinner and another drink, she led him off again to the bedroom. Without making a fuss, she removed his clothes and boots and, when he was naked, she led him to the bed.

He was drunk and getting sleepy. When he opened his eyes at her touch, she stood naked beside the bed. In the sallow light of the lamp, her skin, indeed, was the color of earth. She seemed like some benign Aztec goddess, standing over him.

She slipped in beside him and took him in her arms and soon swept him away with her on a buoyant journey that never seemed to end. The last he remembered was her covering him with a light blanket.

Chapter Eleven

Sunlight streaming through the little window onto his naked skin woke him. He sat up with a jerk, his head pounding. It was late, too late. He should have been in the saddle at daybreak. She lay sleeping beside him, facing the wall, her long, gleaming hair spread over her like a black veil.

Angrily, he kicked her buttocks. "Get up!" he shouted at her. "I have to go. Make me some breakfast."

She woke at once and said nothing, impassively revealing neither surprise nor hurt at the hard kick. She shrugged into a loose dress and padded on bare feet into the kitchen. Groaning, he sat on the side of the bed and held his bursting head with both hands, thinking the *gringos* would be ahead of him by now. Based on what the young Mexican had said in the *cantina*, he felt certain their destination was La Gloria. It wasn't Bavispe, because they had gone into camp early enough yesterday to have reached Bavispe easily. If they were still camped outside San Miguel, he could tell from a nearby mountain where he could look back with binoculars. It was vital that he reach La Gloria before they did, else he would look like the bearer of late news. If they went no farther than San Miguel, it didn't matter. He would be ahead of them, as he alertly had been that time when the company of regular Mexican cavalry had ventured down from Fronteras, and, in the end, had stumbled around in the mountains between Bacerac and La Gloria and found nothing.

By the time he had dressed and washed, Josefa had his breakfast ready. She poured him coffee, which he drank in gulps, and then served him eggs with green chiles and fresh

171

tortillas. A most heartening breakfast. His monstrous headache receded. He ate wolfishly.

Getting up from the table, he gathered his pack and saddlebags and rifle and came back to the kitchen and put a single *peso* on the table. It was niggardly, not nearly enough for all the hospitality he'd enjoyed. He knew it; she knew it. But to him she was only an Indian, a whore to boot, beneath him because of his vaunted Spanish blood. The way he looked at it, he honored her by coming here.

She showed not one flicker of anger or disappointment, her plain Indian features as unreadable as stone, symbolic of her strength. She would have expressed no more emotion if he'd left her nothing. She wouldn't beg. He knew that, too.

There was not even a good bye between them as he lurched out. No word, no touch, no gesture. Inwardly, the pittance of the one *peso* incensed and hurt her to be treated so shamefully, as if she were dirt beneath his polished boots. But the *alcalde* would be here during *siesta,* when the village grew quiet and not many were about to see him come to her house. He was a kind man, always generous. He would help make up for Don Manuel's cruel stinginess, displayed to remind her of her place and his proud Spanish blood.

This was her life, which she had survived by will and a strong body and, above all, her devout faith, which had sustained her since she'd run away as a thirteen-year-old slave from a wealthy *hacendado* in southern Sonora. She loved the Holy Father, and she loved the Virgin Mary and sweet Jesus. Her favorite mind-picture, one that rose before her often when she was alone and gave her strength, was of Mary and baby Jesus, a scene she dearly loved. They would be with her always. She wasn't afraid.

In a secret place in the wall behind a picture of Jesus, she hid money now and then for when she could work no more.

She would put the *peso* there for safekeeping. Sunday she would give it to the church, which was poorer than she was, to cleanse her soul. The mere thought made her feel better, and her anger and hurt softened.

At that moment, as Diego passed the parrot's cage, the bird suddenly squawked: "Jesus loves you."

Startled, he cursed it and hurried on.

Josefa, watching, felt a tiny smile creeping across her impassive face. For her it was a very big smile. *It was strange,* she thought, *how the bird had spoken just as Don Miguel passed, as if Jesus had spoken through the bird.* It was very strange and wonderful. It also made her very happy. She wasn't afraid; she would never be afraid. This was her life.

Mounted, he rode east of town to examine the trail. Many fresh tracks had moved southward this morning. But this late there would be other travelers besides *gringos* on this well-traveled trace linking the river villages. To make certain, he rode to the low mountain and up to a wooded spur. From here San Miguel was plainly visible. Looking through binoculars to where the *gringos* had camped, he saw it was vacant. So they were ahead of him.

He spurred back to the trail and let the gaited saddler settle into a running walk. The brassy fist of the sun was already beginning to hammer him without mercy. Sweat rolled down his face. His stomach churned. His hands shook. His bleary eyes burned. In his hurry, he'd forgotten to fill his canteen, a chore which Josefa should have done. She'd also let him sleep too long. It was all her fault. But what could a man expect of an Indian whore? Now he was paying for his night of indulgence. Grimly, he forced himself to the task at hand. He, Don Manuel Luis Diego, in whose veins flowed the blood of the *conquistadores,* would not be denied.

The miles fell away under the long-striding bay.

The sun stood directly overhead when a feather of dust caught his eye. He rode nearer. Now he saw a low cloud of dust. He halted and reached for the binoculars. His elation soared when he recognized the *gringos,* stepping along in a column of twos. He would follow them at a distance. If they halted at noon, which he expected, he would circle around them. Bacerac was just ahead. They'd probably pass through the village.

Instead, the *gringos* swung around Bacerac. Riding closer, intently observing them, he began to get an impression. These *gringos* seemed to ride with military order. They looked well organized. Civilians would ride loosely, strung out more. There was hardly a gap between the pack mules and the riders. Could they be *soldados?* But they weren't in uniform; besides, American *soldados* were not permitted in Mexico. Hadn't been since the unfortunate war with the *Yanquis* years ago. And there were the picks and shovels. Only miners would carry such tools. They could be miners who'd served in the *Yanqui* Army. He gave a mental shrug.

These rather puzzling and contradictory facts he would report in due time, in advance of the *gringos,* if they rode on to La Gloria. He was feeling much better now. He was in charge of himself and the situation. In recognition of that, he stopped in Bacerac and treated himself to beer and filled his canteen at the village well in the plaza before riding on.

When the *gringos* went into noon camp, he started to pause and wait for them to continue, content to trail them for a while longer. But, after considering the time, he decided to ride by them on into La Gloria, which he would reach well before dark. This time there would be no hurry. He might stay with Lupe several days. Not every whore could say that a man of Spanish blood was among her customers.

He made his saddler switch gaits as he rode by the camp,

aware that in doing so he was drawing the *gringos'* attention.

Major Gordon noticed the rider first. "There he is, boys. I wonder when we got ahead of him?"

"Must have stayed in Bavispe," Jesse said. "That's a fine saddler he's riding. Looks pretty in the running walk."

"Indeed, he does."

"I believe he's switched gaits and the horse is ambling," Jesse said. "You don't see that very often, going from a running walk."

"I much prefer the flat-footed running walk, which can carry a man along at six to eight miles an hour on even ground and is easy on the mount. As your red horse does, and as I've seen done by Tennessee horses." Gordon was sounding more and more like a man who missed saddle-breds and seldom saw them. "Ambling covers ground fast, but is tiring to the horse. The limbs on the right side are raised and lowered simultaneously, the left side alternating."

"He's switched again," Jesse said. "Is that the fox trot he's in now, Major?"

"Yes," came the prompt reply. "It's a four-beat gait, but not as evenly spaced as the running walk. Neither is the stride as long. But mighty pretty to watch. Ah, he's back in the running walk again. He'll probably stay in it if he has a long ride."

La Gloria was a miserable little village groveling at the foot of the mighty Sierra Madre, with the thin blood of the life-giving Bavispe River flowing by from above. As Diego rode into the plaza, it struck him as even more wretched than the other river villages, if possible, and it was. Fewer people lived here and the farming was poorer, if possible, and it was also. Occasionally heavily guarded *conductas* of Mexican mules paused here on the way north to drop off a few goods or take on even less in trade, their coming always brief. Otherwise, the people tilled the lowlands for chiles, corn, beans, and squash, raised some fruit, and hunted deer in the mountains, bred and sold mules, made mescal, and did leather and silver work. He had little or no respect for these toiling people. They were next to nothing to a person of his lineage, being only Indians and *mestizos*.

He rode on through the nearly silent town, even passing up the *cantina* when he could use a drink, and followed the sandy river road. Half a mile out, he took a rocky road that rose gradually into the forbidding mountains. Several hundred yards farther and he approached the stronghold, which occupied a wooded bench that overlooked the river valley, aware by movements on the wall and voices in the guard towers that he was already under observation.

An uneasy excitement gripped him. He felt himself growing tense. It was always like this before they met. He would have to maintain his composure. He always had, but it was still a strain. Why should this meeting be any different from the others? It wasn't. It was just that he always felt a certain sense of ruthless intimidation when he faced the man and talked to him. At the same time, he had always delivered important news which no other person possessed. No one knew the river country and the little towns better than Don Manuel Luis Diego. No one could do what he had done. He was one of a kind.

Stopping before the massive wooden gate hanging on enormous iron hinges, he shouted up to the guard looking down at him from the tower: "I am Don Manuel Luis Diego. Tell the *jefe* that I am here."

"Who'd you say you are?"

Diego started to repeat his name, then checked himself.

He'd had trouble with this upstart guard before for showing lack of respect. The man had boring duty and liked to play games. Because he was a tower guard, he assumed that he was someone of importance.

"You know who I am," Diego said coldly. "Open the gate at once or I'll report to the *jefe* that you delayed me. I have important news."

That did it. They all feared the *jefe*.

He could hear scrambling footsteps as the guard came down the wooden stairs, and the abrasive sounds of a metal bar being lifted. When the creaking gate swung back, he saw a figure running across the courtyard to announce his coming.

El Tigre would be waiting.

Chapter Twelve

A guard took the reins of Diego's saddler with the sheathed rifle at almost the moment he dismounted. Another took his revolver.

He straightened himself and walked across the courtyard. Two guards in high-crowned sombreros and cross bandoleers stood beside the doorway of *El Tigre*'s headquarters in the principal building of the hacienda. They barred his way with raised rifles.

"I am Don Manuel Luis Diego," he informed them in a terse tone, and waited for them to show proper respect and recognition.

They did neither.

What was the matter with these people? He'd been here before. "I have important information for *El Tigre*," he said sharply.

The oldest guard, a sloppy *bandido* with heavy-lidded eyes and a paunch that hung out where the bandoleers crossed, ignored him and strolled inside.

Diego expected a quick entrance. Instead, he waited minute after minute. When the guard strolled back, he said: "Follow me, *señor*."

Diego followed him down a hallway.

The guard stopped at a door and said: "Now I search you, *señor*."

"They took my rifle and revolver. I have no knife."

"Just the same, I search." He went over Diego with both hands, rougher than seemed necessary to Diego, then opened the door and nodded for Diego to enter. When Diego went in, the guard stayed inside by the door.

The vast room, once the office of the *hacendado,* had changed in only one way since Diego's last time here: it held even more weapons. Rifles and carbines were stacked and leaning against the walls, but now there was also a high tier of boxes of ammunition. The room was a virtual arsenal, enough arms here for a hundred or more men.

No man dared mention it, but *El Tigre* harbored an unreasonable distrust and suspicion of mankind. He was constantly looking over his shoulder and all about him when riding. It was the reason he wouldn't sit by a window or with his back to a door. The reason, it was said, he slept in a different room every night and always went armed, even inside the walls of his stronghold. He even made his cook eat a portion of *menudo* before he would touch the steaming mixture of tripe and onions, which he had often for hangovers. Diego searched for the right word from the good schooling he'd had in Mexico City as a youth and had wasted through lewd women, drink, gambling, and fancy horses. *El Tigre* was paranoid. That was it. That and superstitious, which Diego reasoned, could be traced to his primitive Indian blood.

El Tigre had not changed. He sat behind the polished mahogany desk like a bloated toad in a soiled suit of once-white linen. He was short and thick and stood just a little over five feet in height. But the piercing black eyes with their constant threat of menace and the bushy black brows and thick black hair and the large flat nose made him appear much larger than he was — over all, an impression of ruthless strength. As usual, he was drinking *aguardiente,* and, as usual, he would offer Diego none. He had no manners. He was as rude as a mule's kick, as crude as the lowest peon scooping beans with a corn tortilla; but he represented power, and that was all that seemed to matter any more in the vacuum left by the long war between Maximilian's French forces and Juárez's peasant army. It would be years before *El Presidente* could bring order to all of Mexico. Now there was only this, represented by the squat little man before him.

Diego felt a stab of his usual fear, quickly controlled, as he removed his hat, which the bandit chief expected without exception of others in his presence, even of the highly favored *El Hombre Grande,* the former Hussar cavalryman and his chief executioner. Diego halted in front of the desk, standing on a brown carpet which occupied the largest space not stacked with armaments. Why the carpet? It was cheap looking to Diego. Possibly the *jefe,* once a common mule driver and cattle rustler without taste, considered the rug elegant. There were no chairs for others. Everyone stood in the presence of *El Tigre.* Only he was seated. He possessed a high voice that crackled with authority, backed by a wide, yellow-toothed grin. A grin, Diego knew, that was a mask without humor. He never addressed Diego as Don Manuel, which was proper, or as Diego. It was always *hombre.*

"*Jefe,*" Diego said, mixing a tone of respect with the importance of his report, "I have spotted a band of *gringos* on their way to La Gloria. They stopped in San Miguel, camped outside the village last night, and today stopped at noon beyond Bacerac. They should reach La Gloria by late this afternoon."

"So?" the *jefe* asked, looking bored.

"I consider it unusual that a band of *gringos* would come here."

El Tigre leaned forward, black eyes lancing into Diego. "How do you know they'll come to La Gloria? They could camp between La Gloria and Bacerac."

"True, they could, *Jefe,* but they had made noon camp

180

this side of Bacerac. I also saw them in the *cantina* at San Miguel. I heard one say La Gloria was yet ahead of them. In my opinion, they will continue on south."

"How many *gringos* are in this party?"

Ah, facts he liked to report. He prided himself on facts. Facts showed a keen mind. "Exactly nineteen, *Jefe*. I counted them in San Miguel."

"So?" *El Tigre* was still dubious.

Diego tried to bring foreboding into his voice. He raised a dramatic hand. "*Jefe,* these *gringos* are well armed . . . carbines and revolvers."

Obviously a mere nineteen men didn't concern *El Tigre,* who'd been in many skirmishes and battles. "*Hombre,* you forget that Apaches raid through here. Any men riding south would come armed."

"True, *Jefe,* most true. But. . . ."

He was interrupted before he could answer. "What more did you note about these fearsome *gringos?*"

"They rode in a column of twos. A military formation."

"Only fools would ride single file or in little bunches. Even thick-headed *gringos* should know that. What else did you note?" The *jefe* swallowed some brandy and belched as only a mule driver could, Diego thought to himself.

"I took careful note of their mule packs. I saw picks and shovels such as miners use."

Now Diego saw the humorless grin. "Miners, you say? What threat could nineteen miners be to me?"

"I thought the same, *Jefe,* until I noticed US brands on most of the horses and on all the mules."

"You saw US brands?" the *jefe* said, dragging out the words, more interested now. He looked up at the ceiling and pursed moist lips. "You were alert to notice that, *hombre.* Even so, they could not be U.S. *soldados.* It is not allowed." He

181

grunted, which for him was a laugh. To him the reference to the government was most humorous. "What else did you see? The *gringos* couldn't all look alike."

"There is a Mexican with them, a young man of class. I noticed that in the *cantina*. The way he spoke, the way he conducted himself."

"You mean he had manners?" Another grunt. The *jefe* was being sarcastic now. It was his habit to sneer at any mention of class, which meant Spanish. As a common Indian, he had no class in Diego's eyes. Only brute force.

"Mainly, it was how he spoke and dressed."

"So you were impressed?"

"I just noticed that he wasn't a peon."

"It is good that you noticed that, *hombre*. It is very important." Which he didn't mean at all, Diego sensed.

Boot steps sounded behind Diego, and *El Hombre Grande* walked in. He always moved in an aggressive manner, arms swinging, black boots splayed out, the impact of his heels striking the stone floor as loud as gunshots — or, to Diego, like shod hoofs on bridge planking. The Hussar ignored Diego and bowed to the *jefe* as he removed his kepi.

He wore a green jacket with shoulder epaulets from which dangled gold-colored fringe, and dark green trousers with seams the color of gold. The uniform was his own get-up, an amused bandit had told Diego. Revolvers rode on each hip in hand-tooled leather holsters. But the most dominant feature about him was his glossy red beard, which fell to his great chest, and his wavy, shoulder-length hair as red as his handsome beard. Every few seconds he ran his fingers through his beard with undisguised vanity. He had a broad, fleshy face and blue eyes as cold as ice. He'd always treated Diego with disdain, as he did the Mexican bandits, whether of pure Indian stock or *mestizo*. The only man in the bandit band that *El*

Tigre deferred to or really seemed to trust, he commanded the twenty-man bodyguard, composed of ten Hussars and ten carefully chosen Mexicans. All the Hussars were larger than the Mexicans, and *El Hombre Grande* was the largest of them all, broad and towering and threatening, an image he manifestly enjoyed. The Hussars even had their own section of the barracks and did not drink with the Mexicans. Sometimes Diego wondered how the *jefe* held his band together. But he did know. It was partly through fear of him and the Hussar, and partly through their own greed. The *jefe* paid them well in a poor land, as he did Diego, which was why Diego stayed. He wasn't proud of what he did, a spy for ruthless *bandidos* who preyed on *conductas* and travelers and bullied the hapless villagers, a menace nearly equal to the bloodthirsty Apaches; but Diego's needs were expensive, and he had no honor any more, a self-admission that made him ashamed and which he tried not to think about, and the disappointment it caused his proud father.

"This *hombre* has brought us news, *Comandante,*" the *jefe* said, turning to the Hussar. "But, first, come over here and let me touch your hair and beard for good luck."

Diego suddenly remembered the ancient myth: that red hair was seen as good luck by Mexican Indians, and anyone with red hair was related to the sun god, and it was good luck to touch it.

The *jefe* stroked the Hussar's beard and combed his fingers through the long hair. "Good," he said. "Good. My luck will be good for a long time, *Comandante.* The news is that some *gringos* are headed for La Gloria. Eighteen *gringos* and one Mexican of class. They ride good horses, and their mule packs carry picks and shovels such as miners use. All their mules and most of the horses are branded US. *Hombre,* here, thinks they'll arrive late this afternoon."

183

The Hussar wasn't impressed. "How could a few *gringo* miners and one Mexican concern us, *Jefe?*"

"I'm not concerned. But it's always wise to know what's going or coming into La Gloria. You know that."

"I agree, *Jefe*." The Hussar, Diego sensed, knew just how far he could go when disagreeing with *El Tigre*. Sometimes he did all but fawn over his chief.

"The brands bother me, *Comandante*. What do you think about them?"

"When mounts and mules grow old, the Army sells them for a song. The French army does that. So would all armies, I'd think. These men are miners. They must have bought their stock from the *Americano* Army."

"So you are not concerned?"

"Not at the moment. But let's keep an eye on them. As miners, they'll probably go into the *sierras* to look for gold or silver or copper. Who knows?"

El Tigre rose to his feet, somewhat unsteadily. A huge revolver hung on his right hip. Drunk or sober, he never lost his air of being in complete command. *"Hombre,"* he said, his eyes seeming to bore right through Diego, "you will watch these *gringo* miners and the one Mexican of class, as you call him, and see what they are about, and report to me every day."

"Sí, Jefe."

El Tigre then opened a desk drawer, took out a small buckskin bag that clinked of coins, and tossed it like a beanbag to Diego, who caught it deftly. *Or did he toss it as he would a bone to a dog?* That degrading thought flashed through Diego's mind as he greedily grasped the bag and pocketed it.

Dismissed, he turned and walked past the guard, remembering not to put on his hat until he reached the hallway. A bandit waited with his horse and weapons. Another bandit opened the gate, and Diego rode out, his mind now on the coins. In between watching the *gringos* and the Mexican, he would stay with Lupe, the whore in La Gloria, and loaf in the *cantina*, where he would be remembered and respected as Don Manuel. Life was looking up again. And yet, thinking further of the money, he couldn't free himself of feeling cheap and disreputable, a dishonor to his family and Spanish heritage. *There is*, he thought, *a price for all things in life* — and he was paying for them.

Going down the rocky road, he noticed off to the southwest horses and mules moving about in the river timber. Riding closer, he felt a quick elation. The *gringos* had arrived! They were making camp. He would report that tomorrow. *El Tigre* would be pleased that the *hombre* could be trusted to keep him informed.

El Tigre waited until Diego left the room before he spoke to the Hussar. "I didn't tell him about the girl and her *duenna*, *Comandante*. He knows nothing. This is his first report from the north in some weeks. I doubt that even the people in the village know about them, since we ambushed their escort out in the country. But I am concerned that the governor hasn't responded again about the ransom."

"There is still time, *Jefe*," the Hussar said, stroking his beard. "Four days from tomorrow. He won't let his only daughter die."

"He should've offered to make a payment of ample size until he can get all the two million *pesos* together. I've been patient."

"He'll do something. He must love his daughter. She is very beautiful, but her *duenna* has the beauty of a mud wall."

"Remember, two roses off the same bush never look the same."

185

"The *duenna* is not even a rose. More like a weed from the rose garden."

"You are too critical. Maybe her beauty lies within her soul."

The Hussar laughed. "I believe underneath that tough hide of yours we all know about there is the soul of a poet."

The *jefe* grunted, and his eyes even danced for a second, then changed back as direct as before. "No more flattery, *Comandante*. A man who listens to honeyed words becomes weak and makes mistakes."

"It was not mere flattery, *Jefe*. I assure you."

"Whatever, enough of it." His dismissing motion was abrupt. "Tonight, I want you to do something for me again. I am in need. In great need. I'll be generous with you, as I have before."

"You always are. I know what you mean."

"Send me the tall young man with the long blond hair again. I'll be in the northeast room early in the evening. Send him there."

"It will be as you wish, *Jefe*."

"Just what is his nationality? His skin is also fair."

"He is Hungarian, and part German and Dutch. All sorts of men and nationalities served in Maximilian's French Foreign Legion."

"Such as yourself? A man who has fought in many countries and wars?"

The Hussar laughed again. "I believe your description fits."

"Whatever this young man is, he has a perfect body. His mind is of no matter."

"*Sí, Jefe.*"

La Gloria.

Another one-*cantina* town. As the volunteers rode through

the deserted plaza, only a few inhabitants showed themselves. They seemed furtive and fearful, content to take one brief look before they ducked out of sight.

Young Reyes led them about a mile beyond to a wooded area near the river where they bivouacked. They'd made fast time. It was only mid-afternoon. After the stock was watered and put on picket line, Major Gordon called his staff together.

"It occurs to me," he said, "that, if we're going to look like civilians, instead of cavalry, we should take the horses off the line and picket them here and there." Everyone nodded. "And tomorrow some of us will go into town and buy some supplies and let drop that we're miners, and others will start digging a little into the hillside over there, and others of us can appear to be panning for gold in the river." More nods. "In addition, starting tomorrow, we have four days left before the deadline that this *El Tigre,* as he calls himself, has set for the ransom to be paid. So we'll take the horses off the picket line now. You can be sure that not only the villagers but the bandits in the hacienda will be wondering what the hell we're doing here. And when they learn we're miners, they'll still be wondering what the hell. We'll draw many eyes. I don't think there's ever been a gold or silver strike around here, has there, Mister Reyes?"

"Not near La Gloria, but perhaps in the Sierra Madre. In fact, I think copper or silver has been found in the *sierras.* In all, this is very poor country."

Gordon grinned. "That's always the way it is until that first big strike. Then look out. One more thing. Sergeant Bickford, we'll maintain our usual guard duty at night. And since we're in bandit country and have good horses and mules, I want guards posted around the bivouac during the day. But out of casual sight. Nobody marching their post."

"Yes, sir!"

"Corporal Connelly, you will see that our mounts and mules are watered and fed as if on post."

"Yes, sir!"

There were no questions, and, when the meeting broke up, Gordon asked Jesse and Reyes to accompany him, up from the river a way but still in the woods. From there they could see the tiled roofs of the stronghold's main buildings. Shielding everything was the high wall, topped with jagged, broken glass. Guards moved along the parapet and in the towers at both ends of the wall and in the tower by the gate.

"It's evident that they stay alert," Gordon said, casing his binoculars. "I see no way that we can scale that jagged glass and get inside, unless . . . unless the back wall is free of glass. When the moon comes up, Captain, I wish you and Mister Reyes would make a reconnaissance on foot and see what all's back there."

They were in a serious mood as they walked back. *Four days*, Jesse thought, *to do something. What could it be?* They had to take action.

After supper, Bickford detailed the guards for the night, and, when the moon decorated the sky like a golden ornament, Jesse and Reyes made their way on foot up the rocky road leading to the hacienda. Behind it bulked the overawing mass of the mountains. No lights in the towers. They stopped to listen and heard not one sound from within. The high gray wall looked ghostly and even more forbidding in the moon wash.

"A sinister place," Reyes whispered. "I fear for my people."

Jesse laid a hand on the young man's shoulder, then led off to go around the wall. Brush slowed them. Every few steps they paused to listen and heard only their own careful breathing. They reached the corner of the wall and turned toward the rear of the stronghold, walking away from the wall so they could see its top. In the dingy light, it was topped with jagged glass like the front. About fifty yards on they came to another corner. Voices broke the stillness at last as they started along the rear side. A man was laughing in boisterous, drunken Spanish. Another voice answered with a curse. Hard upon that came breaking sounds and a volley of curses.

Jesse stopped. "Sounds like a barracks brawl."

A shot exploded. Then a chorus of high shouts. Boots pounded. Voices again. The voices dropped off. Silence.

They moved on. The underbrush was thicker, greasewood, Spanish bayonet, prickly pear. Here the bench on which the hacienda sat sloped away toward the mountains. Moonlight caught the sheen of broken glass all along the wall's crest. It was like that the entire length. Furthermore, there was no weathered or broken place along the wall where strong-armed troopers might tunnel an opening with picks and shovels. They found the eastern side as formidable as the others as they moved along it.

Reyes tugged suddenly on Jesse's arm when a voice — a girl's sweet voice — floated up in song from the other side of the wall. Both men froze. Her voice was sad and yearning, as supplicating as a prayer. In a way, Jesse thought, it was more prayer than song as he caught words of home and love and family, ending almost as they had begun. But there was no cry, no interrupting sounds to silence her. It was simply a lonely cry for help out of the night.

"Alicia's voice," Reyes hissed in Jesse's ear.

They waited, hoping to hear it again. When it wasn't repeated after several minutes, they went on, slanting away from the wall when they heard men's voices in the corner tower. They had gone no more than a dozen steps when Jesse stopped abruptly and said, low: "I heard a horse stamping."

"So did I," Reyes said. "But where?"

They looked all about. In the flood of light, now sugar white as the moon rose higher, every object stood out starkly: the glistening jagged wall, the tower, and farther on to their left a copse of trees. Jesse supposed they'd heard a loose horse, yet he saw no horse and heard nothing more.

While they walked ahead, the stamping reached them again, this time more distinctly. It seemed to come from the thicket, which stood somewhat below them, where the bench sloped to the east.

They stepped that way. Jesse guessed the horse had caught its halter rope or bridle reins in the brushy timber. A short distance and they came upon a path angling toward the copse from the front side of the hacienda. The path took them down a grassy bank. Following it, they perceived the dark shape of the horse in the trees, which Jesse saw now were junipers and piñons. They entered the thicket, and the horse snorted and pulled back a little, then lifted its head to them, showing it was used to being handled.

Its halter rope wasn't caught but was securely tied to a tree trunk, and beside the trunk was a feed trough for grain, a box-like manger for hay, and a bucket of water. On a stout tree limb hung a saddle, blanket, and bridle. Jesse glanced back toward the hacienda, seeing all this was below the sloping bank. The horse was hidden from view of anyone taking the road to the hacienda. There had to be a purpose behind this. But what?

Major Gordon listened to their reports while they sat around a fire and drank coffee. He said: "Very good. The layout is taking shape. Now we know Alicia and her *duenna* are being held in the east end where the main building is. And we know the men are quartered in the west end. Tomorrow morning, while the boys are doing some ostensible digging and panning, we'll ride into La Gloria and spend a little money, which no doubt will be greatly welcomed, judging by the miserable local conditions." Jesse was impressed again by the man's boundless enthusiasm. Another mark of a good officer. In turn, he could sense his own renewal.

"That is unusual about the horse hidden in the trees east of the stronghold," Gordon mused. "Any guesses?"

"The horse is well fed and watered, and there is a well-trod path from the hacienda to the trees," Reyes said. "So he belongs there."

Gordon poked at the fire. "Usually the only reason to hide out a horse is to save him from thieves or for a quick getaway. And since thieves obviously own the horse and rule the roost around here, there must be another reason."

Reyes shrugged and looked at Jesse, who said: "What would be the advantage of a getaway horse if you had to run out the front gate to get to him in broad daylight? Maybe there's a back door to the place that we didn't see in the dark."

"A ladder could be used to scale the back wall, but it would be a long drop," Reyes pondered.

They quit on those random thoughts and went to their blankets.

Chapter Thirteen

They rode into La Gloria's plaza at mid-morning leading a pack mule — the major, Reyes, and Jesse. A few old people stirred on the dusty streets, the women bent over in *rebozos,* and others moved pokily in and out of time-worn adobes. Others peered at the horsemen from behind murky windows, their faces like copper images. Speckled hens pecked around in the gritty earth. Two gaunt dogs ran out and barked irresolutely at the horses, then gave up. A weather-beaten little church stood defiantly on the far side of the plaza, as if a continuing challenge to the unrelenting elements and man's infidelity. Its door was closed. Its slender bell tower rose high above the humble village, a lone beacon to the lifted eye.

"You men will have to take the lead," Gordon told them. "Let it be known that we are miners, and let's find out when *El Tigre* comes to town. My classroom Spanish of years ago won't do, though I can read it better than I can speak it, and my ear is fairly good."

"I gladly defer to Agustín," Jesse said.

"Don't use your last name," Gordon cautioned. "It might get back to the hacienda, and they'd connect it."

They tied up in front of the one *cantina.* It turned out to be dark and dank, occupied by a lone person, the owner. His round face bore an expression of surprise and welcome, undercut by a wariness. A black mustache fell over his lips. A patch-eyed, stooped man of middle years, he waved them in while his one good eye sized up these strangers.

Did he have any beer? He bowed from the waist. Yes, he had beer. Very good beer, *señores.* So they had beer, and Reyes, under his breath, said: "It tastes as I imagine dishwater would." Nevertheless, they drank it.

"Or as water would out of a cow track," Jesse opined.

"How is business, *señor?*" Reyes asked as they settled in.

"Business, it is bad. So bad I cannot remember when it was good in recent times. If people have money, they spend it for food." His eyes filled with a sad look. "You saw those dogs when you rode up. Well, you can tell how poor a town is by how poor the dogs are. There is not flesh on those dogs. They're all bone and hide. I'm told they have no fleas because there's nothing on them for fleas to feed on. Business, *señor,* is only a memory. Many people, especially the young ones, have gone to bigger towns . . . we are only a village now. It is the sorrow of my life. I was born here. La Gloria is dying. We are too poor to support a church. We have no priest. When someone dies, I, in my poor way, conduct the services, hoping a merciful God will not strike me down for my inadequate efforts."

"Too bad," Reyes said. "Why is this? La Gloria is by the river. It looks like a pleasant place to live near the *sierras.* Cool in the summer. There is firewood in the *sierras* for fuel and fields for planting. It's a stopping place for travelers and *conductas,* going north and south."

"But there are few men left to cut the wood, and many fields lie fallow. Few travelers come here now."

"Why have so many people left?"

He shrugged evasively. "Bad times." But his expressive eyes told what he had not. The three exchanged glances. They understood: the man was afraid to talk. But he might say something if they stayed a while and bought more drinks. Reyes asked if the tequila was good. "It is very good, *señor.* You cannot buy better in all of Mexico."

So they all tried the tequila, hoping the liquor made from

the century plant would kill any enemies of the body lurking in the dirty-looking glasses. The tequila was like the fires of hell, but, instead of complaining, they raised their glasses to the man. *¡Salud!* And a smile actually broke through his melancholy. Jesse even bought a bottle to take along. *"Muy gracis, señor."*

In this stinking hole of a *cantina,* Reyes was at his best: polite and ever gracious, speaking beautiful Castilian Spanish, voicing no complaints at the extortionate prices for the poor quality of the drinks. "Perhaps we can bring good times back to La Gloria," he said. "We are miners from Arizona. I'm their interpreter. Our maps show there may be copper or silver, even gold, in the foothills here or into the Sierra Madre. We've come to town for supplies."

The man's one black eye opened wider. His jaw fell. *"Señores,"* he breathed, "you are like messengers from God."

"That is not to say we're certain to find anything. But we will dig and see."

"Some years ago there was a silver mine higher up in the foothills. La Gloria men worked there. Times were good. But then one day all the silver played out."

"That is encouraging. Perhaps we can find another vein of silver. Has gold ever been found along the river? I mean by panning?"

"Alas, no."

"We won't let that discourage us. We'll keep the old saying in mind . . . 'gold is where you find it.' The same could be said for copper and silver."

The man's reticence seemed to vanish all at once. "It will be a miracle for us here, if you can find something."

"We may need some help. Some person to guide us into the *sierras,* if we fail to find any traces in the foothills." He smiled. "No color, as we miners say when speaking of gold."

"I know of no one in the village, *señor*. All of us are either too old, or, like me, know nothing of the *sierras*."

Reyes stared at his glass. A sudden thought seemed to come to him. "Along the way down, we heard of a *hacendado* living near here. A man of much power and prestige. Perhaps he could furnish us a guide?"

The reticence returned in an instant. "I'm not sure I know the man you mean, *señor*."

"His name" — Reyes looked at Gordon and Jesse — "I believe we were told is very colorful. It's *El Tigre*." They nodded.

"That man . . . I doubt he could help you."

"We were told he's a rancher. Surely he'd have riders who could guide us?"

"He is not a rancher, *señor*. He seems to stay at the headquarters of his hacienda most of the time. Seldom gets out."

"What does he do?"

"I don't know the man personally. But he seems to have interests away from La Gloria."

"I see. So he's not a rancher. Does he ever come to town?"

The man looked relieved. "He comes in every Saturday morning with his men. Exactly at ten o'clock. He always comes here and stays into the afternoon. It's a good day for me. He spends freely."

"Then, perhaps, we could talk to him next Saturday? Being on the trail so long, I've lost track of the days." Reyes looked abashed. "What day is today?"

"Thursday."

"Thank you, *señor*. Then there'll be no delay seeing him. We could ask for his assistance, then."

"*Señor*, I wouldn't count on that."

"Why not?"

A shrug. He turned up the palms of his hands. "*Señor*, you

and your friends have come here to help La Gloria. In turn, I want to be your friend. So I tell you I wouldn't ask *El Tigre*."

"Just why, *señor?*"

Suddenly the words rolled out. "Because I don't think he would help you. It is not . . . within his nature."

They finished their drinks and stood up, and Reyes said in parting: "*Señor,* we thank you. You've helped us."

As they mounted, Reyes said: "I really didn't know what day it is."

"Nor did I," Jesse said.

Gordon quirked his mouth. "I thought it was Tuesday or Wednesday, thereabouts. But now we know when he comes to town. You worked around to that very nicely, Mister Reyes."

They rode to the one store, a sort of sprawling general store, it appeared to be, with strings of red and green *ristras* hanging in front, and some melons lined up side by side under the *ramada*. A pink dress was displayed forlornly in one window, small barrels and implements in the other. A sign in large letters out front read: **HERRERA.**

Near the doorway sat an elderly Mexican, his back against the wall. He nodded courteously. He appeared crippled, one leg bent under him at an odd angle. But he wasn't begging. His arms were folded across his thin chest, and his ragged straw sombrero sat firmly on his head. He smothered a cough and wiped his mouth with a red bandanna. Something about the wasted face, a reflection of hard times and the resolve to work through them, caught Jesse's eyes. High cheekbones set off the proud, black eyes, but under their surface Jesse sensed a resigned bitterness. On impulse, Jesse pressed a silver dollar into the old man's hands.

He was too overcome to speak for a moment. His jaw fell. Then Jesse saw a few tears rise to his eyes as he mumbled —

"Gracias." — over and over. "I no see the shine of silver for a long time. It is beautiful to see again. You are generous, *señor*." He thrust out a strong hand, and Jesse grasped it.

When they went in, a fleshy man in a brown apron met them at once, smiling, bowing, his unctuous eyes eager to please. No doubt he'd seen them coming.

"Welcome, *señores*. I am Herrera."

"We are miners, *Señor* Herrera," Reyes said. "We need supplies."

Another bow, this one sweeping. "I am at your service, *señores*. I have whatever you need. My store is complete in all lines."

Jesse smiled to himself, expecting Herrera to throw in the old sales pitch about there was none better "in all of Mexico." But you couldn't blame these people. It was hard going in this wretchedly poor little village. You had to put on a front when new business came through the doorway. It was survival, and also entertaining. Everyone was being so correct. It was *señor* this and *señor* that. But why not? What was wrong with manners?

Reyes turned to Gordon to detail their needs, and they strolled about the store, taking their time, and after some minutes they bought coffee beans, brown *frijoles*, flour, and dried fruit. The volunteers would welcome it all.

During the transactions, Herrera said: "You are miners. I have picks and shovels. But no powder for blowing up hard places. There's no demand for it."

"Of course. We have the implements, but we need no powder yet. We are looking for likely outcrops and color from the river's sands. Could you order powder for us later?"

"Absolutely, *señor*. I would order it at once out of Hermosillo."

"Thank you, *señor*."

197

"I wish you good luck. It would also be good luck for La Gloria. *Americano* miners have never come here before. Years ago, there was a silver mine in the *sierras,* but it is long gone."

"We've looked at maps," Reyes said, keeping the conversation going. "Besides silver, there could be copper and even gold. Is there any man in La Gloria who worked in the old silver mine? If so, perhaps he could tell us something that might lead us to the paying ore."

Herrera paused in his sacking. "There is one. Old Pablo . . . he's sitting out there now under the *ramada.* He likes to come here every morning to see who passes. Not that many do. All our young people are gone. In a while, his little grandson will come to help him down the street home. They say he was the best miner in La Gloria. They called him The Mole because he could cut the straightest shaft of all, no matter how long."

There was a cough from the *ramada.*

"Unfortunately, old Pablo has the miner's cough," Herrera said. "He's a sick man. Too bad."

"It is. We are sorry to hear that."

"Later, he was injured badly. To this day, he can scarcely walk."

"Injured in the silver mine?" Reyes asked.

"I'm not sure where it was, *señor.* Other shafts were dug, but none had ore." He turned his back, suddenly busy with his hands. Jesse wondered a little. One moment Herrera was only too obliging with information. Another, he'd suddenly quit. Had he let something slip out, recalling the old miner's injury?

"We're told that the man known as *El Tigre* comes to town once a week," Reyes said, still pushing the conversation. "How interesting! We supposed him a rancher, but apparently he is not."

As if courtesy required that he reply, Herrera said: "Sometimes his men from the hacienda come here for supplies. I have never talked to *El Tigre*. Not once. I know nothing about him. The only time I see him is when he rides into town on Saturday with his guards and goes to the *cantina*." Herrera had made that clear: he knew nothing, or claimed he knew nothing. "May I find other supplies for your needs, *señores?*" he asked.

Reyes asked: "You have tobacco?"

"I have Mexican *cigarros* and *cigarrillos*. The *cigarros* are made of the finest black tobacco." He made a face. "Very strong, from Oaxaca. But of excellent taste, I'm told. The best. I smoke *cigarrillos*."

Jesse smiled again. *The best*. But why not?

"I'd like some *cigarros*," Reyes said, and Gordon nodded likewise.

To get the *cigarros*, Herrera went to a case near the front window. He picked up a box, but, as he turned back, an abrupt thought seemed to arrest him. He stepped to the doorway and spoke briefly to old Pablo. Jesse couldn't catch the words, but he could tell they were spoken in a forceful, emphatic manner.

Coming back, Herrera held the box open for them to take what they wished, then asked: "Do you have other needs, *señores?*"

After a glance at Gordon, Reyes said: "That is all. *Gracias* many times over, *Señor* Herrera."

Gordon paid, with Reyes assisting, and they went out with their main purchases in what looked like sacks made of jute or hemp.

Jesse paused by old Pablo and found himself looking down into angry black eyes. *"Señor,"* the old man said, "I am old and weak, but I am not a coward."

199

"What is it, grandfather?" Jesse asked.

Old Pablo shook his head and turned away, his eyes bitter. His mouth was trembling. Jesse waited for him to speak. But when he shook his head again and said no more, they went on to load the mule.

After they had ridden a short way, Jesse said: "I wonder what old Pablo meant when he said he wasn't a coward? And why did Herrera go out and speak to the old man? Was it to warn him, and of what?"

They all looked back. Herrera was talking to the old man again.

Diego rode up to the hacienda's gate and called to the tower guard and gave his full name. There was no reply for fully half a minute. Then the identical half-mocking voice called down: "It's windy up here. I didn't get your name, *señor*. Repeat it, *pronto*."

Furious, Diego kept his calm with effort. "You fool," he said. "You heard my name, and you can see who I am. Now open the gate immediately. I must report to the *jefe*."

When the gate opened after another delay and he saw the swaggering young *bandido,* an arrogant scowl on his pimply face, Diego said: "Are you this slow when *El Hombre Grande* comes to the gate? Are you this insulting? Do you ask him twice what his name is?"

"Think I'm a fool?"

"Yes, a young fool, which is the worst kind, destined for an early grave, and the coyotes will dig up your stinking carcass."

The guard spat after him in his tracks.

A guard took his horse and weapons, and Diego crossed over to headquarters, aware that he was getting weary of the insulting surveillance at every turn, as if he might be a traitor, instead of the trusted scout that he was. The same guard with the hooded eyes searched him roughly as before and asked his business and said he would have to wait.

The wait lasted for about ten minutes, broken when the Hussar walked out. He brushed past Diego without a sign of recognition. Diego's face flamed. Curse the foreign bastard! Diego's resentment grew with each step as the second guard admitted him. He was so worked up that he failed to remove his hat until the last moment.

"What now, *hombre?*" the *jefe* asked, looking no different from the previous day, in the same soiled suit, a glass of brandy at hand. The black Indian eyes seemed bored.

"The *gringos* went into camp yesterday afternoon, *Jefe*. Today they are busy digging here and there, and some are panning in the river."

"What else?"

"Three of them, including the Mexican, rode into town this morning for supplies."

"How do you know they got supplies?"

"I saw them load the mule with several sacks at Herrera's."

"From where did you observe this?" the *jefe* asked curiously.

"From a house between the *cantina* and the store. They went to the *cantina* first and stayed there a while."

"I believe that is a prostitute's house. An old prostitute."

"*Sí, Jefe.*" Yes, Lupe was no longer a girl, but she was good at her profession.

Looking amused, *El Tigre* finished the brandy, opened a drawer and pulled out a bottle and filled his glass and put the bottle back. "Report to me again *only* when you see something suspicious besides *gringos* camping and buying supplies at Herrera's."

"*Sí, Jefe.*"

Diego was dismissed. No money this time. He'd done nothing to earn it. He expected none. But he thought he had impressed on the *jefe* that he was continually alert. He left. He was walking down the hallway, when he heard the measured tread of boot heels striking wood. The tread sounded suddenly louder as the Hussar entered the hallway. Diego looked at him. The Hussar stared past Diego as if no one was there and strode ahead, swinging his arms, his pale eyes like ice.

Diego halted in midstep, feeling not only a tearing anger but a cheapening of himself, an utter humiliation. He, the Spanish-blooded son of a *hacendado* descended from the *conquistadores!* For the first time since he'd entered *El Tigre*'s hire, he realized fully what he'd done to himself, just how far he had diminished himself as a man. He'd become virtually nothing, a man without respect or honor. No better than the poor Indian *peones* he considered beneath him. It was the worst moment of his libidinous life. On that, he went quietly out.

Chapter Fourteen

Major Gordon made no comment until the three reached camp. There he sent an orderly for Bickford and Connelly, the sergeant busy with two men digging on the slope, the corporal on the river with three volunteers energetically pretending to pan for gold. Gordon paced back and forth before he spoke.

For the noncoms' benefit, he said: "At ease. We learned in town that *El Tigre* and his bodyguards ride in every Saturday morning around ten o'clock to the *cantina* and drink until afternoon. This information gives us one hard choice we didn't have before, but it is a choice, since I see no way yet that we can get inside the hacienda. The choice is to wipe out the bandits' leadership by ambush, then try to talk some sense into the remaining bandits at the hacienda to release *Señorita* Reyes and her *duenna*. I don't like the choice. It's too risky for the hostages. The bandits might execute the women in revenge for killing their leaders."

Bickford said: "We might cut down a pine tree, sir, and use it as a battering ram to break down the wooden gate."

"Not a bad plan, Sergeant. That would get us inside. Except they could pick us off from the towers and the walls. We can't take many more losses. But . . . to some extent . . . we might cover the men with the ram by concentrating our fire on the walls and towers."

Jesse said: "We might wipe out the bodyguards, along with *El Hombre Grande,* and capture this *El Tigre* and tell the bandits in the hacienda we'll swap him for the hostages."

"Not a bad plan, either, Captain. But where would we set

up the ambush? Everything's open from the hacienda into town. And how many bodyguards would there be?"

"At least twenty," Reyes said. "Maybe a few more. That's what I learned when I was here before the kidnapping."

"Sir," Connelly said, "why not shoot 'em down when they're in the *cantina* gettin' drunk? Wipe 'em out. Get the horse holders first and run off their mounts. That way them inside would be afoot, and we'd have 'em all in one place."

"If they use horse holders?" Gordon replied. "If they don't, that would be much simpler with everybody inside. But if we killed *El Tigre*, we'd have nothing left to swap for the hostages. Frankly, I wish we could wipe out the entire murderous bunch to the last man. We'd be doing the poor people in this part of Sonora a great favor."

"There is another choice, *Señor* Major," Reyes said. "If all the bandits go inside the *cantina*, we could order them to surrender or we'd open fire."

"Except, Mister Reyes, I shouldn't expect men like the bandit chief and the Hussar to surrender meekly. I think they'd come out shooting. In that event, we'd try to spare *El Tigre* for swapping purposes." He smacked his hands together. "A meeting of minds is helpful . . . clears the air. We've weighed all possible plans. Therefore, we can't set up an ambush in open country between the stronghold and La Gloria. Therefore, we'll have to do it at the *cantina*. We can see *El Tigre*'s bunch from here when they come down the road to town. We'd make a big commotion if we planted the command around the *cantina* too early. One of his spies would see and run to the hacienda. I think Herrera is a spy. He's too oily for me. I don't think the owner of the *cantina* is. I hope he survives this. So it has to be at the *cantina* Saturday morning. At this moment, it strikes me as most feasible to let them get inside the *cantina* before we make our move from here."

"Major," Jesse said, "it would help if we know what *El Tigre* looks like. There'll be a fog of powder smoke. How do we identify him? I believe Agustín gave us a description back at Fort Bowie."

"I was told he's a short, stumpy man," Reyes said eagerly. "Big black mustache and piercing black eyes. And, they say, he always wears a white suit. I don't know much else. I. . . ."

"That's it, right there," Gordon interrupted. "The white suit. For sure, he'll be the only man there in white. Fine, Mister Reyes. Fine, men. Tomorrow morning I'll issue orders in detail."

Bickford and Connelly saluted and left.

Gordon smacked his hands again and started pacing out a circle. Of a sudden, he stopped and said: "I'd much rather get inside the stronghold. Until then, everything's a big gamble. If we kill *El Tigre* in all that smoke, there goes the swap. And he might run out the back door when the shooting starts. Reminds me. Better detail two men there."

"Sir," Jesse said thoughtfully, "I'd like for us to talk to old Pablo when Herrera's not around. Maybe Agustín can get something out of him. At Pablo's house . . . this afternoon. What do you think?"

"Do it," Gordon said, showing his unfailing fervency. "At this stage, we have to follow every possible lead that might help us."

The Hussar ran his fingers through his red beard and looked out his quarters in the barracks across from headquarters. *Siesta.* Now was the time. These primitive Mexicans had to have their rest after the midday meal. Even the *jefe.* One reason why the Mexicans could never measure up to veterans of the French Foreign Legion as fighters. There were some exceptions, he reluctantly admitted. The Juáristas, when properly trained by ex-Confederates, had won some battles and forced the emperor to surrender. Yet, on one occasion, the Juáristas had been badly fooled by superior planning and deception. He looked back with satisfaction to when the Juáristas had massed to attack the big Hussar encampment, led there by a Mexican traitor, while unbeknown to them the Hussars were hitting the Juáristas' camp. A bloody blow to the Juáristas. In war when women and children got in the way, they had to pay the price. He had no qualms about that.

It was a little early yet. Let the two women nap a while. He poured himself another *aguardiente,* poor stuff compared to French brandy and cognac. Another compromise a European had to make living in Mexico. As a Legionnaire, he'd served in many places, some even worse than this, some better. His favorite was Morocco, where he'd had all the women he wanted, especially young ones barely in their teens, and some not that old. Here women were scarce, except for the few worn-out whores in La Gloria.

In a thrust of rueful thought, he realized now that he'd made a mistake when he'd stolen the regimental payroll and deserted in Mexico City. The French had been pulling out of Mexico, headed for Vera Cruz. The emperor had been a prisoner in Querétaro. The lure of easy money had been too much. When most of it had been spent, he'd fled to Sonora to get away from the vengeful bands of roaming Juáristas, taking with him other deserters. The French had known him as First Sergeant Victor Daudet, a name that helped speed his promotions, but his real name was Max Hofer, a Prussian. In a legion of hardened men, many of them criminals from all over Europe, he was known as a taskmaster, which also helped him advance as a noncom. Many men hated him. Weaker ones, like those who had deserted with him, followed him blindly as their one means of survival in a harsh foreign land.

By chance he'd met *El Tigre* in a *cantina,* each strong man wary of the other at first, each with his followers around him. Hofer's men had been outnumbered, but well armed and orderly while drinking. That must have impressed the bandit chief, because he'd sent a bottle of brandy to Hofer's table by the cringing *cantina* proprietor. Hofer, surprised, had thanked him with a wave and, shortly thereafter, had a bottle of brandy sent over to the *jefe.* It had been a beginning that had flourished from that day. They had got drunk together. They had much in common: both ruthless and down on their luck at the time. The leader of each band could use the other's strength. The *jefe* had recently suffered heavy losses in Chihuahua when Mexican regulars had surprised his camp.

In their first joint operation, they had wiped out an entire *conducta. El Tigre* had been so pleased that he had made the giant Hussar *comandante* of the bandits, with instructions to enforce all orders to the letter: shooting deserters and insubordinates. After several examples of what happened to offenders, the Hussar's iron hand wasn't questioned. He ruled by fear. He despised Mexicans as inferiors and relished towering over those of much smaller stature. With the walled hacienda buildings as its stronghold, *El Tigre*'s band was now in its ascendancy in a war-torn land of little order.

He was still not quite ready to go over there. He finished the brandy and got up and stood before a table over which hung a beautiful oval-shaped mirror framed in gold leaf on dark wood, booty from a plundered *conducta.* He ran fingers through his beard and gazed approvingly at himself. Ah, he'd almost forgotten, it had been so long, and he dabbed perfume from a bottle onto his fingertips and patted both sides of his beard. He was ready now.

Striding across the courtyard, he noted that all guards were on the wall, or had better be. He skirted headquarters where two guards stood posted. They stiffened to attention and saluted as he passed. He flicked them a forefinger and strode on.

He came to a small patio at the very end of the east wall, his boot heels resounding on the stone tiles as he turned and strode up to a door and knocked. After some seconds, he thought he heard muted voices.

He knocked again, louder. No voices this time. Only silence. They were trying to ignore him. Would he have to knock down the door? But that would disturb the *jefe*, and the *jefe* didn't like to be disturbed during *siesta*.

He raised his hand to knock again when he heard the bar being lifted, and the door opened a trifle. Instead of the girl, as he expected, it was the *duenna*. She was a dumpy little black-eyed woman with honest eyes that cut him down considerably. She held a shawl in her right hand.

"What do you want?" Her voice was as honest as her eyes, and she wasn't one to be fooled by mere words.

"I want to come in and talk."

The honest eyes snapped at him. "You can't come in. Murderers and thieves aren't welcome here."

"I want to talk to you about your release."

"Not until a member of the Reyes family comes to this door will we know we are freed. Let us alone."

He moved in a step, towering over her, trying to intimidate her.

She stood her ground and sniffed. "You smell like a cheap whore. Go away!"

This insolent Mexican woman! He started to push the door in, but she held it with her stout left arm. "You son of a goat! Go away!"

He pushed her again.

In a flash, she flung the shawl aside and stuck a revolver

208

inches from his leering face. He stepped back, dumbfounded, mouth gaping. He tried to snatch the revolver, but she alertly pulled it back and aimed it at him again.

"Come one more step," she warned, "I'll kill you. I have but one life to give, and I'll gladly spend it for my beloved Alicia. But you will die before we do . . . you *cabrón!*" She leveled the gun even more carefully, this time with both hands, and they didn't shake.

He stood back. She meant what she said, this runty little Mexican woman. He saw that. He was no fool. He said: "I was trying to be kind to you both. To help you. Now I won't. If the ransom's not here in time, you will both die. I will see to that." He flung away, boots pounding.

She slammed the door and slid the bar across. "Alicia, my dear child, I thought it was the cook, who is kind. He promised to bring us some fruit from the valley. I beg your forgiveness that I allowed that *cabrón* to threaten us." She was near tears. She put down the revolver on the table with shaking hands.

"What more could you have done, Rosa? You were so brave . . . far braver than I. I'm so proud of you. I was behind you with this silly broom handle." Glancing at it, they both broke into a cascade of nervous laughter and hugged each other.

Then Rosa held Alicia at arm's length, looking at her, loving her from the day she was born, so tiny and squalling. She was slim and dark, her great eyes like shadowed lights with the long lashes, her sweet, perfect smile, her fine features framed by a wealth of blue-black hair. She was only sixteen. So beautiful. Rosa couldn't love her more were she her own blood.

"Will they ever come, Rosa?" Alicia asked, in that child-like appealing way of hers.

Rosa placed both hands on the points of the girl's shoulders. "They will come, my dear, in answer to our prayers, which rise straight up to heaven. The Reyeses are strong family people. They do not forget their loved ones. And God is on their side against this evil place. They will come." She only wished she felt as confident as her words sounded. If worse came to worse, she would shoot her beloved Alicia, then herself.

Chapter Fifteen

Before they rode into La Gloria, Jesse and Reyes agreed it might be wise not to advertise their presence and likely destination in Herrera's eyes by clattering past the store and on down the street where they understood old Pablo lived. Accordingly, they circled left of the store, past adobes and goat and chicken pens, and came in on the street some distance from Herrera's.

Now, to find Pablo's house. Reyes did the inquiring. At the first house the woman pointed on down the street without saying how far, eyeing the two strangers with open suspicion. But, at least, they were on the right street. The second inquiry brought another woman to a door. She said nothing, just shook her head, as suspicious as the first woman and shut the door in Reyes's face, her fear evident.

"Is there anybody in this place who's not afraid?" Jesse asked.

They weren't far from the street's end when they saw a little boy playing with a black puppy in the front yard of an adobe behind a broken rock wall. Old Pablo had a grandson, Herrera had said. Maybe this was the house.

"Is this where old Pablo lives?" Reyes asked the boy.

The boy nodded.

They tied their mounts to a post and walked into the yard. "I'll give you a *peso* if you'll watch our horses," Reyes told the boy. "Don't go out there. Just stay in the yard and keep an eye on 'em. Can you do that?"

The boy agreed shyly, but his smile was quick while still holding fast to the squirming puppy. He looked about seven or eight, with curious black eyes and black hair cut just above his shoulders.

Reyes gave him the *peso* and asked his name, which he said was Julio.

"That's a good name," Reyes assured him, drawing another smile.

An elderly woman, her face drawn, was at this door. Both men took off their hats. "We're miners, *señora*," Reyes said, bowing. "We'd like to talk to Pablo, if we may?"

She turned uncertainly toward the room. "He is sick. Very sick. I don't know, *señores*. He. . . ."

Before she could say more, a weak voice called out hoarsely: "Invite 'em in. I remember them at the store. The tall *Americano* is the one who gave me the beautiful silver dollar." A cough stopped him.

She let them in, and they nodded to old Pablo, coiled in a chair, his crippled leg half drawn up under him. He seemed down to skin and bones, under a hundred pounds, Jesse thought, down from what once had been a strapping man, judging by the wide cast of his shoulders and his big hands and wrists.

"What can I tell you?" he asked them, clutching a red bandanna. "I'm old and sick."

"*Señor* Herrera said of all the miners you drove the straightest shaft," Reyes began, making talk. "Can you tell us where we might look for ore? Right now we're doing some digging upslope from the river and panning for gold in the river."

Old Pablo cracked up with thin laughter, so hard it brought on coughing. "There was one good vein of silver around here years ago . . . and it wasn't on that slope. It was high up in the Sierra Madre. I was there when it was found . . . a geologist from Hermosillo . . . and I helped drive the main shaft. But you men panning in the river. Hah. There's never been one little grain of gold found there."

"So we're wasting our time?"

"And money," the old man said, laughing through a cough. "Better try the Sierra Madre."

They had to come to the main question sooner or later, Jesse knew, and better soon, judging by old Pablo's waning strength. So, when Reyes paused, after a further run of general talk, Jesse said: "*Señor,* we are more than sorry you were hurt mining. *Señor* Herrera said he didn't know where or how it happened. And when we asked him as a matter of curiosity concerning this *El Tigre* we'd heard about, he said he knew nothing personal about the man. For a merchant who's lived a long time in La Gloria, he seemed to know very little about the town and its people." Old Pablo was listening intently. "Soon after," Jesse continued, "when we were buying supplies, he stepped out on the *ramada* and spoke roughly to you, we thought. We didn't like that. Why did he do that, *Señor* Pablo? Did he threaten you? Why didn't he tell where and how you were injured? We are here as friends. Now you can tell us?"

The old man had straightened in his chair as Jesse spoke. Now his black eyes seemed to smolder. "You are strangers. Why do you ask these things?"

"We're miners like you. We feel for you. If you've been wronged, we'll help you. Why this mystery about your injury?"

A fit of coughing seized old Pablo. He coughed and spat into the bandanna so long that his wife came to his side. When he stopped, she said: "He needs to rest now. He can't talk any more." Her husband was silent. He looked distraught and afraid.

"If you need help," Jesse said, "we're camped down by the river on the other side of town. We'll come. We are friends."

"*Gracias, señor.* It is not good with him."

They rode back down the dusty street a short distance,

then circled around the store to the other side of the village, and continued along in silence, Jesse reflecting on what they hadn't accomplished.

Major Gordon was waiting when they dismounted.

"We found old Pablo," Jesse reported, "but he wouldn't tell us anything. He's afraid. We asked him pointblank what Herrera said to him and where and how he was hurt and why Herrera wouldn't tell us. Pablo's very sick and very afraid, Major. So it didn't pan out."

"Yet it ties to *El Tigre* some way. Part of the prevailing fear here. Why this blanket of silence? Because everything traces to this murderous brute and his cut-throats and their grip on these poor people. Even so, it's most unusual that the man who was injured won't reveal any of the particulars. Well, it was worth your effort."

He thanked them, and then the three walked to the higher woods where they could observe the stronghold through binoculars. In the next hour no one passed in or out. The only visible movements were on the parapet of the wall, the jagged, broken glass glittering viciously in the smoke heat of the afternoon sun.

From there they also could see the patch of timber not far east of the hacienda where the horse was tied, but they couldn't see the horse. The sun was sinking when the stronghold's gate opened and a youthful bandit came out with a sack of feed and a bucket of water. He took the path and vanished in the copse. After a minute or two, he walked back to the hacienda, swinging the bucket. He looked up at the main tower and shouted, and the gate swung open, and he went in, the gate closing fast behind him.

The three traded looks, but no one spoke. After that, a heavy silence seemed to grip the stronghold. Not one sound. Not one voice. Not one ring of metal on metal. Watching,

Jesse couldn't stifle a dark sense of foreboding. He still had it when they walked down to the bivouac.

Little was said around the supper fires. The evening turned somber, a sort of shackled feeling, Jesse sensed, because they were limited to one choice, and that a hazardous one for the hostages if the swap didn't work out. When he heard Bickford set the night's sentries, he looked about his stock and went to his bedroll.

Friday morning after mess, Gordon was working on details of his orders for Saturday when a little Mexican boy burst running into the bivouac.

"It's Julio," Reyes said.

The boy seemed at a loss until he spied Reyes and Jesse. He ran over to them, panting hard, and crying.

"Grandfather say come now. Hurry. Bad sick. Grandmother say come, too. Hurry."

"He's Pablo's grandson," Jesse explained to Gordon. "We'd better go."

The horses saddled, Jesse lifted the boy in front of him, and they took off at a gallop. Again they circled the store, this time sending chickens squawking and flying and rousing dogs to barking, and rushed up to the house.

"I'm afraid he's dying," old Pablo's wife told them, weeping and wringing her hands. "He's so weak." She led them into a tiny room where Pablo lay on a bed, looking even more wasted than the previous day. Eyes like burned embers regarded them. His mouth hung open like a parched bird's as he motioned them to chairs.

"I'm not a coward," he whispered hoarsely, smothering a deep cough. "I won't die a coward. That's why I've asked you to come." He was speaking slowly, choosing his words. "A man shouldn't die with the truth untold, if he's a man."

When he coughed again, his wife brought him a glass of water. He cleared his throat.

"I was injured digging a very curious shaft because it wasn't looking for silver or copper . . . that was three years ago. I dug it straight . . . why they call me The Mole. Y'see, I have a feel for Mother Earth and how she was formed . . . a gift I have." He grew bitter. "Oh, I'd be paid *muchos pesos* if I dug it." He bent over coughing, spat into a bandanna. It pained Jesse to see that Pablo was coughing up blood. Pablo reared onto an elbow, his bitter voice like a rasp. "Just before I finished it, a support fell on my leg . . . crippled me. He wouldn't pay me . . . said I hadn't finished it. Lacked just a few feet more. His own men finished it. Simple. Little Julio could've done it." He reached for a long breath. His eyes seemed to burn. "I dug it for *El Tigre* . . . an escape tunnel that runs from his office, under the wall, to where he keeps a racehorse . . . down on the slope east of the hacienda where there's a patch of timber." He took another long breath, his jaw set, his eyes determined. "There's a trap door in his office, covered by a rug. He said he'd kill me if I ever told anyone about the tunnel . . . that evil man. Herrera knows . . . why he cautioned me not to say how and where I was hurt. Maybe God punished me because I dug that tunnel for a monster. I believe we all pay for our sins in some way." He smothered a cough. "That is my secret, good *señores*. Now why did you want to know?"

Marveling at what he'd heard, Jesse waited for Reyes to answer. When, instead, Reyes turned to him, Jesse said: "We also have a secret, *amigo* Pablo. Before long it will be known. It is good." He dared not say more. "We thank you for sharing yours. We'll honor it and say nothing."

It was time to go. They shook Pablo's hand and left the room.

"Is there anything we can do for you, *señora?*" Jesse asked.

"There is nothing." Her sad eyes thanked him. "I have sent for our daughter in Bavispe. Julio's mother."

"Our heartfelt sympathy," Reyes said.

Jesse nodded. "You can be proud that Pablo is a brave man."

Each threw a hugging arm around her and left money on a table when they walked out. It seemed so paltry after what old Pablo had given them.

Jesse's excitement kept surging as they mounted and swung off at a trot, trying not to move too fast and attract attention leaving Pablo's house, should anyone be watching, then circling and striking out for camp at a run once they'd cleared the village. At last they had a way!

Gordon stood at strict attention, his mouth firming, his eyes lighting up at their report. At the conclusion, he smacked his hands. "By the grace of God and blind persistence, we've got something to go on with more than half a chance."

He immediately summoned his noncoms for orders and explained about the unexpected development of the escape tunnel. Late this afternoon Corporal Connelly would take the entire pack train and swing around the village to a point on the river several miles north where the trail narrowed below a bluff. "A good place to shut off any pursuit. We can't have the train slowing us down getting out of here. Two troopers will be left to guard the packs. This morning we'll cook rations for four days and check the shoes on every horse and mule."

He also detailed Captain Wilder and Mr. Reyes and Sergeant Bickford that afternoon to examine the opening of the tunnel where it came out in the clump of timber on the slope below the hacienda. One question. Could they be spotted from the corner tower? Both Reyes and Jesse said not, if they worked around and kept low, using the bank and the trees

217

for cover between them and the tower.

"Just be sure you make the reconnaissance *after* you see the man come from the hacienda to water and feed the horse," Gordon cautioned. He was thinking of everything, Jesse saw.

Tomorrow morning, Gordon said, after the command had observed *El Tigre* and his bodyguards passing on the road to town and on to the *cantina,* the three aforesaid men and two more troopers would work around to the tunnel entrance. Sergeant Bickford would pick those two, plus another trooper to go into the tunnel with them. The rest of the outfit would mount up and stand to horse at the foot of the slope in the river timber.

"*Señor* Major," Reyes said, "as a matter of honor I'd like to lead us into the tunnel and the hacienda. I feel it is my duty."

"Certainly, Mister Reyes. Request granted. There is another matter I've overlooked. It'll be dark going into the tunnel. You'll have to feel your way. But as Pablo told you, he always cut a straight shaft. Coming out, you'll see the light at the opening. We have no candles, and I don't believe there's a lantern in the outfit. Is there?"

The noncoms shook their heads, no.

"Take hand guns, no carbines. Easier to handle. I estimate there'll be thirty or forty of the enemy still in the hacienda, mainly in the barracks. You may need knives. What about knives?"

They all had knives. Jesse's was in a sheath in his pack. Talking on, they estimated the tunnel's length from thirty to forty yards. They knew Alicia and her *duenna* were near the east wall in the main building, only a general location. To save time, they might have to force a guard to lead them to their quarters.

Presently, Gordon dismissed them.

218

Jesse's first move was to get his knife; next, he and Reyes checked the shoes on their mounts and Chico, the mule. None needed changing. After looking to hand guns and ammunition, they sat in the shade and smoked and talked. After mess, they smoked and napped. In the middle of the afternoon, they climbed the rise to the observation woods with Bickford. The eyes of the binoculars revealed a spiral of lazy smoke and the pacing of the puppet-like sentries on the parapet.

It was later than yesterday when the gate opened and the same young bandit with feed and water materialized. He seemed to be muttering to himself as he walked, kicking at pebbles and tufts of grass. At the thicket he was hardly there before he emerged, swinging the bucket, kicking at things again.

"Life is dull when you're a bandit not wiping out escorts or attacking *conductas*," Reyes said, venting his bitterness.

They waited a while longer and then, keeping low, made for the copse. Not until within ten yards or less could they see the feeding horse. He paid them no mind. The thicket was dense with low-growing brush. They had to look around a bit before they found the tunnel, hidden behind a wall of thick prickly brush and a wooden door. Sliding the door aside, careful not to break any tell-tale brush, they found an opening about five feet high and four feet wide, as well cut as Pablo had said. After looking at the hole and visualizing how the going would be, they placed the door back, and, with backward glances at the corner tower, they angled off the way they had come.

It was nearly dark when they reached the bivouac. By then, the pack train was gone, but the usual mess fires were blazing. There was plenty of coffee to go with dry rations.

As the evening advanced, Jesse began to sense a familiar awareness: a general getting ready and a sense of anticipation and relief, that they were about to embark on their mission in the morning. Major Gordon strolled among the volunteers and stopped to chat. Jesse liked that. A resourceful, fair-minded officer who looked out for his men and their welfare and could project beyond the confines of the bivouac. By now, every man knew what his duties would be.

Morning was much the same, but there were visible signs of the growing tension. Troopers moved a little faster as they watered mounts at the river and led them back to feed from nose bags before grooming and saddling, and rechecking saddle gear and weapons that needed no looking after again. A lookout was poised at the observation point to report when *El Tigre* and his bodyguards and the Hussar left the stronghold. Bickford had picked two volunteers to go as tunnel guards.

Now the waiting. It never seemed to change, Jesse thought, whether back there in his younger marching and fighting years in the Army of Tennessee, which seemed a long time ago, or right here on a river in northern Sonora with Yankee horse soldiers disguised as miners ready to rescue a beautiful Mexican girl and her *duenna*. He had the fleeting picture of himself not unlike an itinerant actor playing different rôles on many stages with fast-changing backdrops. He was sitting, leaning against a tree, resting while he could. Rest while you can, eat while you can, because likely there will be times, day upon day, when you can't do either. His red horse was saddled and rested. He'd tied the Quickloader to the saddle horn and the Spencer rode in a sheath. His knife hung on the left side of his belt, the Colt Navy on his right. His mind kept flitting back and forth to the Hussar, the one the Mexicans called *El Hombre Grande*. A member of the 6th Hussars, which had struck the virtually undefended Juárista camp and wantonly killed so many women and children. He tried to think of the man dispassionately, but could not, feeling grim and vengeful.

The sun had begun to shed waves of smoky heat when the lookout suddenly ran through the woods into camp and reported to the major. "They just left the hacienda, sir. Looks like about twenty or so."

"Good. Get your mount and stand by."

Jesse got up, seeing a stir of dust on the rocky road leading from the stronghold. He focused his field glasses, as others were doing. Some ten bodyguards rode in front, ten behind, all on good horses, each bandit wearing crossed bandoleers and big sombreros. Belted revolvers. Carbines in saddle sheaths. The elite guards. Their arrogance striking even at this distance. Evenly divided between Hussars and Mexicans. In the center rode a thickset little man in a white suit and gray sombrero astride a beautiful white Arabian that kept shaking its majestic head. *So that's the dreaded El Tigre.* Beside him, on his left, rode the Hussar. Green jacket with epaulets, no less. A kepi instead of a sombrero. Jesse could feel himself quicken at the sight. *Retain the Legionnaire look, you brutal bastard. Even out here.* The Hussar filled the saddle and more, dwarfing those around him, looming over them.

Jesse waited for his rush of hot anger; rather, it surged, cold and inflexible, bringing a flood of memories made alive again.

The horsemen trotted on into La Gloria. When Jesse saw them dismount at the *cantina,* tossing reins to horse holders, and troop inside, the bandit chief first, flanked by the Hussar, bodyguards trailing, he looked at Gordon, who waved for the tunnel detail to go.

They started walking fast for the observation woods, the rest of the outfit following with all the mounts, to stand by in the river timber. For the first time, Jesse learned that the

221

fourth man assigned to enter the tunnel was John Webb, charged with cursing and striking an officer. Jesse's impression of the man, gained piecemeal on the march, was of a lank, moody individual, given to reckless talk and arguments with the bantering Irish. Jesse wondered why Bickford had chosen him and wished it were either Connelly or Moriarty. On second thought, there was the rub between Bickford and the corporal, and Moriarty was the sergeant's gadfly.

When the outfit stood posted, the six men ran up the slope to the thicket and past the horse. They parted the bushes, slid back the door, and Reyes entered, followed by Jesse and Bickford and Webb. A few steps and Reyes hesitated, understandably. The heavy, musty air had a palpable feel. Another moment and he plunged ahead, leading them, the four forced to stoop and bend knees.

They moved fast through the stuffy air, Bickford and Webb in the rear. Indeed, old Pablo had dug a straight shaft. Their breathing grew audibly heavy. After a time that seemed longer than it was, they saw a crack of light. They walked faster now. Suddenly they reached the tunnel's end and located the light just above them. They listened for voices and heard none, their breathing the only sound.

Jesse pushed on the trap door with both hands. It gave grudgingly at first, then flipped open, taking a rug or carpet with it. Standing, he found the wooden floor just below his shoulders. With a quick glance around, he pushed up with both hands and gained the floor, then gave Reyes a hand up, and Bickford and Webb.

They were in a room literally jammed with stacks of rifles and carbines and boxes of ammunition. Other rooms opened off the office, all open and unoccupied.

Now where?

Jesse looked questioningly at Reyes, who pointed east, behind the office and toward the wall. As they started out the farthest door, an armed guard approached at a stroll, gazing off across the empty courtyard. They drew back and closed the door. They could hear him coming on at the same even pace. Surely he'd go on. They heard him stop at the door, saw him open it and come in a step, apparently to look around. Before he could pull back, Jesse grabbed him by his shirt front and stuck the Colt Navy in his amazed face. Bickford was there at almost the same instant, grabbing the guard's revolver from his holster.

"Silence," Jesse whispered in Spanish, "or you're dead! Take us to the women prisoners!"

The guard, a stout man with hard-bitten eyes, tried to play dumb. Instantly Bickford grabbed him by his long, greasy hair, jerked his head back, and ran the flat side of his knife across the man's throat. The guard still wouldn't speak. Then Bickford ran the cutting edge of the knife across the man's throat until it drew a line of blood, which he smeared on the man's face. He flinched and gulped.

"Where are they?" Bickford snarled, pressing the knife harder. His rough Spanish was clear enough.

"Back there," the man gulped, nodding vaguely east.

"You're gonna show us where!"

They checked the courtyard first. It was clear. They rushed on, with Bickford still holding the knife at the guard's throat, and Jesse grasping one arm and jabbing the Colt into the man's side. They came to a corner of the building.

"Where?" Bickford snarled.

The man motioned right, and they turned into a small patio near the end of the east wall.

"In there," the man said.

Bickford didn't let go of him.

Reyes stepped to the door, rapped softly, and in a low-pitched voice called Alicia's name.

At least ten seconds passed without a response.

Reyes tapped again and called again, a more urgent note in his voice.

Slowly, uncertainly, bit by bit, the door opened and a determined little Mexican woman of middle age looked at Reyes. Her eyes flew wide, her mouth fell, an expression of utter belief in miracles flashed over her plump face, and she let out a squealed: "Agustín!"

He put a finger to his lips.

An interval of confusion began as Reyes rushed inside amid a clamor of wildly ecstatic voices, quickly hushed. Bickford eased the knife a trifle. Jesse let the Colt drop a little, his attention fixed on the reunion and the urgency to get away from here. Webb stood next to Jesse.

Seeing that momentary laxness, the guard broke free and pulled a knife from his belt and lunged at Jesse, the only one between him and the open courtyard. Webb just stood there, mouth gaping, hands at his side. Before Jesse could turn, the guard was upon him. But Bickford, like a snarling cat, was only half a step behind. He plunged the knife high into the guard's back, so hard it *thunked,* at the same time reaching with his left hand to stifle any outcry. Despite that, the guard got out a shrill — "Haw . . . aw!" — as he dropped the knife and collapsed. Bickford's second slash at his throat cut off further sound.

Damning his own distraction, Jesse met Bickford's eyes just as the sergeant muttered: "We're even now. I'll be beholden to no damned Reb!"

Reyes appeared with the two women, their faces alight with joy now blending with onrushing fear. The three men closed around them, and they started running. They were nearing the open office door when a yellow-haired man came out of a building across the courtyard. He stared at them, puzzled for a moment. Then he shouted and ran toward them, reaching for his sidearm as they darted inside. Jesse and Bickford shut the door behind them.

Going to the gaping tunnel, Jesse said: "Come on, Agustín! Go first! We'll hand the women down to you!"

Reyes jumped down.

The *duenna* went first, then the girl, then Webb.

Jesse and Bickford hesitated, neither willing to be next. Before they could say a word, a paunchy guard burst inside from the hallway, rifle at the ready, shock bulging his hooded eyes.

In that split second of indecision, Jesse shot him twice. The bullets drove him backward and down, screaming and flailing with his arms, the blasts deafening in the room, the blooming powder smoke hanging in the air. They barred the door shut this time and dashed back to the tunnel. Both hesitated again, then both stepped toward the hole simultaneously. It was almost ludicrous. "By God, Sergeant! You go or I go!" Bickford stood rooted, jaw set stubbornly. Jesse said — "Then follow me!" — and dropped down. Bickford followed so fast he nearly landed on Jesse, scarcely a moment's difference in their going.

Bending low, they took off at a fast dog trot. Before long they could see struggling figures, and now more light, and then the tunnel's mouth.

With the two troopers left as guards, the men formed a shield around the women and pressed on through the thicket and down the grassy slope. Behind them they could hear shouts from the hacienda, a rising chorus of shouts.

A jubilant Major Gordon was waiting at the edge of the woods. "This is extraordinary," he greeted them. "Most extraordinary. Most admirable. I salute you all." Which he did.

Sweeping off his hat, he bowed to the women and hurried them to their mounts, while cocking an eye on the noisy stronghold.

The column left at a fast trot. The *duenna* immediately had trouble handling her big cavalry mount, whereupon Reyes took the reins and led the horse. The dark-haired Alicia rode with ease.

Gordon led them past the abandoned camp and on a tight circling course that took them around La Gloria, leaving the hacienda farther behind on their right. Finally, Jesse thought thankfully, they were clear. *But for how long?*

As if in reply, the major increased the pace to a gallop.

Soon afterward, Jesse glanced back and felt the onset of an old tautness when he saw the dusty streak of a rider barreling at a dead run down the road from the hacienda for the village. He pressed his lips together, seeing how all the loose pieces of this nasty fight were coming together, and very fast. How much lead did they have now? He could just about count the minutes.

Close on that hard determination, Gordon called to him: "Captain, I want you and Corporal Connelly to cover our rear. Give us some time. Slow 'em up. Fire and fall back. No heroics. I'll send two more men. Way it looks, we'll have to make a stand where the pack train is."

As Jesse waved and swung away, he knew the major's thinking: concentrated fire and Connelly's long-range marksmanship. *No heroics. Just fire and fall back.* That was all. Already this had echoes of other fighting retreats.

Chapter Sixteen

Diego had overslept this morning. He was eating breakfast with the prostitute, Lupe, when he heard the clatter of horses in front of the *cantina* down the street not far away. Going to the window, he saw the white-suited *El Tigre* and the Hussar and the bodyguards dismount. Their presence reminded him that he hadn't scouted the *gringos'* camp today and observed their movements. He would do so now and report to the *jefe* this afternoon of any suspicious actions. Consistency was important in his line of work. On second thought, he would finish eating and enjoying more coffee before leaving. There was no hurry. The *jefe* wouldn't sleep off his drunk until midafternoon.

Thus, it was some time later when he went out to the shed behind the house and bridled and saddled his horse and rode around to the street. Lupe, always mindful of her customers, growing fewer as the village dwindled, had fed the saddler earlier. He had passed the clamorous *cantina* when a familiar rider from the hacienda raced up. The young bandit looked in a state of fear and near collapse. Recognizing Diego, he blurted out: "The prisoners have escaped! Two guards are dead!"

Diego was puzzled. "What prisoners?"

"The two women the *jefe*'s holding for ransom! The governor's daughter and her *duenna!* Don't you know? They just escaped through the tunnel with some *gringos!* The *jefe* will be furious! He'll kill me for bringing bad news!"

Diego could only listen in open-mouthed amazement.

The rider spurred by, and Diego turned his horse and followed at a trot, thinking: *women prisoners, the governor's daughter, ransom, escape through the tunnel. What tunnel?* Astonishing, but not difficult to believe. *El Tigre* was a brute. He had no scruples.

He saw the rider come down from his horse, hesitate, and with a final dread run inside. He heard a trembling single voice, cut short by a raging shout. Instantly, the *cantina* erupted bodyguards and the *jefe* and the Hussar.

Diego could see *El Tigre* struggling for control. He paced back and forth like a fighting rooster, rage puffing his bloated face. *"Comandante,"* he said, accusation making his voice shrill, "how could this happen? How could the *gringos* have known about the tunnel?"

"There must be a traitor among us, *Jefe*."

"You *will* find him, *Comandante*. But, first, bring everybody here at once. The *gringos* can't be far. They have a pack train. They'll be headed for the border."

"Sí, Jefe." The Hussar flung himself to the saddle and pounded away.

Some villagers had gathered in the street. Herrera left the porch of his store and spoke in a fawning voice: *"Jefe,* a little while ago a boy told me he saw all the *gringos* riding north around town. He saw two women. They rode fast."

"Was there a pack train?"

"He saw none. Just the riders."

"Then the pack train's ahead of them." Pacing again, the *jefe* spotted Diego on his horse. In his fury, he seemed to stand taller. He pointed at Diego. His voice ripped out: *"Hombre,* you had orders to watch the *gringos* . . . report anything suspicious. They must've moved their pack train yesterday. Where were you, *hombre?* Still bedded down with that old whore? You will pay for your neglect, you Spanish-blooded milksop son of a *hacendado!* Today you will ride with us and fight the *gringos!*"

Diego quailed at the words. His breathing seemed to stop. He started to rein his horse away.

"Stop him! Seize him!"

Two bodyguards grabbed his bridle.

"Dismount, *hombre!*"

Diego obeyed, trembling, his knees like water.

"Today, *hombre,* we will show you how to fight like a man!"

Jesse and Connelly and Privates Tim Moriarty and Mike Clancy formed the rear guard. Jesse saw the bandits approaching in a rough column of fours, advancing at a steady trot. At least sixty men, maybe seventy, to the volunteers' nineteen. The range was about half a mile now. Beyond accurate fire. Where were *El Tigre* and the Hussar? He couldn't locate them in that mass with the naked eye. Through the binoculars, he caught the bobbing white. The bandit chief was riding in the center as he had with his bodyguards into La Gloria. The Hussar? He, too, rode deep in the pack.

"Corporal," Jesse said, "you're a good long-distance shot. See if you can pick off *El Tigre.* He's the one in white and rides a white horse. He's in the center of the column, hiding as usual behind his men. His next in command, the Hussar, dressed in green, flanks him."

Connelly raised the sights of his carbine, took aim, fired.

Nothing changed that they could see.

He tried again. Still, nothing happened. "Range is a little too far yet, Cap'n."

They waited, watching the bandits come on at the same relentless pace.

Jesse kept figuring the range. *They think they can overrun us because we're only four.* At what he estimated was about four hundred yards and when he dared not let them come much

229

closer, he said: "Let's all but Connelly concentrate our fire on the lead riders. And keep firing. Corporal, you sight for *El Tigre* and the Hussar back in the middle of the column."

Their carbines banged together, a volley. Powder smoke fogged around them, the air acrid with the hot scent of their firing. Jesse laid down four quick shots and paused.

Suddenly three of the foremost bandits weren't there any longer, and horses were running loose. The column halted, broke apart in confusion as milling riders pulled back and out to get away from the line of steady fire.

Jesse heard Connelly let out: "Son of a bitch! Them two's still back in the pack, Cap'n. I can't get at 'em."

"We're doing all right," Jesse shouted. "Keep firing."

He thought the bandits might possibly hold up now. But, instead, clearly responding to quick commands, knots of riders swept out left and right to form a wide, less vulnerable, front to outflank the volunteers, the maneuver of a skilled commander, Jesse saw. *El Tigre* and the Hussar still rode behind a shield of horsemen. Fire from the bandits was beginning to snarl around the four men, and bullets striking the flinty earth whined and buzzed like bees.

The flanking party on the rear guard's right was nearest when Jesse shouted to turn their fire there. A rider and horse went down, then another rider, whose horse whirled and bolted toward the river. The remaining flankers drew sudden rein. Seeing that, Jesse switched the troopers' fire on the left flankers, now within two hundred yards and coming at a run.

A volley slowed them; another checked them; another broke them.

It was time to fall back, because the bandits' center was beginning to move forward.

As the four wheeled to go, Moriarty jerked with a yell and fell forward on the withers of his mount. Connelly got to him first. With him and Clancy for support, they struck off for the waiting outfit about a mile away.

The Hussar brought the rest of the band into La Gloria on the run. *El Tigre* took command at once, formed them into a column of fours and led them north out of the village at a rapid trot. In the open country, he quickly reformed them, placing veteran subordinates at the head of the column, with orders to pursue and attack. He then dropped back with the Hussar in the column's center, surrounded by his trusty body-guards.

Diego found himself in the second rank of fours, swept along helplessly, a dreadful terror and sense of impending ruin upon him, even death. He still had his rifle and revolver, but, if he tried to flee, he knew he'd be shot. He'd heard the *jefe* give that order. For the first time in many years, he prayed as he had not since as a boy when his good mother and the patient *padres* had instructed him.

When his lips moved, a guard sneered at him: "You pray-ing, you son of a *hacendado?*"

Diego said no word. The guard was just another Mexican Indian without respect for Spanish blood.

"This'll be a lonely fight," the man admitted. "The *jefe* is in a rage. You're to blame. You didn't watch the *gringos.*"

Diego still said nothing.

"If we don't get the women back," the guard warned, "he'll have you shot. If you try to run, I'll shoot you."

Diego kept grimly silent, resigned to whatever might happen to him. Why hadn't he kept closer watch on the *gringos?* He had no one else to blame but himself.

After not many minutes, he saw the dust of the retreating *gringos,* riding very fast. *El Tigre* ordered a halt, his white Arab dancing under tight double reins. He was still furious. His

231

piercing black eyes, darting here and there among his men, seemed to throw off sparks. Around him Diego could hear the low mutters of bandits wondering if he was trying to ferret out the traitor among them who'd told the *gringos* about the secret tunnel.

Now he heard the *jefe* say: "There are the *gringos,* slinking away like coyotes. They're not many. We will kill them to the last man. That is my order. Their bodies will be left to rot for the carrion eaters. Spare no *gringos*. But watch out for the women. Be careful of your aim." His voice struck a final menacing note. "Any man who holds back will be shot on the spot." A few looked away, avoiding his stare. "Now attack them!"

Diego turned his horse with the rest and drew his rifle from its sheath. The lead riders spurred into a quick trot. Ahead, in the shrinking distance, he saw four riders detach from the main body of *gringos* and drop back. They rode only a short way before they halted. *Only four men,* Diego thought. *What could four do?*

Suddenly smoke puffs flowered where the four *gringos* sat their horses, and Diego saw the flashes of their guns. And, as he heard the mingling blasts of their weapons, he also heard bullets striking, and three bandits in the lead four ahead of him either swayed and fell from their mounts or clung to saddles and reined out of line. He yanked up as did those around him, also aware of riders behind him pulling up.

Within seconds, before they could break away completely, *El Tigre*'s arresting voice halted them, bringing order out of confusion. He ordered the column to form a broad front and sent out riders to outflank the four *gringos* on both sides.

Diego rode with the left-going flankers. He had to spur his horse to keep up, afraid to lag with the guard ever at his side. The bandit leading them was a gray-haired man, long a follower of the *jefe*. A scar, which ran from one ear to his mouth, gave him a particularly menacing visage. He made a fast, circling ride, then cut back sharply, which took them in so close Diego could see the *gringos* quite plainly through the drifting balls of cottony powder smoke. The men around Diego fired their rifles. He fired his, but the motion of his horse spoiled his aim, and he really didn't care whether he hit a *gringo* or not. He could think only of how he might slip away and flee for his life.

The *gringos* seemed to catch sight of the flankers almost as soon and started shooting. It was intense, the *gringos* firing volleys. A bandit and his horse went down together. When another bandit dropped from his saddle and his horse bolted toward the river, the other flankers milled and drifted back toward the main body of bandits.

Thinking of escape, Diego spun a glance at the river. But the guard, apparently sensing his desire, was between him and the river, and Diego stayed with those falling back, the guard never far away. Soon after that, he saw the four *gringos'* firing stop the other flankers. Then the *gringos* retreated.

Feeling no letup in his mounting fear, Diego trailed back with the beaten left flankers, the guard still at his side. Across he saw the other repulsed flankers falling back in loose order. He sensed that they rode as the men around him rode, fearful after failure, but afraid not to report to the *jefe*.

As they rode up, the bodyguards opened a path, and *El Tigre* and the Hussar awaited them.

No one moved or spoke. Diego was petrified, caught up in the same paralyzing fear of the cowed men around him. Still, he sensed a ripple of unease. He heard mutters. A young bandit turned his horse and began slipping away to the rear. The Hussar was after him in a second, his revolver out. When the boy faced about with pleading eyes, the Hussar shot him between the eyes, and, as he fell, his brains splattered like broken eggs over his horse's black mane.

All the men just stared, frozen in horror, even the hardened bodyguards.

"No man will turn back," the *jefe* told them in a quieter but distinct voice. "Now we'll go after these *gringos*."

Major Gordon posted his men in the scattered timber at the narrowest point where the broad trail ran between the twisting Bavispe River and a rocky bluff. He went about it without hesitation, Jesse could see, as a veteran field officer who'd thought out the moves beforehand, realizing this was where the fight would be decided, here by the river, the one place where the outnumbered volunteers had a chance to stand off superior numbers. Around a bend some yards beyond, where the pack train and picketed mounts were, the major had sent a trooper with Moriarty who was to be cared for by the women. Jesse bit his lip. Tim Moriarty was dying. There was nothing more they could do for the boy but leave him in tender hands.

Everything was carried out very quickly. No time to fell trees and block the trail or to unload the packs for breastworks.

The idea, Gordon said, walking among the kneeling troopers, was to concentrate their fire at the most telling point of attack. In his heartening way, he told them their position gave them the advantage of a partial angle of enfilading fire, and reminded them that the river and the bluff prevented the enemy from outflanking them. He then posted himself in the center, placing Bickford on his left with others, Jesse and Connelly and Reyes, spaced to his right toward the trail with the rest. The major would give the order to fire.

Jesse finished filling the magazine tubes in the Quickloader.

Connelly kept looking to his carbine sight and off at the bandits. Gordon had suggested that young Reyes stay with the women, but he had declined.

Through binoculars, Jesse saw the bandits' flankers straggling back; they seemed slow about it, which told him much of the fight had been shot out of them. There seemed to be some confusion. But now they were reforming again. He passed on that word to Connelly and Reyes. Another pinch of time slipped by. He briefly glimpsed *El Tigre* and the Hussar — they appeared to be haranguing their men. He heard a distant shot there and saw the puff of white. *Why that? How come?* Now they were forming up . . . back into the column of fours. They were coming on. But the two leaders still rode deep within the column.

He settled himself, conscious of familiar tensions washing over him that never got old, the getting ready, the watching, the waiting for destiny to unfold. He sensed this had the resonance of a fight to the finish.

As if the *jefe* still had eyes on him, Diego felt himself placed again in the second rank of fours beside the guard. They swung out at a brisk trot. Ahead, Diego could see the yellowish bend of the trail, snaking between a high bluff and the river. The *gringos* were there among the trees below the bluff near the trail. He could see moving figures.

For a while they loped along unopposed, through a strange stillness. The *gringos* in the timber had quit moving.

When the *gringos'* first shots started falling, riders in the first rank toppled and the charge slowed, riders colliding as they bunched up. *El Tigre* shouted a command, and the column split in half, each veering away from the other. Now Diego and the guard rode in a column of twos. A backward glance showed the Hussar several riders behind Diego, and the *jefe* commanding the other column.

They rode at a gallop now, the sterile face of the desert rushing by. For a distance they charged unchecked. Everything before Diego came into sharper focus, the trees, the trail, the kneeling shapes. Then Diego saw balls of white smoke shrouding the trees, and he heard the rattle of carbine fire, the ripping sound of a volley. All at once the lead riders dropped, as if swept away. On instinct, he reined to his right, the guard with him. Another volley shook the column, checked its momentum. He could see bandits going down and horses rearing and terrified riderless mounts tearing off.

He angled back, sensing his chance to flee. The Hussar was shouting curses at the men, trying to rally them. He rushed here and there, everywhere, waving his revolver. Some moved forward; most wavered and began to turn back, on the verge of breaking. The *gringos'* concentrated fire was now continuous.

Before Diego could break free, the guard cut him off, and he was caught in a vortex of churning riders. The Hussar waved the revolver at Diego to go forward, calling him a coward. The tip of the waving gun barrel slashed Diego across the face. Blood flew and coursed down to his mouth, with it a numbing pain. He tasted salty blood. Again he heard the Hussar calling him a coward.

Something happened within him, then. It happened quite fast. A welling up. A final gathering of pent-up emotions. A bursting flood. He pointed his rifle at the Hussar and shot him in the chest. He saw the Hussar's utter astonishment as the slug knocked him sprawling from the saddle, his towering body bouncing like a log and rolling when a horse trampled him.

Diego jerked his mount around to flee — at least he was free — but the next he knew the guard blocked his escape, and in the same crush of time he heard and saw the blue flame flashing out the mouth of the guard's rifle. A massive force slammed him backward, and, falling, the saddler's reins loosened in his hands. He struck the ground with a breath-smashing impact and half turned, around him a kaleidoscope of plunging horses and frantic riders. So soon the spinning turquoise sky was beginning to slow and fade, and he knew that he was dying. Yet, strangely, somehow, he felt a certain solace, knowing that he had just redeemed himself and his honor, a man of Spanish blood.

Major Gordon was watching the oncoming columns of charging horsemen through binoculars.

"Fire!"

A volley crashed, and the head of the column seemed to disintegrate all at once.

"Fire at will!"

The column turned into a tangle of horsemen that in seconds found a surprising order; it split, and two lines of riders peeled off, maneuvers that showed an experienced leader. The nearest line came charging straight for the scattered timber, where most of the volunteers lay, the other line for the trail.

Heavy bandit fire was humming and whizzing through the timber. Jesse felt bits and pieces of broken twigs falling on his hat and arms. Cries rose along the line of troopers.

Gordon shouted — "Over here!" — and pointed at the nearest assault.

A shuddering volley followed, then another.

"Keep firing at will!"

The charge faltered, splintered into clots of wavering riders. Among them Jesse caught sight of the Hussar's huge shape. He was trying to rally them. There was a single puff of smoke, then Jesse couldn't see the Hussar any more. Then the entire mass of riders broke. They were fleeing.

At that, the troopers' fire slackened.

It was the major's voice slashing through the din that alerted them to the other column attacking at a run on the trail, the weakest part of the line. Feeding a third tube of shells into the butt of the Spencer, Jesse saw that it was going to be very close. This bunch was riding hell-bent for a break-through. A white figure bobbed up and down in the dusty, headlong column, not far from the lead: *El Tigre. A mad man's charge,* the thought flashed. Now Jesse saw the white Arabian; they were closing that fast. He centered his fire on the front horsemen, working the loading lever and earing back the hammer for each shot.

Connelly was standing beside him. The corporal took aim and followed a moving target to his right. He pinched off a shot and through the smoke Jesse saw *El Tigre* pitch forward.

Connelly whooped like an Indian. "Got the bastard!"

But there was no time for celebrating as the momentum of their charge continued to carry the bandits forward, the riderless white Arabian running with them. Behind them, Jesse glimpsed a white-clad body rolling alongside the trail. It rolled and lay still. Not till the riders saw the loose Arabian did they understand what had happened. They began to shout and pull up and away and point, and abruptly they broke *en masse* to the rear, riding low, scattering like desert quail, some riding Indian fashion on the off side of their mounts to escape fire.

It was over, Jesse saw. It sure as hell was.

Gordon cautioned his men to keep shooting as long as the enemy was in range. That soon ended. Now the usual after-battle letdown. Jesse rose from a kneeling position. His mouth was bitter with powder smoke. His eyes burned. His ears rang, and the Spencer's barrel was so hot that he leaned it against a tree.

Calls for help reached him from the line. They'd taken some hits. Every able-bodied man moved to help. Trooper John Webb lay dead over his carbine, as did James Ryan, the older Irishman. Sam Tate and a trooper named Dick Murphy were wounded, but able to walk and ride. As he gave a hand with the others, Jesse could not help thinking how these men had all stood their ground today. You could ask for no more.

The major ordered pack mules brought up, and, while they were tying on the dead, a trooper brought word that Moriarty also had died.

"We're going on a way," Gordon told his men. "Put this place behind us. They might come at us again, but I don't think they will."

"Corporal Connelly got *El Tigre* for sure," Jesse said, "and I believe the Hussar went down with the first bunch. That's when they turned tail."

"Then they won't be back," Gordon said. "But let's mount up now."

For Jesse there was yet an incompleteness here, a final going back and bringing it forward. "Major," he said, "I'd like a minute or more."

Gordon nodded with understanding. "The Hussar. Take all the time you need, Captain."

Jesse sheathed the Spencer, tied the Quickloader to the saddle horn, and rode out along the hoof-beaten trail, thinking: *veteran leadership, execution, favorable terrain, and stand-up troopers had won the fight against heavy odds.*

He came to *El Tigre*. There in the yellow dust, in the alien dirty white suit, he was no more than a castoff bundle. An evil little man, shrewd and ruthless, yet forceful enough to lead other men to senseless destruction.

Beyond, where the bandits' first charge had died, he found the Hussar, icy blue eyes staring at the flawless blue sky. Near him lay a Mexican whose appearance didn't fit the role of a scruffy bandit. A round-bodied man, well dressed in a dark blue shirt and gray trousers of quality and polished black boots. A man past his youth, but not middle-aged. Something about the full face and heavy mustache pulled at Jesse's memory. A trace of high arrogance in that face. Had he seen the man before?

The impression passed as he dismounted for a closer look at the Hussar, who had taken a bullet in the chest. Jesse noted the gaudy green jacket and gold-fringed epaulets and the meticulously groomed red beard. He wondered why he felt no great sense of revenge or triumph. All he felt was the dragging weariness of war, even though the Hussar possibly had fired the very bullet that took the life of sweet Ana. Certainly the Hussar had been in the raid, likely as a noncom with his imposing stature.

Jesse turned away, realizing something about himself. His war here was finished. But, in another way, it could never be finished.

He mounted and rode back to the outfit.

Chapter Seventeen

They formed quickly. The major posted Jesse and Connelly at rear guard again, Bickford in charge of the wounded and the pack train, and they moved out in close order, retracing their march along the trail they'd followed coming down, Gordon at the point with a single trooper. Reyes and the women rode between the troopers and the pack train. One man, with a picket-line lariat tied to the middle horse, led the three extra mounts, joined together by link straps snapped into bit rings.

Toward mid-afternoon, Gordon halted and called Jesse and the noncoms together. They all knew without speaking what had to be done.

The major pointed to a gentle slope shaded by pines. "It's a pretty place and well above the flood plain," he said. "What do you men think?"

It looked cool and restful, just right for weary horse soldiers.

They nodded in unison.

They would need stone markers, which they found along the river's course. They dug the graves in a deep, neat line, wrapped their comrades in blankets, put back the raw earth, and carefully scratched the names and regiment on the stones. Then Gordon spoke the unadorned words, and they mounted and rode on.

Near dusk they camped by the river. Roaring fires and supper helped dispel the somber bivouac. Afterward, Reyes came over to Jesse and said: "Alicia and Rosa have thanked Major Gordon and Sergeant Bickford, but you've been back with the rear guard. Now they'd like very much to see you."

"Be a little bit," Jesse said, knowing he was dusty and dirty, his face begrimed from powder smoke, and that he smelled like a herd of horses.

"They've wondered about your white hair in a man so young," Reyes said hesitantly. "I told them it was from being in so many wars."

Jesse smiled. "You could say that." He'd never told Agustín when it had happened or why.

When Reyes left him, he went to the river and, stumbling around on the rocks, took off his shirt and washed from the waist up and ran a comb through his tangled hair. That was the best he could do. On that conclusion, he walked up to the Reyes campfire.

"This," Reyes said, making an exaggerated bow, "is *the* Captain Jesse Wilder. You must excuse the brevity of my introductions, Captain. I've already told them all about you, especially when you trained the Juáristas."

Despite the distress of losing the troopers, Jesse could see and feel there the lingering excitement of the rescue and the wish to express their fervent gratitude.

He took off his hat and bowed. "I'm very pleased to see you."

Alicia was swiftly before him, her arms up and around his neck, and a kiss for his cheek. He had to bend to get the kiss. Rosa, smiling, gave him the same greeting.

"We are so grateful to you and all the brave *soldados*," Alicia said earnestly. "We owe you our lives. But we are deeply saddened about those who lost theirs, and the wounded."

She was certainly a fine-looking girl, slim and dark. She had a fine-boned face, enormous dark eyes set wide apart, a wealth of long, blue-black hair, and a full-lipped smile that made Jesse feel instantly at ease and wish to please her many times over. Somehow she'd managed to find a piece of white cloth and tie her hair back on her neck.

"I'm glad to report that we think the two wounded men are going to be all right," he told them. "They'll be able to ride again tomorrow. Maybe even fire a gun, if need be."

"That is good news, after all the sadness," Alicia said, her downcast eyes lifting, smiling again.

At her brother's urging, Jesse began to tell them about Father Garza and how he had organized an army of peasants, and armed and fed them, and how Jesse and his late friend, Cullen, had trained them to march and handle weapons to fight Maximilian's forces.

"At first," Jesse said, "the peasants didn't want to obey officers we'd picked, particularly someone they knew from their own villages. But they learned, after the *padre* lectured them sternly. He was a very persuasive man. Had a wonderful speaking voice. Spoke many languages. Was very humble. Refused to let them call him general. It had to be simply Father Garza."

"Before you trained the Juáristas," Alicia asked, "you were in what Agustín called . . . the Confederation Army?"

"I served in the Army of Tennessee, which was one of the armies of the Confederate States of America. Tennessee is one of the states in the South."

She was just full of eager questions. "What was your *Americano* war called?"

Jesse smiled. "We Southerners called it the War Between the States. The Yankees up North called it the Civil War or the Great Rebellion, and other names."

"And who won the war, Captain?"

"They did."

"Oh, too bad. I wish your side had won."

Jesse smiled broadly. "Thank you, Alicia. But, looking back, I think it was best in the long run that the United States

243

remain one country instead of divided. That way the country will always be stronger. Yet, there wouldn't have been a war with such a terrible loss of lives on both sides if the North had let the South go free. But . . . all that's over now."

Reyes said: "Tell us about President Juárez. My family has always been strong for him. What is he like? A big man with a huge mustache and bandoleers across his chest?"

"Just the opposite," Jesse said. "I saw him only once, at Querétaro. He's a small man, a short man. But he seemed bigger when I talked to him. He impresses you. He dressed plainly, in a dark suit. No uniform. He has penetrating dark eyes. He looks right at you. His face is wide and strong . . . a lot of strength there. His voice . . . as I remember it . . . was deliberate, yet pleasant. My friend, Cullen, told me the president is Zapotec Indian. Anyway, he is a good, honest man and will be good for your country."

Reyes was curious. "Why were you there, Captain?"

"I was at Querétaro to plead for the lives of Maximilian and the two Mexican generals to be executed. Father Garza told me the president was stubborn, and it would do no good. Yet, I went. I told him it was barbaric to execute prisoners . . . that we hadn't done that in our American war, as bloody as it was. He was cordial, but brief and inflexible. He said they'd been found guilty by the courts."

"How could you plead for their lives as a captain?"

"I wasn't pleading as a captain. I'd been a captain in the Army of Tennessee. I was pleading as a citizen general in the patriot army of Mexico, a commission approved by the president."

Reyes's face shone. "A great honor, *Señor* Citizen General Jesse. I am proud. We are all proud of you."

"It was an honor . . . and for a good cause." Jesse smiled. "Cullen said it was the only war we Johnny Rebs won."

They were all visibly impressed, the dark eyes of the women warmly upon him.

"With that," Jesse said, "I think I'd better let all of you rest."

Reyes wouldn't let him go. "President Juárez denied your plea. What did you do, then?"

"The president dismissed me, and I went out where Father Garza was waiting. He knew without asking that the president had denied my plea. Execution was set for three o'clock. We waited in the hot sun. A volley crashed. I saw the *padre* flinch. We said good bye. The war was over. He wished me well. *Un umbrazo, amigo.* Then I got on my horse and headed north."

"Your red horse!" Alicia exclaimed, clapping hands, her expression like that of a delighted child. "He's so beautiful in the sun. His body glistens. He moves like silk, as much as any fancy Arabian I've seen," she said, giving her brother a teasing, sidelong look. "Tell us about him, please."

How could he deny such a request? "He ran as a wild horse on the plains of Texas . . . a *mesteño.* Then a rancher captured him and sold him with a bunch of horses to a dealer in El Paso, where I bought him before I went to Mexico with Cullen. I don't know his breeding. But I think he's descended from horses the early Spaniards brought over. He's very independent. He seems to want to remind me now and then that he used to run wild, and he's letting me ride him just because he's generous. He's a battlefield horse. Has never bolted under fire." Given the chance, nothing like bragging about your horse. Jesse was enjoying this. "His name is *El Soldado.*" He caught himself too late.

"So you named him that because he's a battlefield horse?" Alicia asked.

"No. My late wife, Ana, named him."

A stillness fell upon everyone, including Jesse.

"Did . . . she also wind the pretty red ribbon in *El Soldado*'s black mane?"

"Yes."

"I didn't mean to intrude, *señor*. I'm very sorry."

Suddenly, Jesse felt his tenseness dissolve before these fine people. "You didn't at all, and I'm glad you asked. Ana was killed when the Sixth Hussar regiment raided a Juárista camp. The Hussar killed today was among the raiders. He was one reason I came on this mission. I wanted to get him. Someone else did today. But it was done. Sometimes justice is served in a roundabout way."

That broke the awkward moment. They talked on about other matters: where Juárez was leading Mexico; would the ambitious General Porfirio Díaz be a threat to the president? And on. Jesse felt at ease. All this was good. The fire was down to a few mere coals, and Bickford was posting night sentries when he left.

They were on the trail by daylight in the same tight formation as before. Connelly, low spirited over Moriarty's death, told Jesse: "We're not the same outfit without poor Tim. He could always make a hard march seem better. Besides that, he was the only one who knew how to get under Bull Bickford's hide and not pay for it. Guess he knew just how far he could go. Come to think of it, Cap'n, Tim was one of the few that never fought Bickford. In a way, I think Bickford liked the lad."

"There's one thing that makes losing good men even worse," Jesse said. "It's hearing 'em scream their pain on the way out, and all you can do is to give a man a swig of tepid water from a canteen or take his hand so he'll know he's got somebody at his side when he goes out. You feel helpless and guilty because you've survived and can't share his pain. I believe a soldier fears the agony of unbearable pain far more than he fears death."

"Tim went fast. That was a blessing. Before long, I aim to write his dear old mother back in County Tyrone, where a lot of us are from."

"What part of Ireland is that?"

"Up north. Ulster province. A lot of Scotch-Irish folks. Big families. Not enough land to go around. Hard times. Why so many of us came to America."

The day passed without pursuit or incident.

Buckshot rain pelted them on the third and fourth days. But on the fifth day the sky cleared, and they camped where the volunteers had bivouacked the first day coming down from San Bernardino Springs, in the cool shade of the tributary creek, above its junction with the river of the same name.

That evening, Reyes announced to the women: "This time tomorrow we'll be out of this and at San Bernardino Springs on the border."

Around the supper fires the volunteers expressed the same expectations. One more day and they'd be back on United States soil. The past few days, though uneventful since the fight north of La Gloria, had grown wearisome and depressing while traveling through a lonely land devastated by Apache raids. There was more Apache country ahead, but their luck had held since fighting off *El Tigre*'s band of cut-throats.

In the morning, they formed and moved off smartly, the major following the same order of march.

They hadn't been marching thirty minutes when a trooper loped back to the rear guard. "Major wants you quick, Captain."

Gordon had halted the column, and Bickford was at his side when Jesse rode up.

"We've seen two riders in the last few minutes," Gordon told him. "They seemed to fade back as soon as they saw us."

"Apaches?"

"I don't think so. They vamoosed before I could use the glasses. I have a bad feeling about this, Captain. I fear our luck is about to change. If there's a threat, we'll fall back to the bivouac. We can't expose the women to a running fight. Meanwhile, we'll march on a way and see."

First, he sent Bickford back to close up the column.

Ahead, the thorny desert rose and dipped gently in undulating folds. The column trailed down and up, kicking the ravels of dust.

Jesse and Gordon pulled reins at the same instant. On a rise less than half a mile away, a long line of horsemen blocked the march.

They both knew.

"Blanco!" the major flung out, and immediately sent a trooper back to fetch Bickford and Connelly.

While they watched, six riders dashed out, the lead man waving a white flag. Coming at a gallop, they halted less than ten yards away, and Blanco, flanked by two men, rode forth on his fine bay. The self-styled colonel looked somewhat bedraggled in contrast to their previous meeting, Jesse thought, most probably from effects of the horse herd stampeding through his sleeping camp. Blanco's gray jacket looked dirt smeared and one sleeve was torn. A straw sombrero had replaced his high-crowned cap. But he still wore the same greasy pants and the black boots, still in need of polish. A glob of a purple bruise decorated Blanco's left cheekbone, and his left eye was swollen to a slit. He was furious and remembering, that was evident. Under different conditions his comedown would have approached the comical. Certainly it had incensed him.

"You *Americanos* are back so soon," he said, his accented voice dripping sarcasm with each word. "Did you dig up all the gold and silver in the Sierra Madre, *Señor* Engineer? Did you strike a lode? Whatever you did down there, you paid a price for it, I see, because your men don't count the same."

"That is no concern of yours," Gordon replied.

"This time you have two women along."

"Neither are they any concern of yours."

To explain, Jesse thought, would only complicate matters and possibly encourage the wolfish Blanco to consider ransom.

Blanco gave an impatient toss of his head. "Everything you *Americanos* do concerns Colonel Santa Ana Blanco, of the Sonoran Auxiliary, because you continue to trespass in Mexico."

"You saw our permit from His Excellency, Governor Emanuel Reyes of Sonora."

"*Vah!* I saw it. It is only a piece of paper."

He was being disdainful, Jesse saw, and the man had quite a bagful of fast-changing moods.

"Colonel," Gordon said, "I ask you to move your men aside and let us pass. We want no trouble from you."

A stare of the utmost hurt, Jesse saw, another mood. Then: "You want no more trouble, you say, *Señor* Engineer? Yet you killed my men and stampeded our horses through our camp."

"You brought that on by pursuing and threatening us."

"*Señor* Engineer, you forget that you refused to share medical supplies for my wounded."

"You were going to rob us and kill every man."

Blanco shrugged. "It was a beeg misunderstanding. You do not savvy the ways of my Mexico. Sometimes what seems to you *Americanos* is not as it seems. Perhaps I did not make myself clear. Although I learned your language well as a young student in Mexico City, I do not understand every word as you would."

"The whine of a bullet means the same in any language, Colonel. I ask you again to let us pass."

Blanco brought up a beneficent smile. "I'm a generous man. I will let you pass, *Señor* Engineer. The price is your entire pack train."

"If I did that, you'd only demand more. Our extra horses and our weapons. The answer is no."

"I'm a peaceful man, and peaceful men should be generous. I will give you until the middle of the afternoon to consider my terms."

"My answer will be the same."

Blanco whirled his mount, and they loped back to the line of riders. Without delay, Gordon ordered the column to return to the bivouac in the timber along the stream and take up defensive positions without unsaddling.

In a short time, riders were observed going on picket north and east of the bivouac, while others crossed the creek above the volunteers and circled around, posting themselves at intervals below the bivouac, and still more forded the San Bernardino and spread out in positions to the west, which left the outfit cut off on all sides.

"He's taking no chances this time," Gordon said. "If he hadn't put pickets across the river, and we crossed, we'd still be caught out in the open in a running fight, which is the worst situation we can get into. I like our chances here much better, with a field of fire. If he made one tactical mistake, it was not to overrun us when he might have."

"At a cost, Major," Jesse said. "At a cost."

Around three o'clock Blanco and some riders showed up north of the bivouac and halted and waved a flag. Gordon took Jesse and Connelly along, leaving Bickford in charge.

Blanco was still in his "peaceful mood," Jesse saw, flashing the old piano-keys smile and lolling in the saddle. "What have you decided to do, *Señor* Engineer, about my generous terms to give you safe passage to the border?"

"My answer is the same, Colonel. I can't give up the pack train. You're asking too much."

"What would you give?"

"What else is there?"

"You have forgotten the safety of the two women."

"They are all the more reason for you to let us pass."

Blanco leveled the major a look that spoke of no compromise. "You forget that my men are many and yours are few."

"I'm quite aware of that, Colonel. We are also men of courage and will fight for what is ours. We refuse to be robbed by bandits."

"Bandits?" Blanco had the injured look. "We are irregulars. I am still generous, *Señor* Engineer. You have until daybreak to agree with my terms. Only the pack train will get you through. Meanwhile, if you are wise and consider the safety of the women, send out a rider." He jerked his bay around with a flourish and loped off to the north.

"He's putting us off, hoping you'll give in, knowing he'd have to pay one helluva price to get the train."

"I'd gladly give him the pack train if assured that was all it took," Gordon said. "But we can't trust him. Ever see such a hardscrabble outfit? By comparison, *El Tigre*'s mangy pack of killers look like the royal guard."

When they rode back to the bivouac, Gordon called all the volunteers together, told them that the situation hadn't changed, and that he expected Blanco's main attack to come from the north. The tributary creek, between the bivouac and Blanco's men to the south, should prevent a charge from that direction. Then he directed that packs and saddles be stacked

251

to form a defensive perimeter in the timber. Horses and mules would be hobbled at sundown. When the firing started, he said, the women would be safer below the creek bank. Every man, including himself, would stand guard except Tate and Murphy.

Jesse watered his stock, took the mule's pack out to the perimeter, and came back and unsaddled the red horse and put him on picket. That done, he rested and smoked, reflecting on the damnable luck, like a roll of dice, that had thrown Blanco and his gang of cut-throats in the volunteers' path again. If they'd shot Blanco that day, this wouldn't have happened. Yet, if they had, they'd be no better than the bandits. There was a price for honor as well as for freedom — you had to fight for it.

Gordon joined Jesse and sat down beside him. "Captain," he said, "I've called on you and all the others for a great deal. Every man has come through. Nobody stepped back once."

"These are damned tough horse soldiers, Major, and damned well led, in my opinion."

"Officers always look better with good men." He seemed to ponder something. "I have yet one more asking of you, though it's really not a request, not really an order, since you're not in the U.S. cavalry."

Jesse looked at him, an inkling beginning to take shape in his mind. "Though I'm in U.S. pay as a scout. A man should earn his pay."

"True." Gordon hesitated, which was unlike him, but it was brief as his driving nature took over, and he said: "I'm asking you to ride to San Bernardino Springs tonight . . . get through somehow. Colonel Chilton promised he'd post a troop there soon after we left, with clearance orders to cross the border if necessary. Been plenty of time to do that. How do you view this?"

Jesse didn't reply at once. When he spoke, his voice sounded matter-of-fact: "It's much like on our way down, Major, the outfit posted on that little rocky rise, Blanco in camp . . . when we stampeded his horses. We couldn't just squat there, at his pleasure. We had to do something. Same choice here."

"I considered sending either Bickford or Connelly. But you're a man of much broader experience. I know no man who's fought under the many demanding conditions that you have, on different fields, under different flags. You also have the best horse by far in the outfit, and you're the best armed with the Spencer repeater, which you know how to use effectively. A long ride. I estimate it's thirty miles or more. Close to forty."

"Figured about that comin' down. Be longer, goin' around."

Gordon sat a while in musing silence. "I say it again, Captain, in all honesty. You can refuse. You don't have to go. I really can't order you as a civilian scout."

"I appreciate that, Major. This will take more than a good horse. It calls for a damned good horse . . . a damned tough horse with the bottom to cover a distance of rough ground . . . and some luck. The horse decides it. I think we'd better go, and we will."

No more was said then.

Chapter Eighteen

He went at once to the red horse and fed him grain in the nose bag and, afterward, checked his shoes, which were still tight, and groomed him with extra care. The plaited red ribbon still clung to the black mane, faded and a bit raveled by now, symbolic of the past. He wasn't superstitious, but he thought of it as a good luck charm or talisman, for, indeed, his physical luck had been exceptional since then. He felt of it lightly between his fingers.

The going back pained him, as always. But he put the feelings aside to go out and study all sides of the bivouac. More pickets were riding into position, north and east and south. Westward, across the river, the number of pickets looked about the same as before. He stood a while in thought, calculating his chances, such as they were.

Then a door seemed to open in his mind, and he started walking up the creek. He came to the low barricade of packs and saddles. Past them, the stream was up a little, but not much for what he was considering, and the banks sloped. What lay farther upstream he could only guess. He strolled on through the timber as far as he thought he should, which brought the pickets into closer view. Some were bringing in firewood from the upper reaches of the creek.

He turned back, his decision made, and walked over to Gordon and Reyes, who were busy talking.

"Major," Jesse said, "the only way I see out of here, except for a mad dash through heavy picket fire, is to slip up the creek. What do you think?"

"First, let's look at the map." When the map was unrolled,

Gordon traced out the northeasterly course of the creek a way with a forefinger, then circled northwest to the San Bernardino River. "You'll have to work back to the San Bernardino, which you'll need to lead you on to the springs. Otherwise, you'd be traveling blind, and you could very well miss it."

"I agree."

"It's roundabout, Captain, but it sure as hell beats trying to dash through these tight picket lines."

That settled it.

When it was fully dark, he saddled and made ready to leave, traveling light, thinking of his horse, taking only a sack of grain, two canteens, the Quickloader tied to the saddle horn, the Spencer with a shell in the chamber, making it an eight-foot repeater, and the Colt Navy. One saddlebag contained more carbine shells, the other rations of hardtack and bacon, cooked that afternoon, and his last bottle of tequila. He wore his canvas jacket, for the desert night would be cold, and it was stuffed with shells, a tin box of matches, pipe and tobacco, and his knife.

It was as if the major had gathered his staff for a send-off when he mounted and rode up to the fire where Gordon and Reyes and Bickford and Connelly stood.

"Good luck," Gordon said, and they all wished him luck, and like an afterthought, the major said: "Remember to trust your horse, Captain. His eyesight's better than yours at night."

Jesse waved and rode up the creek.

In the beginning, once past the barricade, he kept to the low, sloping bank, but after a while the bank grew steeper, and the brush thickened and snapped alarmingly as they rode through it, so he took to the water, which rose just below his stirrups. He rode at a careful walk, letting the horse pick his way over the slippery rocks through the timbered darkness. Like a tardy evening guest, the corn-yellow moon was just beginning to show up.

They continued at the slow, even walk. Once the horse checked, and Jesse could hear him sniffing. Then, as if satisfied at whatever had caused him to pause, the horse moved ahead, while the high banks and close timber masked the slow-coming light. Maybe it was better like this, Jesse thought, even if he couldn't see much. Here they were out of sight, and the occasional clack of shod hoofs on rock was muted.

Just above the rim of the banks, to his left and right, he could see campfires burning holes in the early night. A line of fires now. Except for a few lookouts posted west of the river, the many spaced fires told Jesse that Blanco, sure of his advantage, had massed all his rabble in close, especially on the north, enough to overrun the bivouac.

Voices.

He was near enough to campfires that he could hear voices, aware that he and the horse occupied a likely fatal position should someone happen to come to the timber and look down inquiringly at strange noises along the creek.

All at once, they came to a rocky riffle. The rocks were flat, and the horse's shod hoofs rang. The anvil-like sound was startling in the stillness. Jesse pulled up, his eyes jumping.

He froze, the horse standing as still as a statue in a park. When nothing changed, they ventured ahead.

More voices. Distinct voices. Laughter. A strumming guitar. A string broke with a twang, but the strumming went on. A single voice lifted in bawdy song, the singer no better than the strummer.

Another fifty yards, Jesse figured, and they'd be past the nearest picket on his right.

A new sound invaded the night as they groped along. A murmuring that grew louder, filling Jesse's ears, increasing to a low roaring. It was near-blackness before him. Unexpectedly, the horse halted. Jesse tried to heel him on, gently, but the horse wouldn't budge, only stir a little — that was all. *Trust your horse.* Jesse leaned forward, peering, and, as rising amber light bathed the tree cover, he saw what had caused the horse to balk. A waterfall blocked their way, not a big one, but no horse could go over it or around it. They were boxed in. They had to back up and get out of here.

He reined slowly around and back, the horse moving eagerly. In the increasing glow, he searched for a low bank they could climb, but both brushy sides were too high. They groped on, Jesse conscious of their time-killing retreat. Farther on, the south bank didn't look quite so high, yet still too high for a horse to climb on its own. In desperation, he dismounted, feeling the water washing up around his hips. He grabbed a bush and pulled himself up the bank. Digging in with his boot heels, he pulled on the reins for the horse to follow. For a run of seconds the horse balked, not liking this strange business; and then, with Jesse yanking harder, the horse came on with a lunge, digging in, slipping, grunting, splashing — with an abrupt surge, it found footing and topped the bank, breaking brush and simultaneously flattening Jesse.

Stunned, Jesse lay there until his head cleared, hacking for wind. He had taken only a glancing blow, but pain leaped across his chest and up and down his left arm and shoulder. A direct smash by the eight-hundred-pound body would have knocked him out or left him broken, unable to go on. He still held the reins. The horse was trembling. Jesse had a wild thought. *If I hadn't held onto the reins, would the horse have stood by me?* He thought so; it didn't matter now. He staggered up and led the horse to the edge of the timber and peered back at the ground they'd lost: nearly a hundred yards down from the campfire nearest the creek. He studied the figures there. Four or five. Horses on picket nearby.

His head swam as he drew himself to the saddle with pain, pulled the Spencer ready, and, keeping to the timber's edge, rode toward them at a heedful walk.

He smelled coffee. The dreadful music and singing sounded louder. By keeping within the timber's shadows, he might be able to slip by them. He was very close now.

While watching the crouching shapes by the fire, he'd let the eager horse stride a little faster without realizing it until now. That faster sound, faint as it was, must have warned them. Because he saw them suddenly face this way. One man stood up, looking. He reached for a rifle.

On instinct alone, Jesse kicked the horse into a breaking run. The man grabbed the rifle and shouted. The others seemed uncertain. As horse and rider loomed up, they sprang aside. Jesse rode the red horse straight through and over the blazing fire, amid showering coals and flying tinware and sight of the rifleman diving out of the way.

By now the horse was tearing at a dead run. Jesse let him have his head. A shot sounded back there as wild as the night, nowhere close. By God, they were through!

He eased back to the running walk, and they traveled on at that ground-consuming pace until reason reminded Jesse that it was time to change directions. To do that, he had to cross the creek. Reining over there in the strengthening light, he searched for a crossing. But the banks were too high along here. An attempt might injure his horse. It was a while before he found a place; by then he'd lost valuable time, but they were across. Looking to his left, he spotted distant campfires still burning north of the bivouac.

He was starting to hurt all through. So he stopped and took a slug of the cheap tequila, eased the saddle cinch, rested his horse while he smoked a pipeful, cinched up again, and struck out northwest for the San Bernardino River, his guide to the springs.

About an hour passed.

He reached the river without delay, watered his horse, and here he paused. Instead of following the winding course of the river as the outfit had much of the way trailing down, he swung clear of it for faster travel. Thereafter, he rested his horse at regular intervals. Other times, he led the horse. Once he rode to the river for horse water, munched dry rations, and smoked while they rested.

As the night wore on, the clear sky cold and stars blazing, following the twisting band of a road that looked like a pale stream a-winding in the moon wash, he came to the first gloomy devastation of settlements seen days earlier: abandoned adobes and scattered mounds of rocks marked by crude crosses. Through here he heard more coyotes singing than he had all night. Was that because, as sociable animals, they missed the poor people who'd toiled and died here, and the grieving survivors who'd fled farther south to villages along the Bavispe? Several times, unafraid, coyotes crossed in front of the horse and seemed to look back curiously as they dissolved into the night.

He sensed it was after midnight when he approached the springs, aware that his horse was blowing. Several campfires marked the bivouac. Over there by the mesa he made out the dark bulk of the picket line. With time pressing, he approached at a hard lope and called out: "Hello, the camp. Hello."

Instantly a sentry challenged him.

"I'm from Major Gordon's command. It's vital that I see the officer in charge at once."

"Identify yourself."

"Scout Jesse Wilder. Damn it, soldier, hurry. Gordon's outfit's in deep trouble south of here."

A gruff voice shouted: "Guard, let that man through! Bring 'im over here at once!"

"Yes, sir!"

Jesse followed the guard and dismounted when he saw a figure in underwear standing in front of a dog tent. By firelight Jesse recognized no less than Colonel Chilton himself.

"Let's hear it, Wilder."

Jesse reported in quick detail, from the rescue of the women through the tunnel and the bandits' pursuit and the costly fight at the river, to Blanco's interception and demands.

"The command's down to sixteen men, counting two wounded, Reyes and the major," Jesse concluded.

"How far is it?" Chilton said, dressing while he talked.

"About thirty miles or more, as straight as we can go."

"How much time do we have?"

"Till daybreak, Colonel."

"What's the condition of *Señorita* Reyes and her *duenna?*"

"Excellent. Just a bit weary."

"Exactly who is this son-of-a-bitching Blanco you say calls himself colonel?"

"He claims he's in the Sonoran Auxiliary . . . irregulars. But that's just a cover for his banditry. He plays both sides. Gave us trouble goin' down. We got through by stampeding his horse herd one night."

"What's his strength?"

"About sixty or seventy men."

Chilton pulled on his boots with a grunt. "How'd you get through, Captain?"

Jesse told him, succinctly.

"By, God! You're riding a damned good horse, sir. You've covered more than thirty miles, and in fast time. You must cool him out at once. Then light water and feed. That's the right order. Because you have to ride him back. There's time. Take time."

"I intend to, Colonel. You bet."

As Jesse unsaddled, the bivouac came alive. "Boots and Saddles" blew, then the staccato bark of sergeants hurrying the troopers to "pack up." Jesse began walking his horse to the springs and back, not hurrying. Afterward, a quick rub-down, then water, then light grain. The horse had quit blowing. Not many minutes had elapsed. He saddled.

"Stand to horse."

"Prepare to mount."

"Mount."

"Right by twos . . . march!"

As soon as the horses warmed up, Chilton issued a "trot" command.

"We're a troop and a half strong," the colonel told Jesse, "which doesn't leave much at Bowie. But when the President of the United States gives you an order, you'd better throw all you've got into the saddle and hit the grit . . . otherwise, you could very well end up a second lieutenant in some remote post and never be heard of again."

Jesse figured first light was about five hours away — or less. His estimate of the distance was based on the volunteers' daylight search into northern Sonora that first day. On the other hand, since he'd circled around, he thought the red horse, slipping along in the easy running walk at about six miles an hour on level ground, had covered nearly forty miles tonight — maybe more.

When Chilton asked him about casualties, Jesse related how Kaufman had deserted and was found, and how Cramer had died in the Apache attack at the springs, and Maguire, wounded in the same fight, had died at the next bivouac, and Moriarty, Webb, and Ryan, fighting *El Tigre*'s band.

"I tell you, sir, with the exception of Private Kaufman, these men stood up. As for Kaufman, I can't understand why a man would desert in Apache country, even after Apaches had been spotted watching us."

"Kaufman," Chilton said, his voice sharp with loathing, "volunteered so he could desert again. He got what he deserved for quitting his troop when they needed him."

It was soon evident Chilton had no intention of marching "by the book" tonight. Although he halted approximately every hour and rested for ten minutes or less, he was forcing the pace in between. Roughly midway through the march, he watered at the river, ordered girths loosened, rested a short while, tightened girths, and hurried on.

When the first grayish light faintly brushed the eastern sky, it was time to halt again and the colonel said: "Tell me how Major Gordon has drawn up his defensive position."

"The bivouac is this side of the creek in the timber, forted up behind packs and saddles. The major has a field of fire. The creek is to the rear. Blanco has moved pickets around to the east and across the creek to the south and west of the river, which cut us off. His main force is north of the creek."

"I see."

They pressed on. The desert slipped by, dark and formless, and they seemed to make little progress, traveling into a void. Before long, Jesse knew, this would change abruptly, like a drawn curtain.

Chilton ordered the bugler to ride to his left and hastened the command to a faster trot.

Jesse watched the clock of the sky as it changed to a light dove gray. And with that, suddenly time seemed unlocked, unleashed, rushing by, goading them onward. He caught the drift of wood smoke.

It wasn't long, then, until he saw the sky flush pink, and

upon that, before them, low, the crouching light of campfires still burning, and beyond them the dark line of the creek timber where the bivouac lay.

Within moments, the sky parted and bold sunlight burst through, stripping away the night, laying bare everything in detail. In the distance, horses were moving about.

"I believe they're beginning to form a front, Colonel," Jesse said. "Big bunch . . . enough to overrun the bivouac."

"Then we'll hit 'em before they can form," Chilton decided quickly, and threw up a hand to halt and gave the command: "Left front into line."

There followed the faster drumming of hoofs and the squeal of saddle leather and the jingle of chains as the command swung into line.

"Gallop . . . guide right. Sound the charge, bugler!"

Came the quick tat-a-tat-tat notes and the line rushed forward, Jesse riding at a run with Chilton in the center.

In the distance, the forming riders halted and seemed to jerk around in surprise. Carbines started banging along the troopers' charging line.

But the bandits still held. They wheeled about in loose order to face the charge, urged on by a shouting voice. Jesse saw the blue flames of their guns and puffs of powder smoke. As the distance rapidly shortened, the closing action took on sharp clarity before him: faces, gun flashes, horses rearing, riders dropping. He snapped off shots at the bandit center.

The troopers were yelling as they charged, going to revolvers now, but, surprisingly, the bandits hadn't broken. Jesse saw it would soon be a mêlée.

New battle sounds swelled, the rattle of gunfire from the bivouac. Blanco's line, caught between two fires, began to mill and falter. They broke all at once, some riders spurring for the river, others tearing eastward, the troopers in hot pursuit.

Chilton checked his mount to observe the loose ends of the fight, already breaking up into horse races and scattered shooting. The bivouac's fire had ceased. As far as Jesse could tell, Blanco's men south of the creek hadn't attacked.

Chilton ordered the bugler to blow "Recall," and, shortly, the troopers began loping back. Jesse heard one say: "A feller in leather pants on a fine bay plumb outran me to the river, but I got one good shot at 'im. Couldn't tell if he made it across or not. I sure wanted that bay horse."

Chilton rode into the timber where Major Gordon was waiting and dismounted. They shook hands.

"I'd like to suggest, Major, that we get the hell out of here as soon as the boys have had breakfast. I hope you have plenty of coffee. We traveled light."

"We have plenty of coffee, Colonel, and I can assure you that not only will your order be carried out promptly, but that it will meet with wholehearted approval by all concerned."

The command reached Fort Bowie without incident, dragging in on the evening of the sixth day.

Jesse watered and fed his horse and mule, left them in care of the obliging stable sergeant, had his first bath in he didn't know how many days, ate a late supper with the hungry troopers, and slept the night through on a cot in the enlisted men's barracks.

Next morning an orderly came for him, and he found Gordon and Chilton waiting for him. The map was still in place near the colonel's desk. Everything was the same. It gave him a strange sensation of unreality, as if he revolved in a world that went 'round and 'round, and he couldn't get off.

They shook hands.

"As Major Gordon says," Chilton began, "this was an extraordinary mission, undermanned as it was, I admit, and it took extraordinary men to see it through. I've already messaged Washington. We're all deeply appreciative of what you did, Captain. Your name is in the report with the others, with special commendation for the hazardous ride."

Jesse nodded his thanks. "Damned good soldiering, Colonel, and damned good horse soldiers made it possible."

"And one damned good horse," Gordon added.

"Thank you, Major." Jesse was beginning to feel uncomfortable. "He is a good horse."

"Every man's record is cleared," Chilton went on. "Luckily Private Elias Lane is going to make it."

"I'm glad to hear that."

Chilton reached into a desk drawer and drew out a leather money belt. "I'm pleased to pass on to you what was promised . . . one thousand for going, five thousand for a successful mission . . . from the United States government. All in gold." He handed it to Jesse.

"That's a lot of money, sir. More than I'd ever make behind a mule goin' down a cotton patch in Tennessee, or teaching school. I thank you, Colonel."

"You earned far more than that, Captain." Chilton put a forefinger to his chin. "There is one matter." He was smiling as though he was about to divulge a secret. "In addition, I'm offering you the job as post scout, and I sincerely hope you'll take it."

Startled, Jesse didn't know what to say. He looked down and up. "I thank you, Colonel. Right now, it's too early for me to say. I'm very much obliged to you, sir, as we used to say back home." He shook his head. "I may ride on for a while."

"Well, think more about it. There's a place for you here as long as I'm in command, now or later."

"Thank you very much, sir. I appreciate all you've said."

265

A stillness settled over the room. All had been said that was to be said. It was time to let go again. Jesse shook hands again, feeling the pain of saying good bye to good men he'd likely never see again. Why was he doing this? Why was he so driven?

Then, on impulse, because both officers deserved it, he saluted smartly, about-faced, and left the room.

He was surprised to see Reyes, waiting for him just outside headquarters. "You are leaving, *amigo* Jesse, I know," he said accusingly. "I was afraid you'd leave without saying good bye."

"I wouldn't do that. I was going to see you before I left."

Reyes's smile was half hopeful, no more. "I want to invite you to visit our family in Hermosillo. We want to honor you. It's our way of thanking you, *amigo* Jesse, Captain Jesse, *Señor* Citizen General Jesse."

"Thank you, Agustín. Very much."

"Don't wait too long. Mexican girls get married young."

Their glances locked. There were no words left. After hard-hugging *abrazos,* they parted, and Jesse went on to the stables. Chico, the mule, was already packed.

Jesse saddled the red horse and was leading them out when he saw Bickford standing in the stable doorway.

They sized up each other for a long moment, a sort of appraisal, until Jesse said: "You're a damned good horse soldier, Sergeant."

Bickford looked taken aback, but not for long. "Never thought I'd hear that from a Johnny Reb. Well, I never saw you hold back, either." They eyed each other again, hesitating much as they had over the tunnel in *El Tigre*'s office, neither man willing to be first.

Then Bickford said — "Aw, hell, Wilder." — and thrust out his hand. Jesse took it, gripped hard, and led his stock by.

266

Major Gordon was walking east as he looked around. Seeing Bickford, he asked: "Have you seen Captain Wilder, Sergeant?"

"Yes, sir. He just left."

"Did he say where he was going? His destination?"

"No, sir. But he rode west."

THE END

About the Author

Fred Grove has written extensively in the broad field of western fiction, from the Civil War and its postwar effect on the expanding West, to modern quarter horse racing in the Southwest. He has received the Western Writers of American Spur Award five times — for his novels COMANCHE CAPTIVES (which also won the Oklahoma Writing Award at the University of Oklahoma and the Levi Strauss Golden Saddleman Award), THE GREAT HORSE RACE and MATCH RACE, and for his short stories, "Comanche Woman" and "When the *Caballos* Came." His novel, THE BUFFALO RUNNERS, was chosen for a Western Heritage Award by the National Cowboy Hall of Fame, as was the short story, "Comanche Son."

He also received a Distinguished Service Award from Western New Mexico University for his regional fiction on the Apache frontier, including the novels, PHANTOM WARRIOR and A FAR TRUMPET. His recent historical novel, BITTER TRUMPET, followed the bittersweet adventures of ex-Confederate Jesse Wilder training Juáristas in Mexico to fight the mercenaries of the Emperor Maximilian. TRAIL OF ROGUES is a sequel as fortune leads Wilder to the violent New Mexico frontier.

For a number of years Mr. Grove worked on newspapers in Oklahoma and Texas as a sportswriter, straight newsman, and editor. Two of his earlier novels, WARRIOR ROAD and DRUMS WITHOUT WARRIORS, focused on the brutal Osage Murders during the Roaring 'Twenties, a national scandal that brought in the F.B.I. Of Osage descent, the author grew up in Osage County, Oklahoma during the murders. It was while interviewing Oklahoma pioneers that he became interested in Western fiction. He now resides in Tucson, Arizona, with his wife, Lucile. His next **Five Star Western**, INTO THE FAR MOUNTAINS, will continue the saga of Jesse Alden Wilder.